THE LAST MIRACLE

JEWISH STORIES

'The fates of men are nothing to the universe,
Zweig tells us—but he makes us care'
SUNDAY TIMES

'He was capable of making the reader live
other people's deepest experience—which is
a moral education in itself. My advice is that
you should go out at once and buy his books'
TELEGRAPH

'Stefan Zweig's time of oblivion is over
for good... it's good to have him back'
SALMAN RUSHDIE, NEW YORK TIMES

STEFAN ZWEIG was born in 1881 in Vienna, a member of a wealthy Austrian-Jewish family. He studied in Berlin and Vienna and was first known as a translator and later as a biographer. Zweig travelled widely, living in Salzburg between the wars, and enjoying literary fame. His stories and novellas were collected in 1934. In the same year, with the rise of Nazism, he briefly moved to London, where he wrote his only novel, *Beware of Pity*. After a short period in New York, he settled in Brazil. There, in 1942, he and his wife were found dead in an apparent double suicide, the day after he completed his final book, *The World of Yesterday*. Much of his work is available from Pushkin Press.

ANTHEA BELL (1936–2018) was one of the leading literary translators of her time. Her work from German, French and Danish into English encompassed the writings of Kafka, Freud, the Brothers Grimm, Hans Christian Andersen, Georges Simenon, W.G. Sebald, René Goscinny, and more – including many translations of the work of Stefan Zweig for Pushkin Press.

EDEN PAUL (1865–1944) and CEDAR PAUL (1880–1972) together translated dozens of books from French, German, Italian and Russian during their thirty years of marriage. Among them were writings on psychoanalysis and socialist thought, as well as many of the works of Stefan Zweig.

THE LAST MIRACLE

JEWISH STORIES

STEFAN ZWEIG

TRANSLATED FROM THE GERMAN
BY ANTHEA BELL AND
EDEN AND CEDAR PAUL

PUSHKIN PRESS CLASSICS

Pushkin Press
Somerset House, Strand
London WC2R 1LA

Original texts © Williams Verlag AG Zurich

English translations of 'Buchmendel', 'Downfall of the Heart',
'The Miracles of Life' and 'In the Snow' © Anthea Bell

English translation of 'The Buried Candelabrum' © Eden and Cedar Paul

'In the Snow' was first published as 'Im Schnee' in 1901
'The Miracles of Life' was first published as 'Die Wunder des Lebens' in 1903
'Downfall of the Heart' was first published as 'Untergang eines Herzens' in 1927
'Buchmendel' was first published under the same title in 1929
'The Buried Candelabrum' was first published as 'Der begrabene Leuchter' in 1936

First published by Pushkin Press in 2025

ISBN 13: 978-1-80533-183-4

All rights reserved. No part of this publication may be reproduced,
stored in a retrieval system or transmitted in any form or by any
means, electronic, mechanical, photocopying, recording or otherwise,
or for the purpose of training artificial intelligence technologies or
systems without prior permission in writing from Pushkin Press

A CIP catalogue record for this title is available from the British Library

The authorised representative in the EEA is
eucomply OÜ, Pärnu mnt. 139b-14, 11317, Tallinn, Estonia,
hello@eucompliancepartner.com, +33757690241

Designed and typeset by Tetragon, London
Printed and bound in the United Kingdom by Clays Ltd, Elcograf S.p.A.

Pushkin Press is committed to a sustainable future for our
business, our readers and our planet. This book is made from
paper from forests that support responsible forestry.

MIX
Paper | Supporting
responsible forestry
FSC® C018072

www.pushkinpress.com

1 3 5 7 9 8 6 4 2

CONTENTS

Buchmendel	7
Downfall of the Heart	41
The Miracles of Life	79
In the Snow	153
The Buried Candelabrum	169

BUCHMENDEL

B ACK IN VIENNA AGAIN, on my way home from a visit to the outer districts of the city, I was unexpectedly caught in a heavy shower of rain that sent people running from its wet whiplash to take refuge in such shelter as the entrances of buildings, and I myself quickly looked round for a place where I could keep dry. Luckily Vienna has a coffee house on every street corner, so with my hat dripping and my shoulders drenched, I hurried into one that stood directly opposite. Inside, it proved to be a suburban café of the traditional kind, almost a stereotype of a Viennese café, with none of the newfangled features that imitate the inner-city music halls of Germany. It was in the old Viennese bourgeois style, full of ordinary people partaking more lavishly of the free newspapers than the pastries on sale. At this evening hour the air in the café, which would always be stuffy anyway, was thick with ornate blue smoke rings, yet the place looked clean, with velour sofas that were obviously new and a shiny aluminium till. In my haste I hadn't even taken the trouble to read its name outside, and indeed, what would have been the point? Now I was sitting in the warm, looking impatiently through window panes veiled by blue smoke, and wondering when it would suit the vexatious shower to move a few kilometres further on.

So there I sat, with nothing to do, and began to fall under the spell of the passive lethargy that invisibly emanates, with narcotic effect, from every true Viennese coffee house. In that empty, idle mood I looked individually at the customers, to whom the artificial light of the smoke-filled room lent an unhealthy touch of grey shadow round the eyes, and studied the young woman at the till mechanically setting out sugar and a spoon for every cup of coffee served by the waiter; drowsily and without really noticing them I read the posters on the walls, to which I was wholly indifferent, and found myself almost enjoying this kind of apathy. But suddenly, and in a curious way, I was brought out of my drowsy state as a vague impulse began to stir within me. It was like the beginning of a slight toothache, when you don't know yet if it is on the right or the left, if it is starting in the upper or the lower jaw; there was just a certain tension, a mental uneasiness. For all at once—I couldn't have said how—I was aware that I must have been here once before, years ago, and that a memory of some kind was connected with these walls, these chairs, these tables, this smoky room, apparently strange to me.

But the more I tried to pin down that memory, the more refractory and slippery it was as it eluded me—like a luminous jellyfish unconsciously glowing on the lowest level of my mind, yet not to be seized and scrutinized at close quarters. In vain I stared at every item of furnishing; certainly much of it was new to me, for instance the till with the clinking of its automatic calculations, and the brown wallpaper imitating Brazilian rosewood. All that must have been imported later. Nonetheless, I knew I had been here once before, twenty years or more ago, and something of my own old self, long since overgrown, lingered here invisibly, like a nail hidden in wood. I reached out into the room, straining all my senses, and at the same time I searched myself—yet damn it all, I couldn't place that lost memory, drowned in the recesses of my mind.

I was annoyed with myself, as you always are when a failure of some kind makes you aware of the inadequacy and imperfection of your intellectual powers. But I did not give up hope of retrieving the memory after all. I knew I just had to lay hands on some tiny hook, for my memory is an odd one, good and bad at the same time: on the one hand defiant and stubborn, on the other incredibly faithful. It often swallows up what is most important, both incidents and faces, what I read and what I experience, engulfing it entirely in darkness, and will not give anything back from that underworld merely at the call of my will, only under duress. However, I need just some small thing to jog my memory, a picture postcard, a few lines of handwriting on an envelope, a sheet of newsprint faded by smoke, and at once what is forgotten will rise again like a fish on the line from the darkly streaming surface, as large as life. Then I remember every detail about someone, his mouth and the gap between the teeth in it on the left that shows when he laughs, the brittle sound of that laughter, how it makes his moustache twitch, and how another and new face emerges from that laughter—I see all that at once in detail, and I remember over the years every word the man ever said to me. But to see and feel the past so graphically I need some stimulus provided by my senses, a tiny aid from the world of reality. So I closed my eyes to allow me to think harder, to visualize and seize that mysterious hook at the end of the fishing line. Nothing, however, still nothing! All lost and forgotten. And I felt so embittered by the stubborn apparatus of memory between my temples that I could have struck myself on the forehead with my fists, as you might shake a malfunctioning automatic device that is unjustly refusing to do as you ask. No, I couldn't sit calmly here any longer, I was so upset by the failure of my memory, and in my annoyance I stood up to get some air.

But here was a strange thing: I had hardly taken a couple of steps across the room before the first phosphorescent glimmers of light began to dawn in my mind, swirling and sparkling. To the right of the cash desk, I remembered, there would be a way into a windowless room illuminated only by artificial light. And sure enough, I was right. There it was, not with the wallpaper I had known before, but the proportions of that rectangular back room, its contours still indistinct in my memory, were exactly the same. This was the card room. I instinctively looked for individual details, my nerves already joyfully vibrating (soon, I felt, I would remember it all). Two billiard tables stood idle, like silent ponds of green mud; in the corners of the room there were card tables, with two men who looked like civil servants or professors playing chess at one of them. And in the corner, close to the iron stove, where you went to use the telephone, stood a small, square table. Suddenly the realization flashed right through my entire mind. I knew at once, instantly, with a single, warm impulse jogging my memory: my God, that was where Mendel used to sit, Jakob Mendel, Mendel the bibliophile, and after twenty years here I was again in the Café Gluck at the upper end of Alserstrasse, to which he habitually resorted. Jakob Mendel—how could I have forgotten him for such an incredibly long time? That strangest of characters, a legendary man, that esoteric wonder of the world, famous at the university and in a small, eminent circle—how could I have lost my memory of him, the magician who traded in books and sat here from morning to evening every day, a symbol of the knowledge, fame and honour of the Café Gluck?

I had only to turn my vision inwards for that one second, and already his unmistakable figure, in three dimensions, was conjured up by my creatively enlightened blood. I saw him at once as he had been, always sitting at that rectangular table, its dingy grey marble top heaped high at all times with books and other writings. I saw the way he persistently sat there, imperturbable, his eyes behind his glasses hypnotically fixed on a book, humming and muttering as he read, rocking his body and his inadequately polished, freckled bald patch back and forth, a habit acquired in the *cheder*, his Jewish primary school in eastern Europe. He pored over his catalogues and books here, at that table, never sitting anywhere else, singing and swaying quietly, a dark, rocking cradle. For just as a child falls into sleep and is lost to the world by that rhythmically hypnotic rocking movement, in the opinion of pious Jews the spirit passes more easily into the grace of contemplation if one's own idle body rocks and sways at the same time. And indeed, Jakob Mendel saw and heard none of what went on around him. Beside him, the billiards players talked in loud voices, making a great deal of noise; the markers scurried about, the telephone rang, people came to scour the floor and heat the stove—he noticed none of it. Once a hot coal had fallen out of the stove, and was already burning and smoking on the wooden floor two paces away from him; only then did the infernal smell alert another of the guests in the café to the danger, and he made haste to extinguish the smoke. Jakob Mendel himself, however, only a couple of inches away and already affected by the fumes, had noticed nothing. For he read as other people pray, as gamblers gamble, as drunks stare into space, their senses numbed; he read with such touching absorption that the reading of all other persons had always seemed to me profane by comparison. As a young man, I had seen the great mystery of total concentration for the first time in this little Galician book dealer, Jakob Mendel, a kind of concentration in which the artist resembles the scholar, the truly wise resembles the totally deranged. It is the tragic happiness and unhappiness of total obsession.

An older colleague of mine from the university had taken me to see him. At the time I was engaged on research into Mesmer, the Paracelsian doctor and practitioner of magnetism, still too little known today, but I was not having much luck. The standard works on Mesmer proved to be unobtainable, and the librarian to whom I, as a guileless newcomer to the place, applied for information, replied in a surly tone that literary references were my business, not his. That was the occasion when my colleague first mentioned the man's name to me. "I'll go and see Mendel with you," he promised. "He knows everything, he can get hold of anything. He'll find you the most obscure book from the most forgotten of German second-hand bookshops. The ablest man in Vienna, and an original into the bargain, a bibliophilic dinosaur, the last survivor of a dying race from the prehistoric world."

So the two of us went to the Café Gluck, and lo and behold there sat Mendel the bibliophile, bespectacled, sporting a beard that needed trimming, clad in black, and rocking back and forth as he read like a dark bush blown in the wind. We went up to him, and he didn't even notice. He just sat there reading, his torso swaying over the table like a mandarin, and hanging on a hook behind him was his decrepit black overcoat, its pockets stuffed with notes and journals. My friend coughed loudly by way of announcing us. But Mendel, his thick glasses close to his book, still didn't notice us. Finally my friend knocked on the tabletop as loudly and energetically as you might knock at a door—and at last Mendel looked up, automatically pushed his clumsy steel-rimmed glasses up on his forehead, and from under his bushy, ashen grey brows two remarkable eyes gazed keenly at us. They were small, black, watchful eyes, as nimble and sharp as the darting tongue of a snake. My friend introduced me, and I explained my business, first—a trick expressly recommended by my friend—complaining with pretended anger of the librarian who, I said, wouldn't give me any information. Mendel leant back and spat carefully. Then he just laughed, and said with a strong eastern European accent,

"Wouldn't, eh? Not him—couldn't is more like it! He's an ignoramus, a poor old grey-haired ass. I've known him, heaven help me, these twenty years, and in all that time he still hasn't learnt anything. He can pocket his salary, yes, that's all he and his like can do! Those learned doctors—they'd do better to carry bricks than sit over their books."

This forceful venting of his grievances broke the ice, and with a good-natured wave of his hand he invited me, for the first time, to sit at the square marble-topped table covered with notes, that altar of bibliophilic revelations as yet unknown to me. I quickly explained what I wanted: works contemporary with Mesmer himself on magnetism, as well as all later books and polemics for and against his theories. As soon as I had finished, Mendel closed his left eye for a second, just like a marksman before he fires his gun. It was truly for no more than a second that this moment of concentrated attention lasted, and then, as if reading from an invisible catalogue, he fluently enumerated two or three dozen books, each with its place and date of publication and an estimate of its price. I was astonished. Although prepared for it in advance, this was more than I had expected. But my bafflement seemed to please him, for on the keyboard of his memory he immediately played the most wonderful variations on my theme that any librarian could imagine. Did I also want to know about the somnambulists and the first experiments with hypnosis? And about Gassner's exorcisms, and Christian Science, and Madame Blavatsky? Once again names came tumbling out of him, titles and descriptions; only now did I realize what a unique marvel of memory I had found in Jakob Mendel, in truth an encyclopaedia, a universal catalogue on two legs. Absolutely dazed, I stared at this bibliographical phenomenon, washed up here in the shape of an unprepossessing, even slightly grubby little Galician second-hand book dealer who, after reciting some eighty names to me full pelt, apparently without taking much thought, but inwardly pleased to have played his trump card, polished his glasses on what might once have been a white handkerchief. To hide my astonishment a little, I hesitantly asked which of those books he could, if need be, get hold of for me.

"Well, we'll see what can be done," he growled. "You come back here tomorrow, by then old Mendel will have found you a little something, and what can't be found here will turn up elsewhere. A man who knows his way around will have luck."

I thanked him courteously, and in all this civility I stumbled into a great act of folly by suggesting that I could write down the titles of books I wanted on a piece of paper. At the same moment I felt a warning nudge in the ribs from my friend's elbow. But too late! Mendel had already cast me a glance—what a glance!—that was both triumphant and injured, a scornful and superior, a positively regal glance, the Shakespearian glance of Macbeth when Macduff suggests to that invincible hero that he yield without a fight. Then he laughed again, briefly, the big Adam's apple in his throat rolling back and forth in an odd way. Apparently he had bitten back a sharp rejoinder with some difficulty. And good Mendel the bibliophile would have been right to make every imaginable sharp remark, for only a stranger, an ignoramus (*amhorez* is the Yiddish word he used for it) could offer such an insult as to write down the title of a book for him, Jakob Mendel, as if he were a bookseller's apprentice or a servant in a library, as if that incomparable, diamantine bibliophilic brain would ever have needed such a crude aid to his memory. Only later did I realize how much my civil offer must have injured the feelings of such an esoteric genius, for this small, squat Galician Jew, entirely enveloped in his own beard and hunchbacked into the bargain, was a Titan of memory. Behind that chalky, grubby brow, which looked as if it were overgrown by grey moss, there stood in an invisible company, as if stamped in steel, every name and title that had ever been printed on the title page of a book. Whether a work had first been published yesterday or two hundred years ago, he knew at once its exact place of publication, its publisher and the price, both new and second-hand, and at the same time he unfailingly recollected the binding, illustrations and facsimile editions of every book. He saw every work, whether he had held it in his own hands or had only seen it once from a distance, in a window display or a library, with the same optical precision as the creative artist sees the still-invisible forms of his inner world and those of other people. If, say, a book was offered for six marks in the catalogue of a second-hand bookseller in Regensburg, he immediately remembered that another copy of the same book could have been bought for four crowns in an auction in Vienna two years ago, and he also knew who had bought it; indeed, Jakob Mendel never forgot a title or a number, he knew every plant, every micro-organism, every star in the eternally oscillating, constantly changing cosmos of the universe of books. He knew more in every field than the experts in that field, he was more knowledgeable about libraries than the librarians themselves, he knew the stocks of most firms by heart better than their owners, for all their lists and their card indexes, although he had nothing at his command but the magic of memory, nothing but his incomparable faculty of recollection, which could only be truly explained and analysed by citing a hundred separate examples. It was clear that his memory could have been trained and formed to show such demonic infallibility only by the eternal mystery of all perfection: by concentration. This remarkable man knew nothing about the world outside books, for to his mind all the phenomena of existence began to seem truly real to him only when they were cast as letters and assembled as print in a book, a process that, so to speak, had sterilized them. But he read even the books themselves not for their meaning, for their intellectual and narrative content: his sole passion was for their names, prices, forms of publication and original title pages. Unproductive and uncreative in that last point, nothing but a list of hundreds of thousands of titles and names, stamped on the soft cortex of a mammalian brain as if written in a catalogue of books, Jakob Mendel's specifically bibliophilic memory was still, in its unique perfection, no less a phenomenon than Napoleon's memory for faces, Mezzofanti's for languages, the memory of a chess champion like Lasker for opening gambits or of a composer like Busoni for music. In a public place in the context of a seminar, that brain would have instructed and amazed thousands, hundreds of thousands of students and scholars, with results fertile for the sciences, an incomparable gain for those public treasuries that we call libraries. But that higher world was for ever closed to this small, uneducated Galician dealer in books, who had mastered little more than what he was taught in his studies of the Talmud, and consequently his fantastic abilities could take effect only as the secret knowledge shown when he sat at that marble-topped table in the Café Gluck. But some day, when there is a great psychologist who, with patience and persistence equal to Buffon's in arranging and classifying the entire animal kingdom, can do the same for all varieties, species and original forms of the magical power that we call memory, describing them separately and presenting their variants (a work as yet absent from our intellectual world)—then he would be bound to think of Jakob Mendel, that genius of prices and titles, that nameless master of the science of antiquarian books.

By trade, to be sure, Jakob Mendel was known to the ignorant only as a little dealer in second-hand books. Every Sunday the same standard advertisement appeared in the *Neue Freie Presse* and the *Neues Wiener Tagblatt*: "Old books bought, best prices paid, apply to Mendel, Obere Alserstrasse", and then a telephone number which in fact was the number of the Café Gluck. He would search through stockrooms, and every week, with an old servant bearded like the Emperor Joseph, brought back new booty to his headquarters and conveyed it on from there, since he had no licence for a proper bookshop. So he remained a dealer in a small way, not a very lucrative occupation. Students sold him their textbooks, and his hands passed them on from one academic year to the next, while in addition he sought out and acquired any particular work that was wanted, asking a small extra charge. He was free with good advice. But money had no place within his world, for he had never been seen in anything but the same shabby coat, consuming milk and two rolls in the morning, the afternoon and the evening, and at mid-day eating some small dish that they fetched him from the restaurant. He didn't smoke, he didn't gamble, you might even say he didn't live, but the two lively eyes behind his glasses were constantly feeding words, titles and names to this strange being's brain. And the soft, fertile substance of that brain absorbed this wealth of words greedily, like a meadow soaking up thousands upon thousands of raindrops. Human beings did not interest him, and of all the human passions perhaps he knew only one, although that, for sure, is the most human of them all: vanity. If someone came to him for information, after laboriously searching for it elsewhere to no avail, and he could provide it at once, that alone made him feel satisfaction, pleasure; and so too perhaps did the fact that a few dozen people who respected and needed his knowledge lived in and outside Vienna. Every one of those massive conglomerations of millions of people, a place that we would call a metropolis, is sprinkled here and there with several small facets reflecting one and the same universe in miniature, invisible to most and valuable only to the expert, who is related to another expert by virtue of the same passion. And these bibliophiles all knew Jakob Mendel. Just as if you wanted advice on sheet music you turned to Eusebius Mandyczewski at the Viennese Music Association, a friendly presence sitting there in his grey cap among his files and his scores, and he would solve the most difficult problem with a smile as he first looked up at you; just as today everyone wanting to know about the Altwiener Theater and its culture would still turn infallibly to Karl Glossy, who knows all about the subject—so a few devout Viennese bibliophiles, when they had a tough nut to crack, made their pilgrimage to the Café Gluck and Jakob Mendel.

Watching Mendel during one of these conversations gave me, as a young man full of curiosity, a particular kind of pleasure. If you put an inferior book in front of him he would close it scornfully, muttering only, "Two crowns"; but faced with some rarity, or a unique specimen, he would lean respectfully back, place a sheet of paper under it, and you could see that he was suddenly ashamed of his grubby, inky fingers with their black-rimmed nails. Then he would begin leafing tenderly, cautiously and with immense reverence through the rare volume, page by page. No one could disturb him at a moment like that, as little as you can disturb a devout believer at prayer; and indeed that looking, touching, smelling and assessing, each of those single acts, had about it something of the succession of rituals in a religious ceremony. His hunched back shifted to and fro, meanwhile he muttered and growled, scratched his head, uttered curious vowel sounds, a long-drawn-out, almost awe-stricken, "Ah" or "Oh" of captivated admiration, or then again a swift and alarmed, "Oy!" or "Oy vey!" if a page turned out to be missing, or had been nibbled by a woodworm. Finally he would weigh up the thick tome respectfully in his hands, sniff at the large rectangle and absorb its smell with half-closed eyes, as delighted as a sentimental girl enjoying the scent of tuberose. During this rather elaborate procedure, the owner of the book of course had to possess his soul in patience. Having ended his examination, however, Mendel was very happy, indeed positively delighted to give any information, which infallibly came with wide-ranging anecdotes and dramatic accounts of the prices of similar copies. At these moments he seemed to become brighter, younger, livelier, and only one thing could embitter him beyond all measure: that was if a novice tried to offer him money for his opinion. Then he would draw back with an air of injury, for all the world like the distinguished curator of a gallery when an American tourist passing through the city tries to press a tip into his hand.

Holding a precious book meant to Mendel what an assignment with a woman might to another man. These moments were his platonic nights of love. Books had power over him; money never did. Great collectors, including the founder of a collection in Princeton University Library, tried in vain to recruit him as an adviser and buyer for their libraries—Jakob Mendel declined; no one could imagine him anywhere but in the Café Gluck. Thirty-three years ago, when his beard was still soft and black and he had ringlets over his forehead, he had come from the east to Vienna, a crook-backed lad, to study for the rabbinate, but he had soon abandoned Jehovah the harsh One God to give himself up to idolatry in the form of the brilliant, thousand-fold polytheism of books. That was when he had first found his way to the Café Gluck, and gradually it became his workplace, his headquarters, his post office, his world. Like an astronomer alone in his observatory, studying myriads of stars every night through the tiny round lens of the telescope, observing their mysterious courses, their wandering multitude as they are extinguished and then appear again, so Jakob Mendel looked through his glasses out from that rectangular table into the other universe of books, also eternally circling and being reborn in that world above our own.

Of course he was highly esteemed in the Café Gluck, the fame of which was linked, so far as we were concerned, with Mendel at his invisible teacher's lectern rather than with the nominal patronage of that great magician Christoph Willibald Gluck, the composer of *Alceste* and *Iphigénie*. Mendel was as much a part of the fixtures and fittings as the old cherrywood cash desk, the two badly mended cues and the copper coffee pot, and his table was protected like a shrine—for his many customers and seekers after information were always urged by the staff, in a friendly manner, to place an order of some kind, thus ensuring that most of the profits of his knowledge disappeared into the broad leather bag worn at his hip by Deubler the head waiter. In return, Mendel the bibliophile enjoyed many privileges. He was free to use the telephone, his letters were fetched and anything he ordered from the restaurant brought in, the good old lady who looked after the toilets brushed his coat and sewed on buttons, and every week she took a little bundle of washing to the laundry for him. Lunch could be brought over from the nearby restaurant for him alone, and every day Herr Standhartner, the owner of the café, came to his table in person and said good morning (although usually Jakob Mendel, deep in his books, failed to notice the greeting). He arrived promptly at seven-thirty in the morning, and he left the café only when the lights were switched off. He never spoke to the other customers, and when Herr Standhartner once asked him courteously if he didn't find reading better by electric light than in the pallid, fitful illumination from the old Auer gas lamps, he gazed in surprise at the electric light bulbs; in spite of the noise and hammering of an installation lasting several days, this change had entirely passed him by. Only through the twin circles of his glasses, only through those two sparkling lenses that sucked everything in, did the billions of tiny organisms formed by the letters filter into his brain; everything else streamed over him as meaningless noise. In fact he had spent over thirty years, the entire waking part of his life, here at his rectangular table reading, comparing and calculating, in a continual daydream interrupted only by sleep.

So I was overcome by a kind of horror when I saw that the marble-topped table where Jakob Mendel made his oracular utterances now stood in this room as empty as a gravestone. Only now that I was older did I understand how much dies with such a man, first because anything unique is more and more valuable in a world now becoming hopelessly uniform. And then because, out of a deep sense of premonition, the young, inexperienced man I once was had been very fond of Jakob Mendel. In him, I had come close for the first time to the great mystery of the way what is special and overwhelming in our existence is achieved only by an inner concentration of powers, a sublime monomania akin to madness. And I had seen that a pure life of the mind, total abstraction in a single idea, can still be found even today, an immersion no less than that of an Indian yogi or a medieval monk in his cell, and indeed can be found in a café illuminated by electric light and next to a telephone—as a young man, I had sensed it far more in that entirely anonymous little book dealer than in any of our contemporary writers. Yet I had been able to forget him—admittedly in the war years, and in an absorption in my own work not unlike his. Now, however, looking at that empty table, I felt a kind of shame, and at the same time a renewed curiosity.

For where had he gone, what had happened to him? I called the waiter over and asked. No, he was sorry, he didn't know a Herr Mendel, no gentleman of that name frequented the café. But perhaps the head waiter would know. The head waiter ponderously steered his pot belly towards me, hesitated, thought it over. No, he didn't know any Herr Mendel either. But maybe I meant Mandl, Herr Mandl from the haberdashery shop in Florianigasse? A bitter taste rose to my mouth, the taste of transience: what do we live for, if the wind carries away the last trace of us from beneath our feet? For thirty years, perhaps forty, a man had breathed, read, thought and talked in this room of a few square metres, and only three or four years had to pass before there arose up a new king over Egypt, which knew not Joseph. No one in the Café Gluck knew anything now about Jakob Mendel, Mendel the bibliophile! Almost angrily I asked the head waiter if I could speak to Herr Standhartner, or was there anyone else from the old staff left in the house? Oh, Herr Standhartner, oh, dear God, he had sold the café long ago, he had died, and the old head waiter was living on his little property in the town of Krems. No, there was no one from the old staff here now… or yes! Yes, there was—Frau Sporschil was still here, the toilet lady (known in vulgar parlance as the chocolate lady). But he was sure she wouldn't be able to remember individual customers now. I thought at once, you don't forget a man like Jakob Mendel, and I asked her to come and see me.

She came, Frau Sporschil with her untidy white hair, her dropsical feet taking the few steps from her area of responsibility in the background to the front of the café and still hastily rubbing her red hands on a cloth; obviously she had just been sweeping or cleaning the windows of her dismal domain. From her uncertain manner I noticed at once that she felt uneasy to be summoned so suddenly into the smarter part of the café, under the large electric lights—in Vienna ordinary people suspect detectives and the police everywhere, as soon as anyone wants to ask them questions. So she looked at me suspiciously at first, glancing at me from under her brows, a very cautious, surreptitious glance. What good could I want of her? But as soon as I asked about Jakob Mendel she stared at me with full, positively streaming eyes, and her shoulders began to shake.

"Oh, my God, poor Herr Mendel—to think of anyone remembering him now! Yes, poor Herr Mendel"—she was almost weeping, she was so moved in the way of old people when they are reminded of their youth, of some good, forgotten acquaintanceship. I asked if he was still alive.

"Oh, my God, poor Herr Mendel, it must be five or six years he's been dead, no, seven years. Such a kind, good man, and when I think how long I knew him, more than twenty-five years, he was already coming here when I joined the staff. And it was a shame, a real shame, the way they let him die." She was growing more and more agitated, and asked if I was a relation. Because no one had ever troubled about him, she said, no one had ever asked after him—didn't I know what had happened to him?

No, I assured her, I knew nothing, and please would she tell me all about it? The good woman looked shy and embarrassed, and kept wiping her damp hands again and again. I realized that as the toilet lady she felt awkward standing here in the middle of the café, with her untidy white hair and stained apron. In addition, she kept looking anxiously to left and right in case one of the waiters was listening.

So I suggested that we might go into the card room, to Mendel's old table, and she could tell me all about it there. Moved, she nodded to me, grateful for my understanding, and the old lady, already a little unsteady on her feet, went ahead while I followed her. The two waiters stared after us in surprise, sensing some connection, and some of the customers also seemed to be wondering about the unlikely couple we made.

Over at Mendel's table, she told me (another account, at a later date, filled in some of the details for me) about the downfall of Jakob Mendel, Mendel the bibliophile.

Well then, she said, he had gone on coming here even after the beginning of the war, day after day, arriving at seven-thirty in the morning, and he sat there just the same and studied all day, as usual; the fact was they'd all felt, and often said so, that he wasn't even aware there was a war going on. I'd remember, she said, that he never looked at a newspaper and never talked to anyone else, but even when the newsboys were making their murderous racket, announcing special editions, and all the others ran to buy, he never got to his feet or even listened. He didn't so much as notice that Franz the waiter was missing (Franz had fallen at Gorlice), and he didn't know that Herr Standhartner's son had been taken prisoner at Przemyśl, he never said a word when the bread got worse and worse, and they had to serve him fig coffee instead of his usual milk, nasty stuff it was. Just once he did seem surprised because so few students came in now, that was all. "My God, the poor man, nothing gave him pleasure or grief except those books of his."

But then, one day, the worst happened. At eleven in the morning, in broad daylight, a policeman had come in with an officer of the secret police, who had shown the rosette badge in his buttonhole and asked if a man called Jakob Mendel came in here. Then they went straight over to Mendel's table, and he thought, suspecting nothing, they wanted to sell him books or ask for information. But they told him to his face to go with them, and they took him away. It had brought shame on the café; everyone gathered round poor Herr Mendel as he stood there between the two police officers, his glasses pushed up on his forehead, looking back and forth from one to the other of them, not knowing what they really wanted.

Frau Sporschil, however, said that she had instantly told the uniformed policeman this must be a mistake. A man like Herr Mendel wouldn't hurt a fly, but then the secret police officer shouted at her not to interfere in official business. And then, she added, they had taken him away, and it was a long time before he came back, two years. To this day she didn't really know what they'd wanted from him back then. "But I give you my oath," said the old woman, much upset, "Herr Mendel can't have done anything wrong. They made a mistake, I'd swear to it. It was a crime against that poor, innocent man, a real crime!"

And good, kind-hearted Frau Sporschil was right. Our friend Jakob Mendel really had not done anything wrong, only something stupid (and as I said, not until later did I learn all the details)—he had committed a headlong, touching and even in those crazy times entirely improbable act of stupidity, to be explained only by his total self-absorption, the oddity of his unique nature.

This was what had happened. One day the military censorship office, where it was the duty of the officials to supervise all correspondence sent abroad, had intercepted a postcard written and signed by one Jakob Mendel, properly stamped with sufficient postage for a country outside Austria, but—incredible to relate—sent to an enemy nation. The postcard was addressed to Jean Labourdaire, Bookseller, Paris, Quai de Grenelle, and on it the sender, Jakob Mendel, complained that he had not received the last eight numbers of the monthly *Bulletin bibliographique de la France*, in spite of having paid a year's subscription in advance. The junior censorship official who found it, in civil life a high-school teacher by profession and a scholar of Romance languages and literature by private inclination, who now wore the blue uniform of the territorial reserves, was astonished to have such a document in his hands. He thought it must be a silly joke. Among the 2,000 letters that he scanned every week, searching them for dubious comments and turns of phrase that might indicate espionage, he had never come across anything so absurd as someone in Austria addressing a letter to France without another thought, simply posting a card to the enemy country as if the borders had not been fortified by barbed wire since 1914, and as if, on every new day created by God, France, Germany, Austria and Russia were not killing a few thousand of each other's male populations. So at first he put the postcard in his desk drawer as a curio, and did not mention the absurdity to anyone else.

However, a few weeks later another card from the same Jakob Mendel was sent to a bookseller called John Aldridge, at Holborn Square in London, asking if he could procure the latest numbers of *The Antiquarian* for him; and once again it was signed by the same strange individual, Jakob Mendel, who with touching naiveté gave his full address. Now the high-school teacher felt a little uncomfortable in the uniform coat that he was obliged to wear. Was there, after all, some mysteriously coded meaning behind this idiotic joke? Anyway, he stood up, clicked his heels and put the two cards on the major's desk. The major shrugged his shoulders: what an odd case! First he asked the police to find out whether this Jakob Mendel actually existed, and an hour later Jakob Mendel was under arrest and, still stunned with surprise, was brought before the major. The major placed the mysterious postcards in front of him and asked whether he admitted to sending them. Agitated by the major's stern tone, and particularly upset because the police had tracked him down just when he was reading an important catalogue, Mendel said, almost impatiently, that of course he had written those postcards. He supposed a man still had a right to claim value for money paid as an advance subscription. The major turned in his chair and leant over to the lieutenant at the next desk. The two of them exchanged meaningful glances: what an utter idiot! Then the major wondered whether he should just tell this simpleton off in no uncertain terms and send him packing, or whether he ought to take the case seriously. In such difficult circumstances, almost any office will decide that the first thing to do is to write a record of the incident. A record is always a good idea. If it does no great good, it will do no harm either, and one more meaningless sheet of paper among millions will be covered with words.

This time, however, it unfortunately did do harm to a poor, unsuspecting man, for something very fateful emerged in answer to the major's third question. First the man was asked his name: Jakob, originally Jainkeff Mendel. Profession: pedlar (for he had no bookseller's licence, only a certificate allowing him to trade from door to door). The third question was the catastrophe: his place of birth. Jakob Mendel named a small village in Petrikau. The major raised his eyebrows. Petrikau, wasn't that in the Russian part of Poland, near the border? Suspicious! Very suspicious! So he asked more sternly when Mendel had acquired Austrian citizenship. Mendel's glasses stared at him darkly and in surprise: he didn't understand the question. For heaven's sake, asked the major, did he have his papers, his documents, and if so where were they? The only document he had was his permit to trade from door to door. The major's eyebrows rose ever higher. Then would he kindly explain how he came to be an Austrian citizen? What had his father been, Austrian or Russian? Jakob Mendel calmly replied: Russian, of course. And he himself? Oh, to avoid having to serve in the army, he had smuggled himself over the Russian border thirty-three years ago, and he had been living in Vienna ever since. The major was getting increasingly impatient. When, he repeated, had he acquired Austrian citizenship? Why would he bother with that, asked Mendel, he'd never troubled about such things. So he was still a Russian citizen? And Mendel, who was finding all this pointless questioning tedious, replied with indifference, "Yes, I suppose so."

Shocked, the major sat back so brusquely that his chair creaked. To think of such a thing! In Vienna, the capital of Austria, right in the middle of the war at the end of 1915, after Tarnów and the great offensive, here was a Russian walking around with impunity, writing letters to France and England, and the police did nothing about it! And then those fools in the newspapers are surprised that Conrad von Hötzendorf didn't advance directly to Warsaw, and on the general staff they are amazed that all troop movements are reported to Russia by spies. The lieutenant too had risen to his feet and was standing at his desk: the conversation abruptly became an interrogation. Why hadn't he immediately reported to the authorities as a foreigner? Mendel, still unsuspecting, replied in his sing-song Jewish tones, "Why would I want to go and report all of a sudden?" The major saw this reversal of his question as a challenge and asked, menacingly, whether he hadn't read the announcements? No! And didn't he read the newspapers either? Again, no.

The two of them stared at Mendel, who was sweating slightly in his uncertainty, as if the moon had fallen to earth in their office. Then the telephone rang, typewriters tapped busily, orderlies ran back and forth and Jakob Mendel was consigned to the garrison cells, to be moved on to a concentration camp. When he was told to follow two soldiers he stared uncertainly. He didn't understand what they wanted from him, but really he had no great anxiety. What ill, after all, could the man with the gold braid on his collar and the rough voice have in store for him? In his elevated world of books there was no war, no misunderstanding, only eternal knowledge and the desire to know more about numbers and words, titles and names. So he good-naturedly went down the steps with the two soldiers. Only when all the books in his coat pockets were confiscated at the police station, and he had to hand over his briefcase, where he had put a hundred important notes and customers' addresses, did he begin to strike out angrily around him. They had to overcome him, but in the process unfortunately his glasses fell to the floor, and that magic spyglass of his that looked into the intellectual world broke into a thousand pieces. Two days later he was sent, in his thin summer coat, to a concentration camp for civilian Russian prisoners at Komorn.

As for Jakob Mendel's experience of mental horror in those two years in a concentration camp, living without books—his beloved books—without money, with indifferent, coarse and mostly illiterate companions in the midst of this gigantic human dunghill, as for all he suffered there, cut off from his sublime and unique world of books as an eagle with its wings clipped is separated from its ethereal element—there is no testimony to any of it. But the world, waking soberly from its folly, has gradually come to know that of all the cruelties and criminal encroachments of that war, none was more senseless, unnecessary and therefore more morally inexcusable than capturing and imprisoning behind barbed wire unsuspecting civilians long past the age for military service, who had become used to living in a foreign land as if it were their own, and in their belief in the laws of hospitality, which are sacred even to Tungus and Araucanian tribesmen, had neglected to flee in time. It was a crime committed equally unthinkingly in France, Germany and England, in every part of a Europe run mad. And perhaps Jakob Mendel, like hundreds of other innocents penned up in a camp, would have succumbed miserably to madness or dysentery, debility or a mental breakdown, had not a coincidence of a truly Austrian nature brought him back to his own world just in time.

After his disappearance, several letters from distinguished customers had been delivered to his address. Those customers included Count Schönberg, the former governor of Styria and a fanatical collector of heraldic works; the former dean of the theological faculty at the university, Siegenfeld, who was working on a commentary on St Augustine; and the eighty-year-old retired Admiral the Honourable von Pisek, who was still tinkering with his memoirs—all of them, his faithful customers, had repeatedly written to Jakob Mendel at the Café Gluck, and a few of these letters were forwarded to the missing man in the concentration camp. There they fell into the hands of a captain who happened to have his heart in the right place, and who was surprised to discover the names of the distinguished acquaintances of this little half-blind, dirty Jew, who had huddled in a corner like a mole, grey, eyeless and silent, ever since his glasses had been broken (he had no money to buy a new pair). There must, after all, be something special about a man with friends like that. So he allowed Mendel to answer the letters and ask his patrons to put in a good word for him, which they did. With the fervent solidarity of all collectors, His Excellency and the Dean powerfully cranked up their connections, and their united support brought Mendel the bibliophile back to Vienna in the year 1917, after more than two years of confinement, although on condition that he reported daily to the police. However, he could return to the free world, to his old, cramped little attic room, he could walk past the window displays of books again, and above all he could go back to the Café Gluck.

Good Frau Sporschil was able to give me a first-hand account of Mendel's return to the café from an infernal underworld. "One day—Jesus, Mary and Joseph, thinks I, I can't believe my eyes!— one day the door's pushed open, you know what it's like, just a little way, he always came in like that, and there he is stumbling into the café, poor Herr Mendel. He was wearing a much-mended military coat, and something on his head that might once have been a hat someone had thrown away. He didn't have a collar, and he looked like death, grey in the face, grey-haired and pitifully thin. But in he comes, like nothing had happened, he doesn't ask no questions, he doesn't say nothing, he goes to the table over there and takes off his coat, but not so quickly and easily as before, it takes him an effort. And no books with him now, like he always brought—he just sits down there and don't say nothing, he just stares ahead of him with empty, worn-out eyes. It was only little by little, when we'd brought him all the written stuff that had come from Germany for him, he went back to reading. But he was never the same again."

No, he was not the same, he was no longer that *miraculum mundi*, a magical catalogue of all the books in the world. Everyone who saw him at that time sadly told me the same. Something in his otherwise still eyes, eyes that read only as if in his sleep, seemed to be destroyed beyond redemption. Something in him was broken; the terrible red comet of blood must, in its headlong career, have smashed destructively into the remote, peaceful, halcyon star that was his world of books. His eyes, used for decades to the tender, soundless, insect-like letters making up print, must have seen terrible things in that barbed-wire pen into which human beings were herded, for his eyelids cast heavy shadows over his once-swift and ironically sparkling pupils; sleepy and red-rimmed, they shed twilight on his formerly lively eyes as they peered through his glasses, now repaired by being laboriously tied together with thin string. And even more terrible: in the fantastic and elaborate structure of his memory, some prop must have given way, bringing the rest of it down in confusion, for the human brain, that control centre made of the most delicate of substances, a precision instrument in the mechanics of our knowledge, is so finely adjusted that a blocked blood vessel, even a small one, a shattered nerve, an exhausted cell or the shift of a molecule is enough to silence the heavenly harmony of the most magnificently comprehensive mind. And in Mendel's memory, that unique keyboard of knowledge, the keys themselves jammed now that he was back. If someone came in search of information now and then, Mendel would look wearily at him, no longer fully understanding; he heard things wrongly, and forgot what was said to him. Mendel was not Mendel any more, just as the world was no longer the world. Total immersion in reading no longer rocked him back and forth, but he usually sat there perfectly still, his glasses turned only automatically on a book, and you could not tell whether he was reading or only daydreaming. Several times, Frau Sporschil told me, his head dropped heavily on the book and he fell asleep in broad daylight; or he sometimes stared for hours on end at the strange and smelly light of the acetylene lamp they had put on his desk at this time when coal was in short supply. No, Mendel was not the old Mendel, no longer a wonder of the world but a useless collection of beard and clothes, breathing wearily, pointlessly sitting in his once-oracular chair, he was no longer the glory of the Café Gluck but a disgrace, a dirty mark, ill-smelling, a revolting sight, an uncomfortable and unnecessary parasite.

That was how the new owner of the café saw him. This man, Florian Gurtner by name, came from Retz, had made a fortune from shady deals in flour and butter during the starvation year of 1919, and had talked the unsuspecting Herr Standhartner into selling him the Café Gluck for 80,000 crowns in paper money, which swiftly depreciated in value. He set about the place with his firm rustic hands, renovating the old-established café to smarten it up, buying new armchairs for bad money at the right time, installing a marble porch, and he was already negotiating to buy the bar next door and turn it into a dance hall. Naturally enough, the odd little Galician parasite who kept a table occupied all day, and in that time consumed nothing but two cups of coffee and five rolls, was very much in the way of his hastily undertaken project to smarten up the café. Standhartner had, to be sure, specially commended his old customer to the new owner, and had tried to explain what an important man Jakob Mendel was; indeed he had, so to speak, transferred him along with the café's fixtures and fittings as someone with a claim on his goodwill. But along with the new furniture and the shiny aluminium cash register, Florian Gurtner had introduced the approach of a man out to earn all he could, and he was only waiting for an excuse to banish this last, annoying remnant of suburban shabbiness from his now-elegant café.

And a good reason to do so quite soon arose, for Jakob Mendel was in a bad way. The last banknotes he had saved had been pulverized in the paper mill of inflation, and his customers had disappeared. These days he was so exhausted that he lacked the strength to start climbing steps and going from door to door selling books again. There were a hundred little signs of his poverty.

He seldom had something for lunch brought in from the restaurant now, and he was behind with paying the small sums he owed for coffee and rolls, once as much as three weeks behind. At that point the head waiter wanted to turn him out into the street. But good Frau Sporschil, the toilet lady, was sorry for Mendel and said she would pay his debt.

Next month, however, a great misfortune happened. The new head waiter had already noticed, several times, that when he was settling up accounts the money for the baked goods never worked out quite right. More rolls proved to be missing than had been ordered and paid for. His suspicions, naturally, went straight to Mendel, for the decrepit old servant at the café had come to complain, several times, that Mendel had owed him money for six months, and he couldn't get it out of him. So the head waiter kept his eyes open, and two days later, hiding behind the fire screen, he succeeded in catching Jakob Mendel secretly getting up from his table, going into the other front room, quickly taking two rolls from a bread basket and devouring them greedily. When it came to paying for what he had had that day, he denied eating any rolls at all. So that explained the disappearance of the baked goods. The waiter reported the incident at once to Herr Gurtner who, glad of the excuse he had been seeking for so long, shouted at Mendel in front of everyone, accused him of theft and made a great show of magnanimity in not calling the police at once. But he told Mendel to get out of his café immediately and never come back. Jakob Mendel only trembled and said nothing; he got up from where he sat, tottering, and went away.

"Oh, it was a real shame," said Frau Sporschil, describing this departure. "I'll never forget it, the way he stood there, his glasses pushed up on his forehead, white as a sheet. He didn't even take the time to put on his coat, although it was January, and you know what a cold year it was. And in his fright he left his book lying on the table, I didn't notice that until later, and I was going to follow him with it. But he'd already stumbled to the door, and I didn't dare follow him out into the streets, because there was Herr Gurtner himself standing by the door shouting after him so loud that people stopped and crowded together. Yes, I call it a shame, I felt shamed to the heart myself! Such a thing could never have happened when old Herr Standhartner was here, fancy chasing a man away just for a few rolls, with old Herr Standhartner he could have eaten them for free all his life. But folk these days, they've got no hearts. Driving away a man who sat here day after day for over thirty years—a shame, it really was, and I wouldn't like to have to answer to the Lord God for it, not me."

The good woman was greatly agitated, and with the passionate volubility of old age she repeated again and again that it was a real shame, and nothing like it would have happened in Herr Standhartner's day. So finally I had to ask her what had become of our friend Mendel, and whether she had seen him again. At that she pulled herself together, and then went on in even more distress.

"Every day when I passed his table, every time, believe you me, I felt a pang. I always wondered where he might be now, poor Herr Mendel, and if I'd known where he lived I'd have gone there, brought him something hot to eat, because where would he get the money to heat his room and feed himself? And so far as I know he didn't have any family, not a soul in the world. But in the end, when I still never heard a thing, I thought to myself it must all be over, and I'd never see him again. And I was wondering whether I wouldn't get a Mass read for him, because he was a good man, Herr Mendel, and we'd known each other more than twenty-five years.

"But then one day early, half past seven in the morning in February, I'm just polishing up the brass rails at the windows, and suddenly—I mean suddenly, believe you me—the door opens and in comes Herr Mendel. You know the way he always came in, kind of crooked and confused-looking, but this time he was somehow different. I can see it at once, he's torn this way and that, his eyes all glazed, and my God, the way he looked, all beard and bones! I think right away, he don't remember nothing, here he is sleepwalking in broad daylight, he's forgot it all, all about the rolls and Herr Gurtner and how shamefully they threw him out, he don't know nothing about himself. Thank God for it, Herr Gurtner wasn't there yet, and the head waiter had just had his own coffee. So I put my oar in quickly, I tell him he'd better not stay here and get thrown out again by that nasty fellow" (and here she looked timidly around and quickly corrected herself) "I mean by Herr Gurtner. So I call out to him. 'Herr Mendel,' I say. He stares at me. And at that moment, oh my God, terrible it was, at that moment it must all have come back to him, because he gives a start at once and he begins to tremble, but not just his fingers, no, he's trembling all over, you can see it, shoulders and all, and he's stumbling back to the door, he's hurrying, and then he collapsed. We telephoned for the emergency service and they took him away, all feverish like he was. He died that evening. Pneumonia, a bad case, the doctor said, and he said he hadn't really known anything about it, not how he came back to us. It just kind of drove him on, it was like he was sleepwalking. My God, when a man has sat at a table like that every day for thirty-six years, the table is kind of his home."

We talked about him for some time longer; we were the last two to have known that strange man—I, to whom in my youth, despite the minute scope of his own existence, little more than that of a microbe, he had conveyed my first inklings of a perfectly enclosed life of the mind, and she, the poor worn-out toilet lady who had never read a book, and felt bound to this comrade of her poverty-stricken world only because she had brushed his coat and sewn on his buttons for twenty-five years. And yet we understood one another wonderfully well as we sat at his old table, now abandoned, in the company of the shades we had conjured up between us, for memory is always a bond, and every loving memory is a bond twice over. Suddenly, in the midst of her talk, she thought of something. "Jesus, how forgetful I am—I still have that book, the one he left lying on the table here. Where was I to go to take it back to him? And afterwards, when nobody came for it, afterwards I thought I could keep it a memento. There wasn't anything wrong in that, was there?"

She hastily produced it from her cubby hole at the back of the café. And I had difficulty in suppressing a small smile, for the spirit of comedy, always playful and sometimes ironic, likes to mingle maliciously in the most shattering of events. The book was the second volume of Hayn's *Bibliotheca Germanorum Erotica et Curiosa*, the well-known compendium of gallant literature known to every book collector. And this scabrous catalogue—*habent sua fata libelli*—had fallen as the dead magician's last legacy into those work-worn, red and cracked, ignorant hands that had probably never held any other book but her prayer book. As I say, I had difficulty in keeping my lips firmly closed to the smile involuntarily trying to make its way out, and my moment of hesitation confused the good woman. Was it valuable after all, or did I think she could keep it?

I shook her hand with heartfelt goodwill. "Keep it and welcome. Our old friend Mendel would be glad to think that at least one of the many thousands who had him to thank for a book still remembers him." And then I went, feeling ashamed in front of this good old woman, who had remained faithful to the dead man in her simple and yet very human way. For she, unschooled as she was, had at least kept a book so that she could remember him better, whereas I had forgotten Mendel the bibliophile years ago, and I was the one who ought to know that you create books solely to forge links with others even after your own death, thus defending yourself against the inexorable adversary of all life, transience and oblivion.

DOWNFALL OF THE HEART

D ESTINY DOES NOT ALWAYS need the powerful prelude of a sudden violent blow to shake a heart beyond recovery. The unbridled creativity of fate can generate disaster from some small, fleeting incident. In clumsy human language, we call that first slight touch the cause of the catastrophe, and feel surprise in comparing its insignificance with the force, often enormous, that it exerts, but just as the first symptoms of an illness may not show at all, the downfall of a human heart can begin before anything happens to make it visible. Fate has been at work within the victim's mind and his blood long before his soul suffers any outward effects. To know yourself is to defend yourself, but it is usually in vain.

The old man—Salomonsohn was his name, and at home in Germany he could boast of the honorary title of Privy Commercial Councillor—was lying awake in the Gardone hotel where he had taken his family for the Easter holiday. A violent physical pain constricted his chest so that he could hardly breathe. The old man was alarmed; he had troublesome gallstones and often suffered bilious attacks, but instead of following the advice of his doctors and visiting Karlsbad to take the waters there he had decided, for his family's sake, to go further south and stay at this resort on Lake Garda instead. Fearing a dangerous attack of his disorder, he anxiously palpated his broad body, and soon realized with relief, even though he was still in pain, that it was only an ordinary stomach upset, obviously as a result of the unfamiliar Italian food, or the mild food poisoning that was apt to afflict tourists. Feeling less alarmed, he let his shaking hand drop back, but the pressure on his chest continued and kept him from breathing easily. Groaning, the old man made the effort of getting out of bed to move about a little. Sure enough, when he was standing the pressure eased, and even more so when he was walking. But there was not much space to walk about in the dark room, and he was afraid of waking his wife in the other twin bed and causing her unnecessary concern. So he put on his dressing gown and a pair of felt slippers, and groped his way out into the corridor to walk up and down there for a little while and lessen the pain.

As he opened the door into the dark corridor, the sound of the clock in the church tower echoed through the open windows—four chimes, first weighty and then dying softly away over the lake. Four in the morning.

The long corridor lay in complete darkness. But from his clear memory of it in daytime, the old man knew that it was wide and straight, so he walked along it, breathing heavily, from end to end without needing a light, and then again and again, pleased to notice that the tightness in his chest was fading. Almost entirely freed from pain now by this beneficial exercise, he was preparing to return to his room when a sound startled him. He stopped. The sound was a whispering in the darkness somewhere near him, slight yet unmistakable. Woodwork creaked, there were soft voices and movements, a door was opened just a crack and a narrow beam of light cut through the formless darkness. What was it? Instinctively the old man shrank back into a corner, not out of curiosity but obeying a natural sense of awkwardness at being caught by other people engaged in the odd activity of pacing up and down like a sleepwalker. In that one second when the light shone into the corridor, however, he had involuntarily seen, or thought he had seen, a white-clad female figure slipping out of the room and disappearing down the passage. And sure enough, there was a slight click as one of the last doors in the corridor latched shut. Then all was dark and silent again.

The old man suddenly began to sway as if he had suffered a blow to the heart. The only rooms at the far end of the corridor, where the door handle had given away a secret by clicking... the only rooms there were his own, the three-roomed suite that he had booked for his family. He had left his wife asleep and breathing peacefully only a few minutes before, so that female figure—no, he couldn't be mistaken—that figure returning from a venture into a stranger's room could have been no one but his daughter Erna, aged only just nineteen.

The old man was shivering all over with horror. His daughter Erna, his child, that happy, high-spirited child—no, this was impossible, he must be mistaken! But what could she have been doing in a stranger's room if not... Like an injured animal he thrust his own idea away, but the haunting picture of that stealthy figure still haunted his mind, he could not tear it out of his head or banish it. He had to be sure. Panting, he groped his way along the wall of the corridor to her door, which was next to his own bedroom. But he was appalled to see, at this one door in the corridor, a thin line of light showing under the door, and the keyhole was a small dot of treacherous brightness. She still had a light on in her room at four in the morning! And there was more evidence—with a slight crackle from the electric switch the white line of light vanished without trace into darkness. No, it was useless trying to pretend to himself. It was Erna, his daughter, slipping out of a stranger's bed and into her own by night.

The old man was trembling with horror and cold, while at the same time sweat broke out all over his body, flooding the pores of his skin. His first thought was to break in at the shameless girl's door and chastise her with his fists. But his feet were tottering beneath the weight of his broad body. He could hardly summon up the strength to drag himself into his own room and back to bed, where he fell on the pillows like a stricken animal, his senses dulled.

The old man lay motionless in bed. His eyes, wide open, stared at the darkness. He heard his wife breathing easily beside him, without a care in the world. His first thought was to shake her awake, tell her about his dreadful discovery, rage and rant to his heart's content. But how could he express it, how could he put this terrible thing into words? No, such words would never pass his lips. What was he to do, though? What *could* he do?

He tried to think, but his mind was in blind confusion, thoughts flying this way and that like bats in daylight. It was so monstrous— Erna, his tender, well-brought-up child with her melting eyes… How long ago was it, how long ago that he would still find her poring over her schoolbooks, her little pink finger carefully tracing the difficult characters on the page, how long since she used to go straight from school to the confectioner's in her little pale-blue dress, and then he felt her childish kiss with sugar still on her lips? Only yesterday, surely? But no, it was all years ago. Yet how childishly she had begged him yesterday—*really* yesterday—to buy her the blue and gold pullover that looked so pretty in the shop window. "Oh please, dear Papa, please!"—with her hands clasped, with that self-confident, happy smile that he could never resist. And now, now she was stealing away to a strange man's bed by night, not far from his own door, to roll about in it with him, naked and lustful.

My God, my God! thought the old man, instinctively groaning. The shame of it, the shame! My child, my tender, beloved child—an assignation with some man... Who is he? Who can he be? We arrived here in Gardone only three days ago, and she knew none of those spruced-up dandies before—thin-faced Conte Ubaldi, that Italian officer, the baron from Mecklenburg who's a gentleman jockey... they didn't meet on the dance floor until our second day. Has one of them already?... No, he can't have been the first, no... it must have begun earlier, at home, and I knew nothing about it, fool that I am. Poor fool! But what do I know about my wife and daughter anyway? I toil for them every day, I spend fourteen hours a day at my office just to earn money for them, more and more money so that they can have fine dresses and be rich... and when I come home tired in the evening, worn out, they've gone gadding off to the theatre, to balls, out with company, what do I know about them and what they get up to all day long? And now my child with her pure young body has assignations with men by night like a common streetwalker... oh, the shame of it!

The old man groaned again and again. Every new idea deepened his wound and tore it open, as if his brain lay visibly bleeding, with red maggots writhing in it.

But why do I put up with this, he wondered, why do I lie here tormenting myself while she, with her unchaste body, sleeps peacefully? Why didn't I go straight into her room so that she'd know *I* knew her shame? Why didn't I beat her black and blue? Because I'm weak... and a coward... I've always been weak with both of them, I've given way to them in everything, I was proud that I could make their lives easy, even if my own was ruined, I scraped the money together with my fingernails, *pfennig* by *pfennig*, I'd have torn the flesh from my hands to see them content! But as soon as

I'd made them rich they were ashamed of me, I wasn't elegant enough for them any more, too uneducated… where would I have got an education? I was taken out of school aged twelve, I had to earn money, earn and earn, carry cases of samples about from village to village, run agencies in town after town before I could open my own business… and no sooner were they ladies and living in their own house than they didn't like my honourable old name any more. I had to buy the title of Councillor, so that my wife wouldn't be just Frau Salomonsohn, so that she could be Frau Commercial Councillor and put on airs. Put on airs! They laughed at me when I objected to all that putting on airs of distinction, when I objected to what they call high society, when I told them how my mother, God rest her soul, kept house quietly, modestly, just for my father and the rest of us… they called me old-fashioned. "Oh, you're so old-fashioned, Papa!" She was always mocking me… yes, old-fashioned, indeed I am… and now she lies in a strange bed with strange men, my child, my only child! Oh, the shame, the shame of it!

The old man was moaning and sighing in such torment that his wife, in the bed beside his, woke up. "What's the matter?" she drowsily asked. The old man did not move, and held his breath. And so he lay there motionless in the coffin of his torment until morning, with his thoughts eating away at him like worms.

The old man was first at the breakfast table. He sat down with a sigh, unable to face a morsel of food.

Alone again, he thought, always alone! When I go to the office in the morning they're still comfortably asleep, lazily taking their ease after all their dancing and theatre-going… when I come home in the evening they've already gone out to enjoy themselves in company, they don't need me with them. It's the money, the accursed money that's ruined them, made them strangers to me. Fool that I am, I earned it, scraped it together, I stole from myself, made myself poor and them bad with the money... for fifty pointless years I've been toiling, never giving myself a day off, and now I'm all alone...

He felt impatient. Why doesn't she come down, he wondered, I want to talk to her, I have to tell her... we must leave this place at once... why doesn't she come down? I suppose she's too tired, sleeping soundly with a clear conscience while I'm tearing my heart to pieces, old fool that I am... and her mother titivating herself for hours on end, has to take a bath, dress herself, have a manicure, get her hair arranged, she won't be down before eleven, and is it any wonder? How can a child turn out so badly? It's the money, the accursed money...

Light footsteps were approaching behind him. "Good morning, Papa, did you sleep well?" A soft cheek bent down to his side, a light kiss brushed his hammering forehead. Instinctively he drew back; repelled by the sweetly sultry Coty perfume she wore. And then...

"What's the matter, Papa... are you in a cross temper again? Oh, coffee, please, waiter, and ham and eggs... Did you sleep badly, or have you heard bad news?"

The old man restrained himself. He bowed his head—he did not have the courage to look up—and preserved his silence. He saw only her manicured hands on the table, her beloved hands, casually playing with each other like spoilt, slender little greyhounds on the white turf of the tablecloth. He trembled. Timidly, his eyes travelled up the delicate, girlish arms which she had often—but how long ago?—flung around him before she went to sleep. He saw the gentle curve of her breasts moving in time with her breathing under the new pullover. Naked, he thought grimly, stark naked, tossing and turning in bed with a strange man. A man who touched all that, felt it, lavished caresses on it, tasted and enjoyed her… my own flesh and blood, my child… that villainous stranger, oh…

Unconsciously, he had groaned again. "What's the matter with you, Papa?" She moved closer, coaxing him.

What's the matter with me? echoed a voice inside him. A whore for a daughter, and I can't summon up the courage to tell her so.

But he only muttered indistinctly, "Nothing, nothing!" and hastily picked up the newspaper, protecting himself from her questioning gaze behind a barricade of outspread sheets of newsprint. He felt increasingly unable to meet her eyes. His hands were shaking. I ought to tell her now, said his tormented mind, now while we're alone. But his voice failed him; he could not even find the strength to look up.

And suddenly, abruptly, he pushed back his chair and escaped, treading heavily, in the direction of the garden, for he felt a large tear rolling down his cheek against his will, and he didn't want her to see it.

The old man wandered around the garden on his short legs, staring at the lake for a long time. Almost blinded by the unshed tears he was holding back, he still could not help noticing the beauty of the landscape—the hills rose in undulating shades of soft green behind silver light, black-hatched with the thin spires of cypress trees, and beyond the hills were the sterner outlines of the mountains, severe, yet looking down on the beauty of the lake without arrogance, like grave men watching the light-hearted games of beloved children. How mild it all lay there outspread, with open, flowering, hospitable gestures. How it enticed a man to be kindly and happy, that timeless, blessed smile of God at the south he had created! Happy! The old man rocked his heavy head back and forth, confused.

One could be happy here, he thought. I would have liked to be happy myself, just once, feel how beautiful the world of the carefree is for myself, just once, after fifty years of writing and calculating and bargaining and haggling, I would have liked to enjoy a few bright days before they bury me… for sixty-five years, my God, death's hand is in my body now, money is no help and nor are the doctors. I wanted to breathe easily just a little first, have something for myself for once. But my late father always said: contentment is not for the likes of us, we carry our pedlar's packs on our backs to the grave… Yesterday I thought I myself might feel at ease for a change… yesterday I could have been called a happy man, glad of my beautiful, lovely child, glad to give her pleasure… and God has punished me already and taken that away from me. It's all over now for ever… I can't speak to my own child any more, I am ashamed to look her in the eye. I'll always be thinking of this at home, at the office, at night in my bed—where is she now, where has she been, what has she done? I'll never be able to come happily home again, to see her sitting there and then running to meet me, with my heart opening up at the sight of her, so young and lovely… When she kisses me I'll wonder who had her yesterday, who kissed those lips… I'll always live in fear when she's not with me, I'll always be ashamed when I meet her eyes—a man can't live like this, can't live like this…

The old man stumbled back and forth like a drunk, muttering. He kept staring out at the lake, and his tears ran down into his beard. He had to take off his pince-nez and stand there on the narrow path with his moist, short-sighted eyes revealed, looking so foolish that a gardener's boy who was passing stopped in surprise, laughed aloud and called out a few mocking words in Italian at the bewildered old man. That roused him from his turmoil of pain, and he put his pince-nez on and stole aside into the garden to sit on a bench somewhere and hide from the boy.

But as he approached a remote part of the garden, a laugh to his left startled him again... a laugh that he knew and that went to his heart. That laughter had been music to him for nineteen years, the light laughter of her high spirits... for that laughter he had travelled third-class by night to Poland and Hungary so that he could pour out money before them, rich soil from which that carefree merriment grew. He had lived only for that laughter, while inside his body his gall bladder fell sick... just so that that laughter could always ring out from her beloved mouth. And now the same laughter cut him to the heart like a red-hot saw.

Yet it drew him to it despite his reluctance. She was standing on the tennis court, twirling the racket in her bare hand, gracefully throwing it up and catching it again in play. At the same time as the racket flew up, her light-hearted laughter rose to the azure sky. The three gentlemen admiringly watched her, Conte Ubaldi in a loose tennis shirt, the officer in the trim uniform that showed off his muscles, the gentleman jockey in an immaculate pair of breeches, three sharply profiled, statuesque male figures around a plaything fluttering like a butterfly. The old man himself stared, captivated. Good God, how lovely she was in her pale, ankle-length dress, the sun dusting her blonde hair with liquid gold! And how happily her young limbs felt their own lightness as she leapt and ran, intoxicated and intoxicating as her joints responded to the free-and-easy rhythm of her movements. Now she flung the white tennis ball merrily up to the sky, then a second and a third after it, it was wonderful to see how the slender wand of her girlish body bent and stretched, leaping up now to catch the last ball. He had never seen her like that before, incandescent with high spirits, an elusive, wavering flame, the silvery trill of her laughter above the blazing of her body, like a virginal goddess escaped in panic from the southern garden with its clinging ivy and the gentle surface of the lake. At home she never stretched that slender, sinewy body in such a wild dance or played competitive games. No, he had never seen her like this within the sombre walls of the crowded city, had never heard her voice rise like lark-song set free from the earthly confines of her throat in merriment that was almost song, not indoors and not in the street. She had never been so beautiful. The old man stared and stared. He had forgotten everything, he just watched and watched that white, elusive flame. And he would have stood like that, endlessly absorbing her image with a passionate gaze, if she had not finally caught the last of the balls she was juggling with a breathless, fluttering leap, turning nimbly, and pressed them to her breast breathing fast, face flushed, but with a proud and laughing gaze. "*Brava, brava!*" cried the three gentlemen, who had been intently watching her clever juggling of the balls, applauding as if she had finished an operatic aria. Their guttural voices roused the old man from his enchantment, and he stared grimly at them.

So there they are, the villains, he thought, his heart thudding. There they are—but which of them is it? Which of those three has had her? Oh yes, how finely rigged out they are, shaved and perfumed, idle dandies... while men like me still sit in offices in their old age, in shabby trousers, wearing down the heels of their shoes visiting customers... and for all I know the fathers of these fine fellows may still be toiling away today, wearing their hands out so that their sons can travel the world, wasting time at their leisure, their faces browned and carefree, their impudent eyes bright. Easy for them to be cheerful, they only have to throw a silly, vain child a few sweet words and she'll fall into bed... But which of the three is it, which is it? One of them, I know, is seeing her naked through her dress and smacking his lips. I've had her, he's thinking, he's known her hot and naked, we'll do it again this evening, he thinks, winking at her—oh, the bastard, the dog, yes, if only I could whip him like a dog!

And now they had noticed him standing there. His daughter swung up her racket in a salutation, and smiled at him, the gentlemen wished him good day. He did not thank them, only stared at his daughter's smiling lips with brimming, bloodshot eyes. To think that you can laugh like that, he thought, you shameless creature... and one of those men may be laughing to himself, telling himself—there goes the stupid old Jew who lies snoring in bed all night... if only he knew, the old fool! Oh yes, I do know, you fine fellows laugh, you tread me underfoot like dirt... but my daughter, so pretty and willing, she'll tumble into bed with you... and as for her mother, she's a little stout now, but she goes about all dolled up with her face painted, and if you were to make eyes at her, who knows, she might yet venture to dance a step or so with you... You're right, you dogs, you're right when they run after you, those shameless women, women on heat... what's it to you that another man's heart is breaking so long as you can have your fun, fun with those shameless females... someone should take a revolver and shoot you down, you deserve to be horsewhipped... but yes, you're right, so long as no one does anything, so long as I swallow my rage like a dog returning to his vomit... you're right, if a father is so cowardly, so shockingly cowardly... if he doesn't go to the shameless girl, take hold of her, drag her away from you... if he just stands there saying nothing, bitter gall in his mouth, a coward, a coward, a coward...

The old man clutched the balustrade as helpless rage shook him. And suddenly he spat on the ground in front of his feet and staggered out of the garden.

The old man made his way unsteadily into the little town. Suddenly he stopped in front of a display window full of all kinds of things for tourists' needs—shirts and nets, blouses and angling equipment, ties, books, tins of biscuits, not in chance confusion but built up into artificial pyramids and colourfully arranged on shelves. However, his gaze went to just one object, lying disregarded amidst this elegant jumble—a gnarled walking stick, stout and solid with an iron tip, heavy in the hand; it would probably come down with a good thump. Strike him down, thought the old man, strike the dog down! The idea transported him into a confused, almost lustful turmoil of feeling which sent him into the shop, and he bought the stout stick quite cheaply. And no sooner was the weighty, heavy, menacing thing in his hand than he felt stronger. A weapon always makes the physically weak more sure of themselves. It was as if the handle of the stick tensed and tautened his muscles. "Strike him down... strike the dog down!" he muttered to himself, and unconsciously his heavy, stumbling gait turned to a firmer, more upright, faster rhythm. He walked, even ran up and down the path by the shores of the lake, breathing hard and sweating, but more from the passion spreading through him than because of his accelerated pace. For his hand was clutching the heavy handle of the stick more and more tightly.

Armed with this weapon, he entered the blue, cool shadows of the hotel lobby, his angry eyes searching for the invisible enemy. And sure enough, there in the corner they were sitting together on comfortable wicker chairs, drinking whisky and soda through straws, talking cheerfully in idle good fellowship—his wife, his daughter and the inevitable trio of gentlemen. Which of them is it, he wondered, which of them is it? And his fist clenched around the handle of the heavy stick. Whose skull do I smash in, whose, whose? But Erna, misunderstanding his restless, searching glances, was already jumping up and running to him. "So here you are, Papa! We've been looking for you everywhere. Guess what, Baron von Medwitz is going to take us for a drive in his Fiat, we're going to drive all along the lake to Desenzano!" And she affectionately led him to their table, as if he ought to thank the gentlemen for the invitation.

They had risen politely and were offering him their hands. The old man trembled. But the girl's warm presence, placating him, lay soft and intoxicating against his arm. His will was paralysed as he shook the three hands one by one, sat down in silence, took out a cigar and bit grimly into the soft end of it. Above him, the casual conversation went on, in French, with much high-spirited laughter from several voices.

The old man sat there, silent and hunched, biting the end of his cigar until his teeth were brown with tobacco juice. They're right, he thought, they're right, I deserve to be spat at... now I've shaken their hands! Shaken hands with all three, and I know that one of them's the villain. Here I am sitting quietly at the same table with him, and I don't strike him down, no, I don't strike him down, I shake hands with him civilly... they're right, quite right if they laugh at me... and see the way they talk, ignoring me as if I weren't here at all! I might already be underground... and they both know, Erna and my wife, that I don't understand a word of French. They both know that, both of them, but no one asked me whether I minded, if only for form's sake, just because I sit here so foolishly, feeling so ridiculous. I might be thin air to them, nothing but thin air, a nuisance, a hanger-on, something in the way of their fun... someone to be ashamed of, they tolerate me only because I make so much money. Money, money, always that wretched, filthy lucre, the money I've spent indulging them, money with God's curse on it. They don't say a word to me, my wife, my own child, they talk away to these idlers, their eyes are all for those smooth, smartly rigged-out dandies... see how they smile at those fine gentlemen, it tickles their fancy, as if they felt their hands on bare female flesh. And I put up with it all. I sit here listening to their laughter, I don't understand what they say, and yet I sit here instead of striking out with my fists, thrashing them with my stick, driving them apart before they begin coupling before my very eyes. I let it all pass... I sit here silent, stupid, a coward, coward, coward...

"Will you allow me?" asked the Italian officer, in laborious German, reaching for his lighter.

Startled out of his heated thoughts, the old man sat up very erect and stared grimly at the unsuspecting young officer. Anger was seething inside him. For a moment his hand clutched the handle of the stick convulsively. But then he let the corners of his mouth turn down again, stretching it into a senseless grin. "Oh, I'll allow you!" he sardonically repeated. "To be sure I'll allow you, ha ha, I'll allow you anything you want—ha ha!—anything I have is entirely at your disposal... you can do just as you like."

The bewildered officer stared at him. With his poor command of German, he had not quite understood, but that wry, grinning smile made him uneasy. The gentleman jockey from Germany sat up straight, startled, the two women went white as a sheet—for a split second the air among them all was breathless and motionless, as electric as the tiny pause between a flash of lightning and the thunder that follows.

But then the fierce distortion of his face relaxed, the stick slid out of his clutch. Like a beaten dog, the old man retreated into his own thoughts and coughed awkwardly, alarmed by his own boldness. Trying to smooth over the embarrassing tension, Erna returned to her light conversational tone, the German baron replied, obviously anxious to maintain the cheerful mood, and within a few minutes the interrupted tide of words was in full flow once more.

The old man sat among the others as they chattered, entirely withdrawn; and you might have thought he was asleep. His heavy stick, now that the clutch of his hands was relaxed, dangled useless between his legs. His head, propped on one hand, sank lower and lower. But no one paid him any more attention, the wave of chatter rolled over his silence, sometimes laughter sprayed up, sparkling, at a joking remark, but he was lying motionless below it all in endless darkness, drowned in shame and pain.

The three gentlemen rose to their feet, Erna followed readily, her mother more slowly; in obedience to someone's light-hearted suggestion they were going into the music room next door, and did not think it necessary to ask the old man drowsing away there to come with them. Only when he suddenly became aware of the emptiness around him did he wake, like a sleeping man roused by the cold when his blanket has slipped off the bed in the night, and cold air blows over his naked body. Instinctively his eyes went to the chairs they had left, but jazzy music was already coming from the room next door, syncopated and garish. He heard laughter and cries of encouragement. They were dancing next door. Yes, dancing, always dancing, they could do that all right! Always stirring up the blood, always rubbing avidly against each other, chafing until the dish was cooked and ready. Dancing in the evening, at night, in bright daylight, idlers, gentlemen of leisure with time on their hands, that was how they charmed the women.

Bitterly, he picked up his stout stick again and dragged himself after them. At the door he stopped. The German baron, the gentleman jockey, was sitting at the piano, half turned away from the keyboard so that he could watch the dancers at the same time as he rattled out an American hit song on the keys, a tune he obviously knew more or less by heart. Erna was dancing with the officer; the long-legged Conte Ubaldi was rhythmically pushing her strong, sturdy mother forward and back, not without some difficulty. But the old man had eyes for no one but Erna and her partner. How that slender greyhound of a man laid his hands, soft and flattering, on her delicate shoulders, as if she belonged to him entirely! How her body, swaying, following his lead, pressed close to his, as if promising herself, how they danced, intertwined, before his very eyes, with passion that they had difficulty in restraining! Yes, he was the man—for in those two bodies moving as one there burnt a sense of familiarity, something in common already in their blood. He was the one—it could only be he, he read it from her eyes, half-closed and yet brimming over, in that fleeting, hovering movement reflecting the memory of lustful moments already enjoyed—he was the man, he was the thief who came by night to seize and ardently penetrate what his child, his own child, now concealed in her thin, semi-transparent, flowing dress! Instinctively he stepped closer to tear her away from the man. But she didn't even notice him. With every movement of the rhythm, giving herself up to the guiding touch of the dancer, the seducer leading her, with her head thrown back and her moist mouth open, she swayed softly to the beat of the music, with no sense of space or time or of the man, the trembling, panting old man who was staring at her in a frenzied ecstasy of rage, his eyes bloodshot. She felt only herself, her own young limbs as she unresistingly followed the syncopation of the breathlessly swirling dance music. She felt only herself, and the fact that a male creature so close to her desired her, his strong arm surrounded her, and she must preserve her balance and not fall against him with greedy lips, hotly inhaling his breath as she abandoned herself to him. And all this was magically known to the old man in his own blood, his own shattered being—always, whenever the dance swept her away from him, he felt as if she were sinking for ever.

Suddenly, as if the string of an instrument had broken, the music stopped in the middle of a bar. The German baron jumped up. "*Assez joué pour vous*," he laughed. "*Maintenant je veux danser moi-même.*"—"You've had your fun. Now I want to dance myself!" They all cheerfully agreed, the group stopped dancing in couples and moved into an informal, fluttering dance all together.

The old man came back to his senses—how he wanted to do something now, say something! Not just stand about so foolishly, so pitifully superfluous! His wife was dancing by, gasping slightly from exertion but warm with contentment. Anger brought him to a sudden decision. He stepped into her path. "Come with me," he said brusquely. "I have to talk to you."

She looked at him in surprise. Little beads of sweat moistened his pale brow, his eyes were staring wildly around. What did he want? Why disturb her just now? An excuse was already forming on her lips, but there was something so convulsive, so dangerous in his demeanour that, suddenly remembering the grim outburst over the lighter just now, she reluctantly followed him.

"*Excusez, messieurs, un instant!*" she said, turning back apologetically to the gentlemen. So she'll apologize to *them*, thought the agitated old man grimly, she didn't apologize to me when she got up from the table. I'm no more than a dog to her, a doormat to be trodden on. But they're right, oh yes, they're right if I put up with it.

She was waiting, her eyebrows sternly raised; he stood before her, his lip quivering, like a schoolboy facing his teacher.

"Well?" she finally asked.

"I don't want… I don't want…" he stammered awkwardly. "I don't want you—you and Erna—I don't want you mixing with those people."

"With what people?" Deliberately pretending not to understand, she looked up indignantly, as if he had insulted her personally.

"With those men in there." Angrily, he jerked his chin in the direction of the music room. "I don't like it… I don't want you to…"

"And why not, may I ask?"

Always that inquisitorial tone, he thought bitterly, as if I were a servant. Still more agitated, he stammered, "I have my reasons… I don't like it. I don't want Erna talking to those men. I don't have to tell you everything."

"Then I'm sorry," she said, flaring up, "but I consider all three gentlemen extremely well-brought up, far more distinguished company than we keep at home."

"Distinguished company! Those idlers, those… those…" Rage was throttling him more intolerably than ever. And suddenly he stamped his foot. "I don't want it, I forbid it! Do you understand that?"

"No," she said coldly. "I don't understand any of what you say. I don't know why I should spoil the girl's pleasure…"

"Her pleasure… her pleasure!" He was staggering as if under a heavy blow, his face red, his forehead streaming with sweat. His hand groped in the air for his heavy stick, either to support himself or to hit out with it. But he had left it behind. That brought him back to his senses. He forced himself to keep calm as a wave of heat suddenly passed over his heart. He went closer to his wife, as if to take her hand. His voice was low now, almost pleading. "You... you don't understand. It's not for myself... I'm begging you only because... it's the first thing I've asked you for years, let's go away from here. Just away, to Florence, to Rome, anywhere you want, I don't mind. You can decide it all, just as you like. I only want to get away from here, please, away... away, today, this very day. I... I can't bear it any longer, I can't."

"Today?" Surprised, dismissively, she frowned. "Go away today? What a ridiculous idea! Just because you don't happen to like those gentlemen. Well, you don't have to mingle with them."

He was still standing there, hands raised pleadingly. "I can't bear it, I told you... I can't, I can't. Don't ask me any more, please... but believe me, I can't bear it, I can't. Do this for me, just for once, do something for me..."

In the music room someone had begun hammering at the piano again. She looked up, touched by his cry despite herself, but how very ridiculous he looked, that short fat man, his face red as if he had suffered a stroke, his eyes wild and swollen, his hands emerging from sleeves too short for him and trembling in the air. It was embarrassing to see him standing there in such a pitiful state. Her milder feelings froze.

"That's impossible," she informed him. "We've agreed to go out for that drive today, and as for leaving tomorrow when we've booked for three weeks... why, we'd make ourselves look ridiculous. I can't see the faintest reason for leaving early. I am staying here, and so is Erna, we are not—"

"And I can go, you're saying? I'm only in the way here, spoiling your... pleasure."

With that sombre cry he cut her short in mid-sentence. His hunched, massive body had reared up, he had clenched his hands into fists, a vein was trembling alarmingly on his forehead in anger. He wanted to get something else out, a word or a blow. But he turned abruptly, stumbled to the stairs, moving faster and faster on his heavy legs, and hurried up them like a man pursued.

Gasping, the old man went hastily up the stairs; he wanted only to be in his room now, alone, try to control himself, take care not to do anything silly! He had already reached the first floor when—there it came, the pain, as if a burning claw were tearing open his guts from the inside. He suddenly stumbled back against the wall, white as a sheet. Oh, that raging, burning pain kneading away at him; he had to grit his teeth to keep himself from crying out loud. Groaning, his tormented body writhed.

He knew at once what was wrong—it was his gall bladder, one of those fearful attacks that had often plagued him recently, but had never before tortured him so cruelly. Next moment, in the middle of his pain, he remembered that the doctor had prescribed "no agitation". Through the pain he grimly mocked himself. Easily said, he thought, no agitation—my dear good Professor, can you tell me how to avoid agitation when... oh, oh...

The old man was whimpering as the invisible, red-hot claw worked away inside his poor body. With difficulty, he dragged himself to the door of the sitting room of the suite, pushed it open, and fell on the ottoman, stuffing the cushions into his mouth. As he lay there the pain immediately lessened slightly; the hot nails of that claw were no longer reaching so infernally deep into his sore guts. I ought to make myself a compress, he remembered, I must take those drops, then it will soon be better.

But there was no one there to help him, no one. And he himself had no strength to drag himself into the next room, or even reach the bell.

There's no one here, he thought bitterly, I shall die like a dog sooner or later, because I know what it is that hurts, it's not my gall bladder, it's Death growing in me. I know it, I'm a defeated man, no professors, no drinking the waters at spas can help me… you don't recover from this sort of thing, not at sixty-five. I know what's piercing me and tearing me from the inside, it's Death, and the few years I have left will not be life, just dying, dying. But when did I ever really live? Live my own life, for myself? What kind of life have I had, scraping money together all the time, always for other people, and now, what help is it to me now? I've had a wife, I married her as a girl, I knew her body and she bore me a child. Year after year we lay together in the same bed… and now, where is she now? I don't recognize her face any more… she speaks so strangely to me, and never thinks of my life, of all I feel and think and suffer… she's been a stranger to me for years now… Where has my life gone, where did it go?… And I had a child, watched her grow up, I thought I'd begin to live again through her, a brighter, happier life than was granted to me, in her I wouldn't entirely die… and now she steals away by night to throw herself at men. There's only me, I shall die alone, all alone… I'm already dead to those two. My God, my God, I was never so much alone…

The claw sometimes closed grimly inside him and then let go again. But another pain was hammering deeper and deeper into his temples; his thoughts, harsh, sharp, were like mercilessly hot gravel in his forehead, he mustn't think just now, mustn't think! The old man had torn open his jacket and waistcoat—his bloated body quivered, plump and shapeless, under his billowing shirt. Cautiously he pressed his hand to the painful place. All that hurts there is me, he felt, it's only me, only this piece of hot skin... and only what's clawing around in it there still belongs to me, it is *my* illness, *my* death... I am all it is... I am not a Privy Commercial Councillor any more, with a wife and child and money and a house and a business... this is all I really am, what I feel with my fingers, my body and the heat inside it hurting me. Everything else is folly, makes no sense now... because what hurts in there hurts only me, what concerns me concerns me alone. They don't understand me any more, and I don't understand them... you are all alone with yourself in the end. I never felt it so much before... But now I know, now I lie here feeling Death under my skin, too late now in my sixty-fifth year, just before dying, now while they dance and go for walks or drift aimlessly about, those shameless women... now I know it, I lived only for them, not that they thank me for it, and never for myself, not for an hour. But what do I care for them now... what do I care for them... why think of them when they never think of me? Better die than accept their pity... what do I care for them now?...

Gradually receding, the pain ebbed away; the cruel hand did not grasp into the suffering man with such red-hot claws. But it left behind a dull, sombre feeling, barely perceptible as pain now, yet something alien pressing and pushing, tunnelling away inside him. The old man lay with his eyes closed, attending carefully to this soft pushing and pulling; he felt as if a strange, unknown power were hollowing something out in him, first with sharp tools, then with blunter ones. It was like something coming adrift, fibre by fibre, within his body. The tearing was not so fierce now, and did not hurt any more. But there was something quietly smouldering and rotting inside him, something beginning to die.

All he had lived through, all he had loved, was lost in that slowly consuming flame, burning black before it fell apart, crumbling and charred, into the lukewarm mire of indifference. Something was happening, he knew it vaguely, something was happening while he lay like this, reflecting passionately on his life. Something was coming to an end. What was it? He listened and listened to what was going on inside him.

And slowly his heart began to fail him.

The old man lay in the twilight of the room with his eyes closed. He was still half awake, half already dreaming. And then, between sleeping and waking, it seemed to him in the confusion of his feelings as if, from somewhere or other, something moist and hot was seeping softly into him from a wound that did not hurt and that he was unaware of having suffered. It was like being drained of his own blood. It did not hurt, that invisible flow, it did not run very strongly. The drops fell only slowly, like warm tears trickling down, and each of them struck him in the middle of the heart. But his heart, his dark heart, made no sound and quietly soaked up that strange torrent. Soaked it up like a sponge, became heavier and heavier with it, his heart was already swelling with it, brimming over, it was spilling into the narrow frame of his chest. Gradually filling up, overflowing with its own weight, whatever it was began gently pulling to expand itself, pulling at taut muscles, pressing harder and harder and forcing his painful heart, gigantic by now, down after its own weight. And now (oh, how this hurt!) now the weight came loose from the fibres of flesh—very slowly, not like a stone or a falling fruit, no, like a sponge soaked with moisture it sank deeper and ever deeper into a warm void, down into something without being that was outside himself, into vast and endless night. All at once it was terribly still in the place where that warm, brimming heart had been a moment ago. What yawned empty there now was uncanny and cold. No sensation of thudding any more, no dripping now, all was very still and perfectly dead inside him. And his shuddering breast surrounded that silent and incomprehensible void like a hollow black coffin.

So strong was this dreamlike feeling, so deep his confusion, that when the old man began to wake he instinctively put his hand to the left side of his chest to see whether his heart was still here. But thank God, he felt a pulse, a hollow, rhythmical pulse beating below his groping fingers, and yet it might have been beating mutely in a vacuum, as if his heart was really gone. For strange to say, it suddenly seemed as if his body had left him of its own accord. No pain wrenched at it any more, no memory twitched painfully, all was silent in there, fixed and turned to stone. What's this, he wondered, when just now I felt such pain, such hot pressure, when every fibre was twitching? What has happened to me? He listened, as if to the sounds in a cavern, to find out whether what had been there before was still moving. But those rushing sounds, the dripping, the thudding, they were far away. He listened and listened, no echo came, none at all. Nothing hurt him any more, nothing was swelling up to torment him; it must be as empty and black in there as a hollow, burnt-out tree. And all at once he felt as if he had already died, or something in him had died, his blood was so sluggish and silent. His own body lay under him cold as a corpse, and he was afraid to feel it with his warm hand.

There in his room the old man, listening to what was happening to him, did not hear the sound of church clocks down by the lake striking the hours, each hour bringing deeper twilight. The night was already gathering around him, darkness fell on the things in the room as it flowed away into the night, at last even the pale sky visible in the rectangle of the window was immersed in total darkness. The old man never noticed, but only stared at the blackness in himself, listening to the void there as if to his own death.

Then, at last, there was exuberant laughter in the room next door. A switch was pressed, and light came through the crack of the doorway, for the door was only ajar. The old man roused himself with a start—his wife, his daughter! They would find him here on the day bed and ask questions. He hastily buttoned up his jacket and waistcoat; why should they know about the attack he had suffered, what business of theirs was it?

But the two women had not come in search of him. They were obviously in a hurry; the imperious gong was striking for the third time. They seemed to be dressing for dinner; listening, he could hear every movement through the half-open doorway. Now they were opening the shutters, now they were putting their rings down on the washstand with a light chink, now shoes were tapping on the floor, and from time to time they talked to each other. Every word, every syllable came to the old man's ears with cruel clarity. First they talked about the gentlemen, mocking them a little, about a chance incident on the drive, light, inconsequent remarks as they washed and moved around, dressing and titivating themselves. Then, suddenly, the conversation turned to him.

"Where's Papa?" Erna asked, sounding surprised that he had occurred to her so late.

"How should I know?" That was her mother's voice, instantly irritated by the mere mention of him. "Probably waiting for us down in the lobby, reading the stock prices in the Frankfurt newspaper for the hundredth time—they're all he's interested in.

Do you think he's even looked at the lake? He doesn't like it here, he told me so at mid-day. He wanted us to leave today."

"Leave today? But why?" Erna's voice again.

"I really don't know. Who can tell what he has in mind? He doesn't like the other guests here, the company of those gentlemen doesn't suit him—probably he feels how little his company suits them. Really, the way he goes around here is disgraceful, with his clothes all crumpled, his collar open... you should suggest that he might look a little more *soigné*, at least in the evenings, he'll listen to you. And this morning... I thought I'd sink into the ground to hear him flare up at the lieutenant when he wanted to borrow Papa's lighter."

"Yes, Mama, what was that all about? I wanted to ask you, what was the matter with Papa? I've never seen him like that before... I was really shocked."

"Oh, he was just in a bad temper. I expect prices on the stock exchange have fallen. Or perhaps it was because we were speaking French. He can't bear other people to have a nice time. You didn't notice, but while we were dancing he was standing at the door of the music room like a murderer lurking behind a tree. Leave today! Leave on the spot! Just because that's what he suddenly feels like doing. Well, if he doesn't like it here, there's no need for him to grudge us our pleasure... but I'm not going to bother with his whims any more, whatever he says and does."

The conversation ended. Obviously they had finished dressing for dinner. Yes, the door was opened, they were leaving the room, he heard the click of the switch, and the light went out.

The old man sat perfectly still on the ottoman. He had heard every word. But strange to say, it no longer hurt, it did not hurt at all. The clockwork in his breast that had been hammering and tearing at him fiercely not so long ago had come to a standstill;

it must be broken. He had felt no reaction to the sharp touch of their remarks. No anger, no hatred… nothing, nothing. Calmly, he buttoned up his clothes, cautiously made his way downstairs, and sat down at the dinner table with them as if they were strangers.

He did not speak to them that evening, and for their part they did not notice his silence, which was as concentrated as a clenched fist. After dinner he went back to his room, again without a word, lay down on the bed and put out the light. Only much later did his wife come up from the evening's cheerful entertainment, and thinking he was asleep she undressed in the dark. Soon he heard her heavy, easy breathing.

The old man, alone with himself, stared open-eyed at the endless void of the night. Beside him something lay in the dark, breathing deeply; he made an effort to remember that the body drawing in the same air in the same room was the woman whom he had known when she was young and ardent, who had borne him a child, a body bound to him through the deepest mystery of the blood; he kept forcing himself to think that the warm, soft body there—he had only to put out a hand to touch it—had once been a life that was part of his own. But strangely, the memory aroused no feelings in him any more. And he heard her regular breathing only like the murmuring of little waves coming through the open window as they broke softly on the pebbles near the shore. It was all far away and unreal, something strange was lying beside him only by chance—it was over, over for ever.

Once he found himself trembling very slightly, and stole to his daughter's door. So she was out of her room again tonight. He did feel a small, sharp pang in the heart he had thought dead.

For a second, something twitched there like a nerve before it died away entirely. That was over now as well. Let her do as she likes, he thought, what is it to me?

And the old man lay back on his pillow again. Once more the darkness closed in on his aching head, and that cool, blue sensation seeped into his blood—a beneficial feeling. Soon light slumber cast its shadow over his exhausted senses.

When his wife woke up in the morning she saw her husband already in his coat and hat. "What are you doing?" she asked, still drowsy from sleep.

The old man did not turn around. He was calmly packing his night things in a small suitcase. "You know what I'm doing. I'm going home. I'm taking only the necessities; you can have the rest sent after me."

His wife took fright. What was all this? She had never heard his voice like that before, bringing each word out cold and hard. She swung both legs out of bed. "You're not going away, surely? Wait… we'll come with you, I've already told Erna that…"

He only waved this vigorously away. "No, no, don't let it disturb you." And without looking back he made his way to the door. He had to put the suitcase down on the floor for a moment in order to press down the door handle. And in that one fitful second a memory came back—a memory of thousands of times when he had put down his case of samples like that as he left the doors of strangers with a servile bow, ingratiating himself with an eye to further business. But he had no business here and now, so he omitted any greeting. Without a look or a word he picked up his suitcase again and closed the door firmly between himself and his old life.

Neither mother nor daughter understood what had happened. But the strikingly abrupt and determined nature of his departure made them both uneasy. They wrote to him back at home in south Germany at once, elaborately explaining that they assumed there had been some misunderstanding, writing almost affectionately, asking with concern how his journey had been, and whether he had arrived safely. Suddenly compliant, they expressed themselves ready and willing to break off their holiday at any time. There was no reply. They wrote again, more urgently, they sent telegrams, but there was still no reply. Only the sum of money that they had said they needed in one of the letters arrived—a postal remittance bearing the stamp of his firm, without a word or greeting of his own.

Such an inexplicable and oppressive state of affairs made them bring their own return home forward. Although they had sent a telegram in advance, there was no one to meet them at the station, and they found everything unprepared at home. In an absent-minded moment, so the servants told them, the master had left the telegram lying on the table and had gone out, without leaving any instructions. In the evening, when they were already sitting down to eat, they heard the sound of the front door at last. They jumped up and ran to meet him. He looked at them in surprise—obviously he had forgotten the telegram—patiently accepted his daughter's embrace, but without any particular expression of feeling, let them lead him to the dining room and tell him about their journey. However, he asked no questions, smoked his cigar in silence, sometimes answered briefly, sometimes did not notice what they said at all; it was as if he were asleep with his eyes open. Then he got up ponderously and went to his room.

And it was the same for the next few days. His anxious wife tried to get him to talk to her, but in vain; the more she pressed him, the more evasively he reacted. Some place inside him was barred to her, inaccessible, an entrance had been walled up. He still ate with them, sat with them for a while when callers came, but in silence, absorbed in his own thoughts. However, he took no part in their lives any more, and when guests happened to look into his eyes in the middle of a conversation, they had the unpleasant feeling that a dead man's dull and shallow gaze was looking past them.

Even those who hardly knew him soon noticed the increasing oddity of the old man's behaviour. Acquaintances began to nudge each other on the sly if they met him in the street—there went the old man, one of the richest men in the city, slinking along by the wall like a beggar, his hat dented and set at a crooked angle on his head, his coat dusted with cigar ash, reeling in a peculiar way at every step and usually muttering aloud under his breath. If people greeted him, he looked up in surprise; if they addressed him he stared at them vacantly, and forgot to shake hands. At first a number of acquaintances thought he must have gone deaf, and repeated what they had said in louder tones. He was not deaf, but it always took him time to wake himself, as it were, from his internal sleep, and then he would lapse back into a strange state of abstraction in the middle of the conversation. All of a sudden the light would go out of his eyes, he would break off the discussion hastily and stumble on, without noticing the surprise of the person who had spoken to him. He always seemed to have emerged from a dark dream, from a cloudy state of self-absorption; other people, it was obvious, no longer existed for him. He never asked how anyone was; even in his own home he did not notice his wife's gloomy desperation or his daughter's baffled questions. He read no newspapers, listened to no conversations; not a word, not a question penetrated his dull and overcast indifference for a moment. Even what was closest to him became strange. He sometimes went to his office to sign letters. But if his secretary came back an hour later to fetch them, duly signed, he found the old man just as he had left him, lost in reverie over the unread letters and with the same vacant look in his eyes. In the end he himself realized that he was only in the way at the office, and stayed away entirely.

But the strangest and most surprising thing about the old man, to the whole city, was the fact that although he had never been among the most devoutly observant members of its Jewish community he suddenly became pious. Indifferent to all else, often unpunctual at meals and meetings, he never failed to be at the synagogue at the appointed hour. He stood there in his black silk cap, his prayer shawl around his shoulders, always at the same place, where his father once used to stand, rocking his weary head back and forth as he chanted psalms. Here, in the dim light of the room where the words echoed around him, dark and strange, he was most alone with himself. A kind of peace descended on his confused mind here, responding to the darkness in his own breast. However, when prayers were read for the dead, and he saw the families, children and friends of the departed dutifully bowing down and calling on the mercy of God for those who had left this world, his eyes were sometimes clouded. He was the last of his line, and he knew it. No one would say a prayer for him. And so he devoutly murmured the words with the congregation, thinking of himself as one might think of the dead.

Once, late in the evening, he was coming back from wandering the city in a daze, and was halfway home when rain began to fall. As usual, the old man had forgotten his umbrella. There were cabs for hire quite cheaply, entrances to buildings and glazed porches offered shelter from the torrential rain that was soon pouring down, but the strange old man swayed and stumbled on through the wet weather. A puddle collected in the dent in his hat and seeped through, rivulets streamed down from his own dripping sleeves; he took no notice but trudged on, the only person out and about in the deserted street. And so, drenched and dripping, looking more like a tramp than the master of a handsome villa, he reached the entrance of his house just at the moment when a car with its headlights on stopped right beside him, flinging up more muddy water on the inattentive pedestrian. The door swung open, and his wife hastily got out of the brightly lit the interior, followed by some distinguished visitor or other holding an umbrella over her, and then a second man. He drew level with them just outside the door. His wife recognized him and was horrified to see him in such a state, dripping wet, his clothes crumpled, looking like a bundle of something pulled out of the water, and instinctively she turned her eyes away. The old man understood at once—she was ashamed of him in front of her guests. And without emotion or bitterness, he walked a little further as if he were a stranger, to spare her the embarrassment of an introduction, and turned humbly in at the servants' entrance.

From that day on the old man always used the servants' stairs in his own house. He was sure not to meet anyone here, he was in no one's way and no one was in his. He stayed away from meals—an old maidservant brought something to his room. If his wife or daughter tried to get in to speak to him, he would send them away again with a vague murmur that was none the less clearly a refusal to see them. In the end they left him alone, and gradually stopped asking how he was, nor did he enquire after anyone or anything. He sometimes heard music and laughter coming through the walls from the other rooms in the house, which were already strange to him, he heard vehicles pass by until late at night, but he was so indifferent to everything that he did not even look out of the window. What was it to do with him? Only the dog sometimes came up and lay down by his forgotten master's bed.

Nothing hurt in his dead heart now, but the black mole was tunnelling on inside his body, tearing a bloodstained path into quivering flesh. His attacks grew more frequent from week to week, and at last, in agony, he gave way to his doctor's urging to have himself thoroughly examined. The professor looked grave. Carefully preparing the way, he said he thought that at this point an operation was essential. But the old man did not take fright, he only smiled wearily. Thank God, now it was coming to an end. An end to dying, and now came the good part, death. He would not let the doctor say a word to his family, the day was decided, and he made ready. For the last time, he went to his firm (where no one expected to see him any more, and they all looked at him as if he were a stranger), sat down once more in the old black leather chair where he had sat for thirty years, a whole lifetime, for thousands and thousands of hours, told them to bring him a cheque book and made out a cheque. He took it to the rabbi of the synagogue, who was almost frightened by the size of the sum. It was for charitable works and for his grave, he said, and to avoid all thanks he hastily stumbled out, losing his hat, but he did not even bend to pick it up. And so, bareheaded, eyes dull in his wrinkled face, now yellow with sickness, he went on his way, followed by surprised glances, to his parents' grave in the cemetery. There a few idlers gazed at the old man, and were surprised to hear him talk out loud and at length to the mouldering tombstones as if they were human beings. Was he announcing his imminent arrival to them, or asking for their blessing? No one could hear the words, but his lips moved, murmuring, and his shaking head was bowed deeper and deeper in prayer. At the way out of the cemetery beggars, who knew him well by sight, crowded around him. He hastily took all the coins and notes out of his pockets, and had distributed them when a wrinkled old woman limped up, later than the rest, begging for something for herself. In confusion, he searched his pockets, but there was nothing left. However, he still had something strange and heavy on his finger—his gold wedding ring. Some kind of memory came to him—he quickly took it off and gave it to the startled old woman.

And so, impoverished, empty and alone, he went under the surgeon's knife.

When the old man came round from the anaesthetic, the doctors, seeing the dangerous state he was in, called his wife and daughter, now informed of the operation, into the room. With difficulty, his eyes looked out from lids surrounded by blue shadows. "Where am I?" He stared at the strange white room that he had never seen before.

Then, to show him her affection, his daughter leant over his poor sunken face. And suddenly a glimmer of recognition came into the blindly searching eyes. A light, a small one, was kindled in their pupils—that was her, his child, his beloved child, that was his beautiful and tender child Erna! Very, very slowly the bitterly compressed lips relaxed. A smile, a very small smile that had not come to his closed mouth for a long time, cautiously began to show. And shaken by that joy, expressed as it was with such difficulty, she bent closer to kiss her father's bloodless cheeks.

But there it was—the sweet perfume that aroused a memory, or was it his half-numbed brain remembering forgotten moments?—and suddenly a terrible change came over the features that had looked happy only just now. His colourless lips were grimly tightened again, rejecting her. His hand worked its way out from under the blanket, and he tried to raise it as if to push something repellent away, his whole sore body quivering in agitation. "Get away!… Get away!" he babbled. The words on his pale lips were almost inarticulate, yet clear enough. And so terribly did a look of aversion form on the face of the old man, who could not get away, that the doctor anxiously urged the women to stand aside. "He's delirious," he whispered. "You had better leave him alone now."

As soon as the two women had gone, the distorted features relaxed wearily again into final drowsiness. Breath was still escaping, although more and more stertorously, as he struggled for the heavy air of life. But soon his breast tired of the struggle to drink in that bitter nourishment of humanity. And when the doctor felt for the old man's heart, it had already ceased to hurt him.

THE MIRACLES OF LIFE

To my dear friend Hans Müller

GREY MIST LAY LOW over Antwerp, enveloping the city entirely in its dense and heavy swathes. The shapes of houses were blurred in the fine, smoky vapour, and you could not see to the end of the street, but overhead there was ringing in the air, a deep sound like the word of God coming out of the clouds, for the muted voices of the bells in the church towers, calling their congregations to prayer, had also merged in the great, wild sea of mist filling the city and the countryside around, and encompassing the restless, softly roaring waters of the sea far away in the harbour. Here and there a faint gleam struggled against the damp grey mist, trying to light up a gaudy shop sign, but only muffled noise and throaty laughter told you where to find the taverns in which freezing customers gathered, complaining of the weather. The alleys seemed empty, and any passers-by were seen only as fleeting impressions that soon dissolved into the mist. It was a dismal, depressing Sunday morning.

Only the bells called and pealed as if desperately, while the mist stifled their cries. For the devout were few and far between; foreign heresy had found a foothold in this land, and even those who had not abandoned their old faith were less assiduous and zealous in the service of the Lord. Heavy morning mists were enough to keep many away from their devotions. Wrinkled old women busily telling their beads, poor folk in their plain Sunday best stood looking lost in the long, dark aisles of the churches, where the shining gold of altars and chapels and the priests' bright chasubles shone like a mild and gentle flame. But the mist seemed to have seeped through the high walls, for here, too, the chilly and sad mood of the deserted streets prevailed. The morning sermon itself was cold and austere, without a ray of sunlight to brighten it. It was preached against the Protestants, and the driving force behind it was furious rage, hatred along with a strong sense of power, for the time for moderation was over, and good news from Spain had reached the clerics—the new king served the work of the Church with admirable fervour. In his sermon, the preacher united graphic descriptions of the Last Judgement with dark words of admonition for the immediate future. If there had been a large congregation, his words might have been passed on by the faithful murmuring in their pews to a great crowd of hearers, but as it was they dropped into the dark void with a dull echo, as if frozen in the moist, chilly air.

During the storm two men had quickly entered the main porch of the cathedral, their faces obscured at first by windblown hair and voluminous coats with collars turned up high. The taller man shed his damp coat to reveal the honest but not especially striking features of a portly man in the rich clothing suitable for a merchant. The other was a stranger figure, although not because of anything unusual in his clothing; his gentle, unhurried movements and his rather big-boned, rustic but kindly face, surrounded by abundant waving white hair, lent him the mild aspect of an evangelist. They both said a short prayer, and then the merchant signed to his older companion to follow him. They went slowly, with measured steps, into the side aisle, which was almost entirely in darkness because dank air made the candles gutter, and heavy clouds that refused to lift still obscured the bright face of the sun. The merchant stopped at one of the small side chapels, most of which contained devotional items promised to the Church as donations by the old families of the city, and pointing to one of the little altars he said, "Here it is."

The other man came closer and shaded his eyes with his hand to see it better in the dim light. One wing of the altarpiece was occupied by a painting in clear colours made even softer by the twilight, and it immediately caught the old painter's eye. It showed the Virgin Mary, her heart transfixed by a sword, and despite the pain and sorrow of the subject it was a gentle work with an aura of reconciliation about it. Mary had a strangely sweet face, not so much that of the Mother of God as of a dreaming girl in the bloom of youth, but with the idea of pain tingeing the smiling beauty of a playful, carefree nature. Thick black hair tumbling down softly surrounded a small, pale but radiant face with very red lips, glowing like a crimson wound. The features were wonderfully delicate, and many of the brushstrokes, for instance in the assured, slender curve of the eyebrows, gave an almost yearning expression to the beauty of the tender face. The Virgin's dark eyes were deep in thought, as if dreaming of another brighter and sweeter world from which her pain was stealing her away. The hands were folded in gentle devotion, and her breast still seemed to be quivering with slight fear at the cold touch of the sword piercing her. Blood from her wound ran along it. All this was bathed in a wonderful radiance surrounding her head with golden flame, and even her heart glowed like the mystical light of the chalice in the stained glass of the church windows when sunlight fell through them. And the twilight around it took the last touch of worldliness from this picture, so that the halo around the sweet girlish face shone with the true radiance of transfiguration.

Almost abruptly, the painter tore himself away from his lengthy admiration of the picture. "None of our countrymen painted this," he said.

The merchant nodded in agreement.

"No, it is by an Italian. A young painter at the time. But there's quite a long story behind it. I will tell it all to you from the beginning, and then, as you know, I want you to complete the altarpiece by putting the keystone in place. Look, the sermon is over. We should find a better place to tell stories than this church, well as it may suit our joint efforts. Let's go."

The painter lingered for a moment longer before turning his eyes away from the picture. It seemed even more radiant as the smoky darkness outside the windows lifted, and the mist took on a golden hue. He almost felt that if he stayed here, rapt in devout contemplation of the gentle pain on those childish lips, they would smile and reveal new loveliness. But his companion had gone ahead of him already, and he had to quicken his pace to catch up with the merchant in the porch. They left the cathedral together, as they had come.

The heavy cloak of mist thrown over the city by the early spring morning had given way to a dull, silvery light caught like a cobweb among the gabled roofs. The close-set cobblestones had a steely, damp gleam, and the first of the flickering sunlight was beginning to cast its gold on them. The two men made their way down narrow, winding alleys to the clear air of the harbour, where the merchant lived. And as they slowly walked towards it at their leisure, deep in thought and lost in memory, the merchant's story gathered pace.

"As I have told you already," he began, "I spent some time in Venice in my youth. And to cut a long story short, my conduct there was not very Christian. Instead of managing my father's business in the city, I sat in taverns with young men who spent all day carousing and making merry, drinking, gambling, often bawling out some bawdy song or uttering bitter curses, and I was just as bad as the others. I had no intention of going home. I took life easy and ignored my father's letters when he wrote to me more and more urgently and sternly, warning me that people in Venice who knew me had told him that my licentious life would be the end of me. I only laughed, sometimes with annoyance, and a quick draught of sweet, dark wine washed all my bitterness away, or if not that then the kiss of a wanton girl. I tore up my father's letters, I had abandoned myself entirely to a life of intoxicated frenzy, and I did not intend to give it up. But one evening I was suddenly free of it all. It was very strange, and sometimes I still feel as if a miracle had cleared my path. I was sitting in my usual tavern; I can still see it today, with its smoke and vapours and my drinking companions. There were girls of easy virtue there as well, one of them very beautiful, and we seldom made merrier than that night, a stormy and very strange one. Suddenly, just as a lewd story aroused roars of laughter, my servant came in with a letter for me brought by the courier from Flanders. I was displeased. I did not like receiving my father's letters, which were always admonishing me to do my duty and be a good Christian, two notions that I had long ago drowned in wine. But I was about to take it from the servant when up jumped one of my drinking companions, a handsome, clever fellow, a master of all the arts of chivalry. 'Never mind the croaking old toad. What's it to you?' he cried, throwing the letter up in the air, swiftly drawing his sword, neatly spearing the letter as it fluttered down and pinning it to the wall. The supple blue blade quivered as it stuck there. He carefully withdrew the sword, and the letter, still unopened, stayed where it was. 'There clings the black bat!' he laughed. The others applauded, the girls clustered happily around him, they drank his health. I laughed myself, drank with them, and forgetting the letter and my father, God and myself, I forced myself into wild merriment. I gave the letter not a thought, and we went on to another tavern, where our merriment turned to outright folly. I was drunk as never before, and one of those girls was as beautiful as sin."

The merchant instinctively stopped and passed his hand several times over his brow, as if to banish an unwelcome image from his mind. The painter was quick to realize that this was a painful memory, and did not look at him, but let his eyes rest with apparent interest on a galleon under full sail, swiftly approaching the harbour that the two men had reached, and where they now stood amidst all its colourful hurry and bustle. The merchant's silence did not last long, and he soon continued his tale.

"You can guess how it was. I was young and bewildered, she was beautiful and bold. We came together, and I was full of urgent desire. But a strange thing happened. As I lay in her amorous embrace, with her mouth pressed to mine, I did not feel the kiss as a wild gesture of affection willingly returned. Instead, I was miraculously reminded of the gentle evening kisses we exchanged in my parental home. All at once, strange to say, even as I lay in the whore's arms I thought of my father's crumpled, mistreated, unread letter, and it was as if I felt my drinking companion's sword-thrust in my own bleeding breast. I sat up, so suddenly and looking so pale that the girl asked in alarm what the matter was. However, I was ashamed of my foolish fears, ashamed in front of this woman, a stranger, in whose bed I lay and whose beauty I had been enjoying. I did not want to tell her the foolish thoughts of that moment. Yet my life changed there and then, and today I still feel, as I felt at the time, that only the grace of God can bring such a change. I threw the girl some money, which she took reluctantly because she was afraid I despised her, and she called me a German fool. But I listened to no more from her, and instead stormed away on that cold, rainy night, calling like a desperate man over the dark canals for a gondola. At last one came along, and the price the gondolier asked was high, but my heart was beating with such sudden, merciless, incomprehensible fear that I could think of nothing but the letter, miraculously reminded of it as I suddenly was. By the time I reached the tavern my desire to read it was like a devouring fever; I raced into the place like a madman, ignoring the cheerful, surprised cries of my companions, jumped up on a table, making the glasses on it clink, tore the letter down from the wall and ran out again, taking no notice of the derision and angry curses behind me. At the first corner I unfolded the letter with trembling hands. Rain was pouring down from the overcast sky, and the wind tore at the sheet of paper in my hands. However, I did not stop reading until, with overflowing eyes, I had deciphered the whole of the letter. Not that the words in it were many—they told me that my mother was sick and likely to die, and asked me to come home. Not a word of the usual blame or reproach. But how my heart burnt with shame when I saw that the sword blade had pierced my mother's name..."

"A miracle indeed, an obvious miracle, one to be understood not by everyone but certainly by the man affected," murmured the painter as the merchant, deeply moved, lapsed into silence. For a while they walked along side by side without a word. The merchant's fine house was already visible in the distance, and when he looked up and saw it he quickly went on with his tale.

"I will be brief. I will not tell you what pain and remorseful madness I felt that night. I will say only that next morning found me kneeling on the steps of St Mark's in ardent prayer, vowing to donate an altar to the Mother of God if she would grant me the grace to see my mother again alive and receive her forgiveness. I set off that same day, travelling for many days and hours in despair and fear to Antwerp, where I hurried in wild desperation to my parental home. At the gate stood my mother herself, looking pale and older, but restored to good health. On seeing me she opened her arms to me, rejoicing, and in her embrace I wept tears of sorrow pent up over many days and many shamefully wasted nights. My life was different after that, and I may almost say it was a life well lived. I have buried that letter, the dearest thing I had, under the foundation stone of this house, built by the fruits of my own labour, and I did my best to keep my vow. Soon after my return here I had the altar that you have seen erected, and adorned as well as I could. However, as I knew nothing of those mysteries by which you painters judge your art, and wanted to dedicate a worthy picture to the Mother of God, who had worked a miracle for me, I wrote to a good friend in Venice asking him to send me the best of the painters he knew, to paint me the work that my heart desired.

"Months passed by. One day a young man came to my door, told me what his calling was, and brought me greetings and a letter from my friend. This Italian painter, whose remarkable and strangely sad face I well remember to this day, was not at all like the boastful, noisy drinking companions of my days in Venice. You might have thought him a monk rather than a painter, for he wore a long, black robe, his hair was cut in a plain style, and his face showed the spiritual pallor of asceticism and night watches. The letter merely confirmed my favourable impression, and dispelled any doubts aroused in me by the youthfulness of this Italian master. The older painters of Italy, wrote my friend, were prouder than princes, and even the most tempting offer could not lure them away from their native land, where they were surrounded by great lords and ladies as well as the common people. He had chosen this young master because, for some reason he did not know, the young man's wish to leave Italy weighed more with him than any offer of money, but the young painter's talent was valued highly and honoured in his own country.

"The man my friend had sent was quiet and reserved. I never learnt anything about his life beyond hints that a beautiful woman had played a painful part in his story, and it was because of her that he had left his native Italy. And although I have no proof of it, and such an idea seems heretical and unchristian, I think that the picture you have seen, which he painted within a few weeks without a model, working with careful preparation from memory, bears the features of the woman he had loved. Whenever I came to see him at work I found him painting another version of that same sweet face again, or lost in dreamy contemplation of it. Once the painting was finished, I felt secretly afraid of the godlessness of painting a woman who might be a courtesan as the Mother of God, and asked him to choose a different model for the companion piece that I also wanted. He did not reply, and when I went to see him next day he had left without a word of goodbye. I had some scruples about adorning the altar with that picture, but the priest whom I consulted felt no such doubt in accepting it."

"And he was right," interrupted the painter, almost vehemently. "For how can we imagine the beauty of Our Lady if not from looking at the woman we see in the picture? Are we not made in God's image? If so, such a portrayal, if only a faint copy of the unseen original, must be the closest to perfection that we can offer to human eyes. Now, listen—you want me to paint that second picture. I am one of those poor souls who cannot paint without a living model. I do not have the gift of painting only from within myself, I work from nature in trying to show what is true in it. I would not choose a woman whom I myself loved to model for a portrait worthy of the Mother of God—it would be sinful to see the immaculate Virgin through her face—but I would look for a lovely model and paint the woman whose features seem to me to show the face of the Mother of God as I have seen it in devout dreams. And believe me, although those may be the features of a sinful human woman, if the work is done in pious devotion none of the dross of desire and sin will be left. The magic of such purity, like a miraculous sign, can often be expressed in a woman's face. I think I have often seen that miracle myself."

"Well, however that may be, I trust you. You are a mature man, you have endured and experienced much, and if you see no sin in it…"

"Far from it! I consider it laudable. Only Protestants and other sectarians denounce the adornment of God's house."

"You are right. But I would like you to begin the picture soon, because my vow, still only half-fulfilled, still burns in me like a sin. For twenty years I forgot about the second picture in the altarpiece. Then, quite recently, when I saw my wife's sorrowful face as she wept by our child's sickbed, I thought of the debt I owed and renewed my vow. And as you are aware, once again the Mother of God worked a miracle of healing, when all the doctors had given up in despair. I beg you not to leave it too long before you start work."

"I will do what I can, but to be honest with you, never in my long career as an artist has anything struck me as so difficult. If my picture is not to look a poor daub, carelessly constructed, beside the painting of that young master—and I long to know more about his work—then I shall need to have the hand of God with me."

"God never fails those who are loyal to him. Goodbye, then, and go cheerfully to work. I hope you will soon bring good news to my house."

The merchant shook hands cordially with the painter once again outside the door of his house, looking confidently into the artist's clear eyes, set in his honest German, angular face like the waters of a bright mountain lake surrounded by weathered peaks and rough rocks. The painter had another parting remark on his lips, but left it unspoken and firmly clasped the hand offered to him. The two parted in perfect accord with each other.

The painter walked slowly along beside the harbour, as he always liked to do when his art did not keep him to his studio. He loved the busy, colourful scene presented by the place, with the hurry and bustle of work at the waterside, and sometimes he sat down on a bollard to sketch the curious physical posture of a labourer, or practice the difficult knack of foreshortening a path only a foot wide. He was not at all disturbed by the loud cries of the seamen, the rattling of carts and the monotonous sound of the sea breaking on shore. He had been granted those insights that do not reflect images seen only in the mind's eye, but can recognize in every living thing, however humble or indifferent, the ray of light to illuminate a work of art. For that reason he always liked places where life was at its most colourful, offering a confusing abundance of different delights. He walked among the sailors slowly, with a questing eye, and no one dared to laugh at him, for among all the noisy, useless folk who gather in a harbour, just as the beach is covered with empty shells and pebbles, he stood out with his calm bearing and the dignity of his appearance.

This time, however, he soon gave up his search and got to his feet. The merchant's story had moved him deeply. It touched lightly upon an incident in his own life, and even his usual devotion to the magic of art failed him today. The mild radiance of that picture of the Virgin painted by the young Italian master seemed to illuminate the faces of all the women he saw today, even if they were only stout fishwives. Dreaming and thoughtful, he wandered indecisively for a while past the crowd in its Sunday best, but then he stopped trying to resist his longing to go back to the cathedral and look at the strange portrayal of that beautiful woman again.

A few weeks had passed since the conversation in which the painter agreed to his friend's request for a second picture to complete the altarpiece for the Mother of God, and still the blank canvas in his studio looked reproachfully at the old master. He almost began to fear it, and spent a good deal of time out and about in the streets of the city to keep himself from brooding on its stern admonition and his own despondency. In a life full of busy work—perhaps he had in fact worked *too* hard, failing to keep an enquiring eye on his true self—a change had come over the painter since he first set eyes on the young Italian's picture. Future and past had been wrenched abruptly apart, and looked at him like an empty mirror reflecting only darkness and shadows. And nothing is more terrible than to feel that your life's final peak of achievement already lies just ahead if only you stride on boldly, and then be assailed by a brooding fear that you have taken the wrong path, you have lost your power, you cannot take the last, least step forward. All at once the artist, who had painted hundreds of sacred pictures in the course of his life, seemed to have lost his ability to portray a human face well enough for him to think it worthy of a divine subject. He had looked at women who sold their faces as artist's models to be copied by the hour, at others who sold their bodies, at citizens' wives and gentle girls with the light of inner purity shining in their faces, but whenever they were close to him, and he was on the point of painting the first brushstroke on the canvas, he was aware of their humanity. He saw the blonde, greedy plump figure of one, he saw another's wild addiction to the game of love; he sensed the smooth emptiness behind the brief gleam of a girlish brow, and was disconcerted by the bold gait of whores and the immodest way they swung their hips. Suddenly a world full of such people seemed a bleak place. He felt that the breath of the divine had been extinguished, quenched by the exuberant flesh of these desirable women who knew nothing about mystical virginity, or the tremor of awe in immaculate devotion to dreams of another world. He was ashamed to open the portfolios containing his own work, for it seemed to him as if he had, so to speak, made himself unworthy to live on this earth, had committed a sin in painting pictures where sturdy country folk modelled for the Saviour's disciples and stout countrywomen as the women who served him. His mood became more and more sombre and oppressive. He remembered himself as a young man following his father's plough, long before he took to art instead, he saw his hard peasant hands thrusting the harrow through the black earth, and wondered if he would not have done better to sow yellow seed corn and work to support a family, instead of touching secrets and miraculous signs, mysteries not meant for him, with his clumsy fingers. His whole life seemed to be turned upside down, he had run aground on the fleeting vision of an hour when he saw an image that came back to him in his dreams, and was both torment and blessing in his waking moments. For he could no longer see the Mother of God in his prayers except as she was in the picture that presented so lovely a portrayal of her. It was so different from the beauty of all the earthly women he met, transfigured in the light of feminine humility touched with a presentiment of the divine. In the deceptive twilight of memory, the images of all the women he had ever loved came together in that wonderful figure. And when he tried, for the first time, to ignore reality and create a Mother of God out of the figure of Mary with her child that hovered before his mind's eye, smiling gently in happy, unclouded bliss, then his fingers, wielding the brush, sank powerless as if numbed by cramp. The current was drying up, the skill of his fingers in interpreting the words spoken by the eye seemed helpless in the face of his bright dream, although he saw as clearly in his imagination as if it were painted on a solid wall. His inability to give shape to the fairest and truest of his dreams and bring it into reality was pain that burnt like fire now that reality itself, in all its abundance, did not help him to build a bridge. And he asked himself a terrible question—could he still call himself an artist if such a thing could happen to him, had he been only a hardworking craftsman all his life, fitting colours together as a labourer constructs a building out of stones?

Such self-tormenting reflections gave him not a day's rest, and drove him with compelling power out of his studio, where the empty canvas and carefully prepared tools of his trade reproached him like mocking voices. Several times he thought of confessing his dilemma to the merchant, but he was afraid that the latter, while a pious and well-disposed man, would never understand him, and would think it more of a clumsy excuse than real inability to begin such a work. After all, he had already painted many sacred pictures, to the general acclaim of laymen and master painters alike. So he made it his habit to wander the streets, restless and at his wits' end, secretly alarmed when chance or a hidden magic made him wake from his wandering dreams again and again, finding himself outside the cathedral with the altarpiece in its chapel, as if there were an invisible link between him and the picture, or a divine power ruled his soul even in dreams. Sometimes he went in, half-hoping to find some flaw in the picture and thus break free of its spell, but in front of it he entirely forgot to assess the young artist's creation enviously, judging its art and skill. Instead, he felt the rushing of wings around him, bearing him up into spheres of calm, transfigured contemplation. It was not until he left the cathedral and began thinking of himself and his own efforts that he felt the old pain again, redoubled.

One afternoon he had been wandering through the colourful streets once more, and this time he felt that his tormenting doubt was eased. The first breath of spring wind had begun to blow from the south, bringing with it the brightness, if not the warmth, of many fine spring days to come. For the first time the dull grey gloom that his own cares had cast over the world seemed to leave the painter, and a sense of the grace of God poured into his heart, as it always did when fleeting signs of spring announced the great miracle of resurrection. A clear March sun washed all the rooftops and streets clean, brightly coloured pennants fluttered down in the harbour, the water shone blue between the ships rocking gently there, and the never-ending noise of the city was like jubilant song. A troop of Spanish cavalry trotted over the main square. No hostile glances were cast at them today; the townsfolk enjoyed the sight of the sun reflected from their armour and shining helmets. Women's white headdresses, tugged wilfully back by the wind, revealed fresh, highly coloured complexions. Wooden clogs clattered on the cobblestones as children danced in a ring, holding hands and singing.

And in the usually dark alleys of the harbour district, to which the artist now turned feeling ever lighter at heart, something shimmering flickered like a falling rain of light. The sun could not quite show its bright face between the gabled roofs here as they leant towards each other, densely crowded together, black and crumpled like the hoods of a couple of little old women standing there chattering, one each side of the street. But the light was reflected from window to window, as if sparkling hands were waving in the air, passing back and forth in a high-spirited game. In many places the light remained soft and muted, like a dreaming eye in the first evening twilight. Down below in the street lay darkness where it had lain for years, hidden only occasionally in winter by a cloak of snow. Those who lived there had the sad gloom of constant dusk in their eyes, but the children who longed for light and brightness trusted the enticement of these first rays of spring, playing in their thin clothing on the dirty, potholed streets. The narrow strip of blue sky showing between the rooftops, the golden dance of the sunlight above made them deeply, instinctively happy.

The painter walked on and on, never tiring. He felt as if he, too, were granted secret reasons to rejoice, as if every spark of sunlight was the fleeting reflection of the radiance of God's grace going to his heart. All the bitterness had left his face. It now shone with such a mild and kindly light that the children playing their games were amazed, and greeted him with awe, thinking that he must be a priest. He walked on and on, with never a thought for where he was going. The new force of springtime was in his limbs, just as flower buds tap hopefully at the bast holding old, weather-beaten trees together, willing it to let their young strength shoot out into the light. His step was as spry and light as a young man's, and he seemed to be feeling fresher and livelier even though he had been walking for hours, putting stretches of the road behind him at a faster and more flexible pace.

Suddenly the painter stopped as if turned to stone and shaded his eyes with his hand to protect them, like a man dazzled by a flashing light or some awesome, incredible event. Looking up at a window, he had felt the full beam of sunlight reflected back from it strike his eyes painfully, but through the crimson and gold mist forming in front of them a strange apparition, a wonderful illusion had appeared—there was the Madonna painted by that young Italian master, leaning back dreamily and with a touch of sorrow as she did in the picture. A shudder ran through him as the terrible fear of disappointment united with the trembling ecstasy of a man granted grace, one who had seen a vision of the Mother of God not in the darkness of a dream but in bright daylight. That was a miracle of the kind to which many had borne witness, but few had really seen it! He dared not look up yet, his trembling shoulders did not feel strong enough to bear the shattering effect of finding that he was wrong, and he was afraid that this one moment could crush his life even more cruelly than the merciless self-torment of his despairing heart. Only when his pulse was beating more steadily and slowly, and he no longer felt it like a hammer blow in his throat, did he pull himself together and look up slowly from the shelter of his hand at the window where he had seen that seductive image framed.

He had been mistaken. It was not the girl from the young master's Madonna. Yet all the same, his raised hand did not sink despondently. What he saw also appeared to him a miracle, if a sweeter, milder, more human one than a divine apparition seen in the radiant light of a blessed hour. This girl, looking thoughtfully out of the sunlit window frame, bore only a distant resemblance to the altarpiece in the chapel—her face too was framed by black hair, she too had a delicate complexion of mysterious, fantastic pallor, but her features were harder, sharper, almost angry, and around the mouth there was a tearful defiance that was not moderated even by the lost expression of her dreaming eyes, which held an old, deep grief. There was a childlike wilfulness and a legacy of hidden sorrow in their bright restlessness, which she seemed to control only with difficulty. He felt that her silent composure could dissolve into abrupt and angry movement at any time, and her mood of gentle reverie did not hide it. The painter felt a certain tension in her features, suggesting that this child would grow to be one of those women who live in their dreams and are at one with their longings, whose souls cling to what they love with every fibre of their being, and who die if they are forced away from it. But he marvelled not so much at all this strangeness in her face as at the miraculous play of nature that made the sunny glow behind her head, reflected in the window, look like a saint's halo lying around her hair until it shone like black steel. And he thought he clearly felt here the divine hand showing him how to complete his work in a manner worthy of the subject and pleasing to God.

A carter roughly jostled the painter as he stood in the middle of the street, lost in thought. "God's wrath, can't you watch out, old man, or are you so taken with the lovely Jew girl that you stand there gaping like an idiot and blocking my way?"

The painter started with surprise, but took no offence at the man's rough tone, and indeed he had scarcely noticed it in the light of the information provided by this gruff and heavily clad fellow. "Is she Jewish?" he asked in great surprise.

"So it's said, but I don't know. Anyway, she's not the child of the folk here, they found her or came by her somehow. What's it to me? I've never felt curious about it, and I won't neither. Ask the master of the house himself if you like. He'll know better than me, for sure, how she comes to be here."

The "master" to whom he referred was an innkeeper, landlord of one of those dark, smoky taverns where the liveliness and noise never quite died down, because it was frequented by so many gamblers and seamen, soldiers and idlers that the place was seldom left entirely empty. Broad-built, with a fleshy but kindly face, he stood in the narrow doorway like an inn sign inviting custom. On impulse the painter approached him. They went into the tavern, and the painter sat down in a corner at a smeared wooden table. He still felt rather agitated, and when the landlord put the glass he had ordered in front of him, he asked him to sit at the table with him for a few moments. Quietly, so as not to attract the attention of a couple of slightly tipsy sailors bawling out songs at the next table, he asked his question. He told the man briefly but with deep feeling of the miraculous sign that had appeared to him—the landlord listened in surprise as his slow understanding, somewhat clouded by wine, tried to follow the painter—and finally asked if he would allow him to paint his daughter as the model for a picture of the Virgin Mary. He did not forget to mention that by giving permission her father too would be taking part in a devout work, and pointed out several times that he would be ready to pay the girl good money for her services.

The innkeeper did not answer at once, but kept rubbing his broad nostrils with a fat finger. At last he began.

"Well, sir, you mustn't take me for a bad Christian, by God no, but it's not as easy as you think. If I was her father and I could say to my daughter, off you go and do as I say, well, sir, the bargain would soon be struck. But with that child, it's different... Good God, what's the matter?"

He had jumped up angrily, for he did not like to be disturbed as he talked. At another table a man was hammering his empty tankard on the bench and demanding another. Roughly, the landlord snatched the tankard from his hand and refilled it, suppressing a curse. At the same time he picked up a glass and bottle, went back to join his new guest, sat down and filled glasses for them both. His own was soon gulped down, and as if well refreshed he wiped his bristling moustache and began his tale.

"I'll tell you how I came by that Jewish girl, sir. I was a soldier, fighting first in Italy, then in Germany. A bad trade, I can tell you, never worse than today, and it was bad enough even back then. I'd had enough of it, I was on my way home through Germany to take up some honest calling, because I didn't have much left to call my own. The money you get as loot in warfare runs through your fingers like water, and I was never a skinflint. So I was in some German town or other, I'd only just arrived, when I heard a great to-do that evening. What set it off I don't know, but the townsfolk had ganged up together to attack the local Jews and I went along with them, partly hoping to pick something up, partly out of curiosity to see what happened. The townsfolk went to work with a will, there was storming of houses, killing, robbing, raping, and the men of the town were roaring with greed and lust. I'd soon had enough of that kind of thing, and I left them to it. I wasn't going to sully my honourable sword with women's blood, or wrestle with whores for what loot I could find. Well then, as I'm about to go back down a side alley, I see an old Jew with his long beard a-quiver, his face distorted, holding in his arms a small child just woken from sleep. He runs to me and stammers out a torrent of words I can't make out. All I understood of his Yiddish German was that he'd give me a good sum of money in return for saving the pair of them. I felt sorry for the child, looking at me all alarmed with her big eyes. And it didn't seem a bad bargain, so I threw my cloak over the old man and took them to my lodgings. There were a few people standing in the alleys, looking like they were inclined to go for the old man, but I'd drawn my sword, and they let all three of us pass. I took them to the inn where I was staying, and when the old man went on his knees to plead with me we left the town that same evening, while the fire-raising and murder went on into the night. We could still see the firelight when we were far away, and the old man stared at it in despair, but the child, she just slept on calmly. The three of us weren't together for long. After a few days the old man fell mortally sick, and he died on the way. But first he gave me all the money he'd brought away with him, and a piece of paper written in strange letters—I was to give a broker in Antwerp, he said, and he told me the man's name. He commended his granddaughter to my care as he died. Well, I came here to Antwerp and showed that piece of paper, and a strange effect it had too—the broker gave me a handsome sum of money, more than I'd have expected. I was glad of it, for now I could be free of the wandering life, so I bought this house and the tavern with the money and soon forgot the war. I kept the child. I was sorry for her, and then I hoped that as she grew up she'd do the work about the place for me, old bachelor that I am. But it didn't turn out like that.

"You saw her just now, and that's the way she is all day. She looks out of the window at empty air, she speaks to no one, she gives timid answers as if she was ducking down expecting someone to hit her. She never speaks to men. At first I thought she'd be an asset here in the tavern, bringing in the guests, like the landlord's young daughter over the road, she'll joke with his customers and encourage them to drink glass after glass. But our girl here's not bold, and if anyone so much as touches her she screams and runs out of the door like a whirlwind. And then if I go looking for her she's sure to be sitting huddled in a corner somewhere, crying fit to break your heart, you'd think God know what harm had come to her. Strange folk, the Jews!"

"Tell me," said the painter, interrupting the storyteller, who was getting more and more thoughtful as he went on, "tell me, is she still of the Jewish religion, or has she converted to the true faith?"

The landlord scratched his head in embarrassment. "Well, sir," he said, "I was a soldier. I couldn't say too much about my own Christianity. I seldom went to church and I don't often go now, though I'm sorry, and as for converting the child, I never felt clever enough for that. I didn't really try, seemed to me it would be a waste of time with that truculent little thing. Folk set the priest on me once, and he read me a right lecture, but I was putting it off until the child reached the age of reason. Still, I reckon we'll be waiting a long time yet for that, although she's past fifteen years old now, but she's so strange and wilful. Odd folk, these Jews, who knows much about them? Her old grandfather seemed to me a good man, and she's not a bad girl, hard as it is to get close to her. And as for your idea, sir, I like it well enough, I think an honest Christian can never do too much for the salvation of his soul, and everything we do will be judged one day... but I'll tell you straight, I have no real power over the child. When she looks at you with those big black eyes you don't have the heart to do anything that might hurt her. But see for yourself. I'll call her down."

He stood up, poured himself another glass, drained it standing there with his legs apart, and then marched across the tavern to some sailors who had just come in and were puffing at their short-stemmed white clay pipes, filling the place with thick smoke. He shook hands with them in friendly fashion, filled their glasses and joked with them. Then he remembered what he was on his way to do, and the painter heard him make his way up the stairs with a heavy tread.

He felt strangely disturbed. The wonderful confidence he had drawn from that happy moment of emotion on seeing the girl began to cloud over in the murky light of this tavern. The dust of the street and the dark smoke were imposed on the shining image he remembered. And back came his sombre fear that it was a sin to take the solid, animal humanity that could not be separated from earthly women, mingling it with sublime ideas and elevating it to the throne of his pious dreams. He shuddered, wondering from what hands he was to receive the gift to which miraculous signs, both secret and revealed, had pointed his way.

The landlord came back into the tavern, and in his heavy, broad black shadow the painter saw the figure of the girl, standing in the doorway indecisively, seeming to be alarmed by the noise and the smoke, holding the doorpost with her slender hands as if seeking for help. An impatient word from the landlord telling her to hurry up alarmed her, and sent her shrinking further back into the darkness of the stairway, but the painter had already risen to approach her. He took her hands in his—old and rough as they were, they were also very gentle—and asked quietly and kindly, looking into her eyes, "Won't you sit down with me for a moment?"

The girl looked at him, astonished by the kindness and affection in the deep, bell-like sound of his voice on hearing it for the first time there in the dark, smoky tavern. She felt how gentle his hands were, and saw the tender goodness in his eyes with the sweet diffidence of a girl who has been hungering for affection for weeks and years, and is amazed to receive it. When she saw his snow-white head and kindly features, the image of her dead grandfather's face rose suddenly before her mind's eye, and forgotten notes sounded in her heart, chiming with loud jubilation through her veins and up into her throat, so that she could not say a word in reply, but blushed and nodded vigorously—almost as if she were angry, so harshly abrupt was the sudden movement. Timidly, she followed him to his table and perched on the edge of the bench beside him.

The painter looked affectionately down at her without saying a word. Before the old man's clear gaze, the tragic loneliness and proud sense of difference that had been present in this child from an early age flared up suddenly in her eyes. He would have liked to draw her close and press a reassuring kiss of benediction on her brow, but he was afraid of alarming her, and he feared the eyes of the other guests, who were pointing the strange couple out to each other and laughing. Before even hearing a word from this child he understood her very well, and warm sympathy rose in him, flowing freely, for he understood the painful defiance, harsh and brusque and defensive, of someone who wants to give an infinite wealth of love, yet who feels rejected. He gently asked, "What is your name, child?"

She looked up at him with trust, but in confusion. All this was still too strange and alien to her. Her voice shook shyly as she replied quietly, half turning away, "Esther."

The old man sensed that she trusted him but dared not show it yet. He began, in a quiet voice, "I am a painter, Esther, and I would like to paint a picture of you. Nothing bad will happen to you, you will see a great many beautiful things in my studio, and perhaps we will sometimes talk to each other like good friends. It will only be for one or two hours a day, as long as you please and no more. Will you come to my studio and let me paint you, Esther?"

The girl blushed even more rosily and did not know what to say. Dark riddles suddenly opened up before her, and she could not find her way to them. Finally she looked at the landlord, who was standing curiously by, with an uneasy, questioning glance.

"Your father will allow it and likes the idea," the painter made haste to say. "The decision is yours alone, for I cannot and do not want to force you into it. So will you let me paint you, Esther?"

He held out his large, brown, rustic hand invitingly. She hesitated for a moment, and then, bashfully and without a word, placed her own small white hand in the painter's to show her consent. His hand enclosed hers for a moment, as if it were prey he had caught. Then he let it go with a kindly look. The landlord, amazed to see the bargain so quickly concluded, called over some of the sailors from the other tables to point out this extraordinary event. But the girl, ashamed to be at the centre of attention, quickly jumped up and ran out of the door like lightning. The whole company watched her go in surprise.

"Good heavens above," said the astonished landlord, "that was a masterstroke, sir. I'd never have expected that shy little thing to agree."

And as if to confirm this statement he poured another glassful down his throat. The painter, who was beginning to feel ill at ease in the company here as it slowly lost its awe of him, threw some money on the table, discussed further details with the landlord, and warmly shook his hand. However, he made haste to leave the tavern; he did not care for its musty air and all the noise, and the drunk, bawling customers repelled him.

When he came out into the street the sun had just set, and only a dull pink twilight lingered in the sky. The evening was mild and pure. Walking slowly, the old man went home musing on events that seemed to him as strange and yet as pleasing as a dream. There was reverence in his heart, and it trembled as happily as when the first bell rang from the church tower calling the congregation to prayers, to be answered by the bells of all the other towers nearby, their voices deep and high, muffled and joyful, chiming and murmuring, like human beings calling out in joy and sorrow and pain. It seemed to him extraordinary that after following a sober and straightforward path all his life, his heart should be inflamed at this late hour by the soft radiance of divine miracles, but he dared not doubt it, and he carried the grace of that radiance for which he had longed home through the dark streets, blessedly awake and yet in a wonderful dream.

Days had passed by, and still the blank canvas stood on the painter's easel. Now, however, it was not despondency paralysing his hands, but a sure inner confidence that no longer counted the days, was in no hurry, and instead waited in serene silence while he held his powers in restraint. Esther had been timid and shy when she first visited the studio, but she soon became more forthcoming, gentler and less timid, basking in his fatherly warmth as he bestowed it on the simple, frightened girl. They spent these days merely talking to each other, like friends meeting after long years apart who have to get acquainted again before putting ardent feeling into heartfelt words and reviving their old intimacy. And soon there was a secret bond between these two people, so dissimilar and yet so like each other in a certain simplicity—one of them a man who had learnt that clarity and silence are at the heart of life, an experienced man schooled in simplicity by long days and years; the other a girl who had never yet truly felt alive, but had dreamt her days away as if surrounded by darkness, and who now felt the first ray from a world of light reach her heart, reflecting it back in a glow of radiance. The difference between the sexes meant nothing to the two of them; such thoughts were now extinguished in him and merely cast the evening light of memory into his life, and as for the girl, her dim sense of her own femininity had not fully awoken and was expressed only as vague, restless longing that had no aim as yet. A barrier still stood between them, but might soon give way—their different races and religions, the discipline of blood that has learnt to see itself as strange and hostile, nurturing distrust that only a moment of great love will overcome. Without that unconscious idea in her mind the girl, whose heart was full of pent-up affection, would long ago have thrown herself in tears on the old man's breast, confessing her secret terrors and growing longings, the pains and joys of her lonely existence. As it was, however, she showed her feelings only in glances and silences, restless gestures and hints. Whenever she felt everything in her trying to flow towards the light and express itself in clear, fluent words of ardent emotion, a secret power took hold of her like a dark, invisible hand and stifled them. And the old man did not forget that all his life he had regarded Jews if not with hatred, at least with a sense that they were alien. He hesitated to begin his picture because he hoped that the girl had been placed in his path only to be converted to the true faith. The miracle was not to be worked for him; he was to work it for her. He wanted to see in her eyes the same deep longing for the Saviour that the Mother of God must herself have felt when she trembled in blessed expectation of his coming. He would like to fill her with faith before painting a Madonna who still felt the awe of the Annunciation, but had already united it with the sweet confidence of coming fulfilment. And around his Madonna he imagined a mild landscape, a day just before the coming of spring, with white clouds moving through the air like swans drawing the warm weather along on invisible threads, with the first tender green showing as the moment of resurrection approached, flowers opening their buds to announce the coming of blessed spring as if in high, childlike voices. But the girl's eyes still seemed to him too timid and humble. He could not yet kindle the mystic flame of the Virgin's Annunciation and her devotion to a sombre promise in those restless glances; the deep, veiled suffering of her race still showed there, and sometimes he sensed the defiance of the Chosen People at odds with their God. They did not yet know humility and gentle, unearthly love.

With care and caution he tried to find ways to bring the Christian faith closer to her heart, knowing that if he showed it to her glowing in all its brightness, like a monstrance with the sun sparkling in it to show a thousand colours, she would not sink down before it in awe but turn brusquely away, seeing it as a hostile sign. There were many pictures taken from the Scriptures in his portfolios, works painted when he was an apprentice and sometimes copied again later when he was overcome by emotion. He took them out now and looked at the pictures side by side, and soon he felt the deep impression that many of them made on his mind in the trembling of his hands, and the warmth of his breath on his cheeks as it came faster. A bright world of beauty suddenly lay before the eyes of the lonely girl, who for years had seen only the swollen figures of guests at the tavern, the wrinkled faces of old, black-clad women, the grubby children shouting and tussling with each other in the street. But here were gentlewomen of enchanting beauty wearing wonderful dresses, ladies proud and sad, dreamy and desirable, knights in armour with long and gorgeous robes laughing or talking to the ladies, kings with flowing white locks on which golden crowns shone, handsome young men who had suffered martyrdom, sinking to the ground pierced by arrows or bleeding to death under torture. And a strange land that she did not know, although it touched her heart sweetly like an unconscious memory of home, opened up before her—a land of green palms and tall cypress trees, with a bright blue sky, always the same deep hue, above deserts and mountains, cities and distant prospects. Its radiant glow seemed much lighter and happier than this northern sky of eternal grey cloud.

Gradually he began telling her little stories about the pictures, explaining the simple, poetic legends of the Bible, speaking of the signs and wonders of that holy time with such enthusiasm that he forgot his own intentions, and he described, in ecstatic terms, the confidence in his faith that had brought him grace so recently. And the old man's deeply felt faith touched the girl's heart; she felt as if a wonderful country were suddenly revealed to her, opening its gates in the dark. She was less and less certain of herself as her life woke from the depths of the dark to see crimson light. She herself was feeling so strange that nothing seemed to her incredible—not the story of the silver star followed by three kings from distant lands, with their horses and camels bearing bright burdens of precious things—nor the idea that a dead man, touched by a hand in blessing, might wake to life again. After all, she felt the same wonderful power at work in herself. Soon the pictures were forgotten. The old man told her about his own life, connecting the old legends with many signs from God. He was bringing to light much that he had thought and dreamt of in his old age, and he himself was surprised by his own eloquence, as if it were something strange taken from another's hand to be tested. He was like a preacher who begins with a text from the word of God, meaning to explain and interpret it, and who then suddenly forgets his hearers and his intentions and gives himself up to the pleasure of letting all the springs of his heart flow into a deep torrent of words, as if into a goblet containing all the sweetness and sanctity of life. And then the preacher's words rise higher and higher above the heads of the humble members of his congregation, who cannot reach up to the world he now inhabits, but murmur and stare at him as he approaches the heavens in his bold dream, forgetting the force of gravity that will weigh down his wings again…

The painter suddenly looked around him as if still surrounded by the rosy mists of his inspired words. Reality showed him its cold and ordered structure once more. But what he saw was itself as beautiful as a dream.

Esther was sitting at his feet looking up at him. Gently leaning on his arm, gazing into the still, blue, clear eyes that suddenly seemed so full of light, she had gradually sunk down beside him, and in his devout emotion he had never noticed. She was crouching at his knees, her eyes turned up to him. Old words from her own childhood were suddenly present in her confused mind, words that her father, wearing his solemn black robe and frayed white bands, had often read from an old and venerable book. Those words too had been so full of resonant ceremony and ardent piety. A world that she had lost, a world of which she now knew little came back to life in muted colours, filling her with poignant longing and bringing the gleam of tears to her eyes. When the old man bent down to those sad eyes and kissed her forehead, he felt a sob shaking her tender, childlike frame in a wild fever. And he misunderstood her. He thought the miracle had happened, and God, in a wonderful moment, had given his usually plain and simple manner of speech the glowing, fiery tongue of eloquence as he once gave it to the prophets when they went out to his people. He thought this awe was the shy, still timorous happiness of one who was on her way home to the true faith, in which all bliss was to be found, and she was trembling and swaying like a flame suddenly lit, still feeling its way up into the air before settling into a clear, steady glow. His heart rejoiced at his mistake; he thought that he was suddenly close to his aim. He spoke to her solemnly.

"I have told you about miracles, Esther. Many say that miracles only happened long ago, but I feel and I tell you now that they still happen today. However, they are quiet miracles, and are only to be found in the souls of those who are ready for them. What has happened here is a miracle—my words and your tears, rising from our blind hearts, have become a miracle of enlightenment worked by an invisible hand. Now that you have understood me you are one of us; at the moment when God gave you those tears you became a Christian…"

He stopped in surprise. When he uttered that word Esther had risen from where she knelt at his feet, putting out her hands to ward off the mere idea. There was horror in her eyes, and the angry, wild truculence that her foster father had mentioned. At that moment, when the severity of her features turned to anger, the lines around her mouth were as sharp as the cut of a knife, and she stood in a defensive attitude like a cat about to pounce. All the ardour in her broke out in that moment of wild self-defence.

Then she calmed down. But the barrier between them was high and dark again, no longer irradiated by supernatural light. Her eyes were cold, restless and ashamed, no longer angry, but no longer full of mystic awe; only reality was in them. Her hands hung limp like wings broken in soaring too high. Life was still a mystery of strange beauty to her, but she dared not love the dream from which she had been so shatteringly woken.

The old painter too felt that his hasty confidence had deceived him, but it was not the first disappointment in his long and questing life of faith and trust. So he felt no pain, only surprise, and then again almost joy to see how quickly *she* felt ashamed. He gently took her two childish hands, still feverishly burning as they were. "Esther, your sudden outburst almost alarmed me. But I do not hold it against you... is that what you are thinking?"

Ashamed, she shook her head, only to raise it again next moment. Again her words were almost defiant.

"But I don't want to be a Christian. I don't want to. I—" She choked on the words for some time before saying, in a muted voice. "I... I hate Christians. I don't know them but I hate them. What you told me about love embracing everything is more beautiful than anything I have ever heard in my life. But the people in the tavern say that they are Christians too, although they are rough and violent. And... I don't even remember it clearly, it's all so long ago... but when they talked about Christians at home, there was fear and hatred in their voices. Everyone hated the Christians. I hate them too... when I was little and went out with my father they shouted at us, and once they threw stones at us. One of the stones hit me and made me bleed and cry, but my father made me go on, he was afraid, and when I shouted for help... I don't remember any more about all that. Or yes, I do. Our alleys were dark and narrow, like the one where I live here. And only Jews lived there. But higher up, the town was beautiful. I once looked down at it from the top of a house... there was a river flowing through it, so blue and clear, and a broad bridge over the river with people crossing it in brightly coloured clothes like the ones you showed me in the pictures. And the houses were decorated with statues and with gilding and gable ends. Among them there were tall, tall towers, where bells rang, and the sun shone all the way down into the streets there. It was all so lovely. But when I told my father he ought to go and see the lovely town with me he looked very serious and said, 'No, Esther, the Christians would kill us.' That frightened me... and ever since then I have hated the Christians."

She stopped in the middle of her dreams, for all around her seemed bright again. What she had forgotten long ago, leaving it to lie dusty and veiled in her soul, was sparkling once again. She was back there walking down the dark alleys of the ghetto to the house she was visiting. And suddenly everything connected and was clear, and she realized that what she sometimes thought was a dream had been reality in her past life. Her words came tumbling out in pursuit of the images hurrying through her mind.

"And then there was that evening... I was suddenly snatched up out of my bed... I saw my grandfather, he was holding me in his arms, his face was pale and trembling… the whole house was in uproar, shaking, there was shouting and noise. Oh, now it's coming back to me. I hear what they were shouting again—it's the others, they were saying, it's the Christians. My father was shouting it, or my mother, or… I don't remember. My grandfather carried me down into the darkness, through black streets and alleys… and there was always that noise and the same shouting—the others, the Christians! How could I have forgotten? And then we went away with a man… when I woke up we were far out in the country, my grandfather and the man I live with now… I never saw that town again, but the sky was very red back where we had come from… and we travelled on…"

Again she stopped. The pictures seemed to be disappearing, getting slowly darker.

"I had three sisters. They were very beautiful, and every evening they came to my bedside to kiss me goodnight… and my father was tall, I couldn't reach up to him, so he often carried me in his arms. And my mother… I never saw her again. I don't know what happened to them, because my grandfather looked away and wouldn't tell me when I asked him. And when he died there was no one I dared to ask."

She stopped once more, and a painful, violent sob burst from her throat. Very quietly, she added, "But now I know it all. How could it all be so dark to me? I feel as if my father were standing beside me saying the words he used to say at that time, it is all so clear in my ears. I won't ask anyone again…"

Her words turned to sobs, to silent, miserable weeping that died away in deep, sad silence. Only a few minutes ago life had shown her an enticing image; now it lay dark and sombre before her again. And the old man had long ago forgotten his intention of converting her as he watched her pain. He stood there in silence, feeling as sad himself as if he must sit down and weep with her, for there were some things that he could not put into words, and with his great love of humanity he felt guilty for unknowingly arousing such pain in her. Shuddering, he felt the fullness of blessing and the weight of a burden to be borne, both coming at the same hour; it was as if heavy waves were rising and falling, and he did not know whether they would raise his life or drag it down into the menacing deeps. But wearily, he felt neither fear nor hope, only pity for this young life with so many different paths opening up before it. He tried to find words; but they were all as heavy as lead and had the ring of false coin. What was all they could express, in the face of such a painful memory?

Sadly, he stroked the hair on her trembling head. She looked up, confused and distracted; then mechanically tidied her hair and rose, her eyes wandering this way and that as if getting used to reality again. Her features became wearier, less tense, and there was only darkness now in her eyes. Abruptly, she pulled herself together, and quickly said, to hide the sobs still rising inside her, "I must go now. It's late. And my father is expecting me."

With a brusque gesture of farewell she shook her head, picked up her skirts and turned to leave. But the old man, who had been watching her with his steady, understanding gaze, called after her. She turned back reluctantly, for there were still tears in her eyes. And again the old man took both her hands in his forceful manner and looked at her. "Esther, I know that you want to go now and not come back again. You do not and will not believe me, because a secret fear deceives you."

He felt her hands relax in his gently, softer now. He went on more confidently, "Come back another day, Esther! We will forget all of this, the happy and the sad part of it alike. Tomorrow we will begin on my picture, and I feel as if it will succeed. And don't be sad any more, let the past rest, don't brood on it. Tomorrow we will begin a new work with new hope—won't we, Esther?"

In tears, she nodded. And she went home again, still timid and uncertain, but with a new and deeper awareness of many things.

The old man stayed there, lost in thought. His belief in miracles had not deserted him, but they had seemed more solemn before; were they only a case of a divine hand playing with life? He abandoned the idea of seeing faith in a mystical promise light up a face when perhaps its owner's soul was too desperate to believe. He would no longer presume to bring God and his own ideas to anyone, he would only be a simple servant of the Lord painting a picture as well as he could, and laying it humbly on God's altar as another man might bring a gift. He felt that it was a mistake to look for signs and portents instead of waiting until they were revealed to him in their own good time.

Humbled, his heart sank to new depths. Why had he wanted to work a miracle on this child when no one had asked him to? Wasn't it enough that when his life was taking bleak and meaningless root, like the trunk of an old tree with only its branches aspiring to reach the sky, another life, a young life full of fear, had come to cling trustfully to him? One of life's miracles, he felt, had happened to him; he had been granted the grace to give and teach the love that still burnt in him in his old age, to sow it like a seed that may yet come to wonderful flower. Hadn't life given him enough with that? And hadn't God shown him the way to serve him? He had wanted a female figure in his picture, and the model for it had come to meet him, wasn't it God's will for him to paint her likeness, and not try converting her to a faith that she might never be able to understand? Lower and lower sank his heart.

Evening and darkness came into his room. The old man stood up, feeling a restlessness unusual to him in his late days, for they were usually as mild as cool rays of autumn sunlight. He slowly kindled a light. Then he went to the cupboard and looked for an old book. His heart was weary of restlessness. He took the Bible, kissed it ardently, and then opened it and read until late into the night.

He began work on the picture. Esther sat leaning thoughtfully back in a soft, comfortable armchair, sometimes listening to the old man as he told her all kinds of stories from his own life and the lives of others, trying to while away the monotonous hours of sitting still for her. Sometimes she just sat calmly dreaming in the large room where the tapestries, pictures and drawings adorning the walls attracted her gaze. The painter's progress was slow. He felt that the studies he was doing of Esther were only first attempts, and had not yet caught the final conviction that he wanted. There was still something lacking in the idea behind his sketches; he could not put it into words, but he felt it deep within him so clearly that feverish haste often drove him on from sketch to sketch, and then, comparing them with each other, he was still not content, faithful as his likenesses of Esther were. He did not mention it to the girl, but he felt as if the harsh set of her lips, a look that never entirely left them even when she was gently dreaming, would detract from the serene expectation that was to transfigure his Madonna. There was too much childish defiance in her for her mood to turn to sweet contemplation of motherhood. He did not think any words would really dispel that darkness in her; it could change only from within. But the soft, feminine emotion he wanted would not come to her face, even when the first spring days cast red-gold sunlight into the room through every window and the whole world stirred as it revived, when all colours seemed to be even softer and deeper, like the warm air wafting through the streets. Finally the painter grew weary. He was an experienced old man, he knew the limits of his art, and he knew he could not overcome them by force. Obeying the insistent voice of sudden intuition, he soon gave up his original plan for the painting. And after weighing up the possibilities, he decided not to paint Esther as the Madonna absorbed in thoughts of the Annunciation, since her face showed no signs of devoutly awakening femininity, but as the most straightforward but deeply felt symbol of his faith, the Madonna with her child. And he wanted to begin it at once, because hesitation was making inroads on his soul, again now that the radiance of the miracle he had dreamt of was fading, and had almost disappeared entirely into darkness. Without telling Esther, he removed the canvas, which bore a few fleeting traces of overhasty sketches, and replaced it with a fresh one as he tried to give free rein to his new idea.

When Esther sat down in her usual way next day and waited, leaning gently back, for him to begin his work—not an unwelcome prospect to her, since it brought inspiring words and happy moments into the bleakness of her lonely day—she was surprised to hear the painter's voice in the next room, in friendly conversation with a woman whose rough, rustic voice she did not recognize. Curious, she pricked up her ears, but she could not hear what they were saying distinctly. Soon the woman's voice died away, a door latched, and the old man came in and went over to her carrying something pale in his arms. She did not realize at once what it was. He carefully placed a small, naked, sturdy child a few months old on her lap. At first the baby wriggled, then he lay still. Esther stared wide-eyed at the old man—she had not expected him to play such a strange trick on her. But he only smiled and said nothing. When he saw that her anxious, questioning eyes were still fixed on him, he calmly explained, in a tone that asked her approval, his intention of painting her with the child on her lap. All the warm kindliness of his eyes went into that request. The deep fatherly love that he had come to feel for this strange girl, and his confidence in her restless heart, shone through his words and even his eloquent silence.

Esther's face had flushed rosy red. A great sense of shame tormented her. She hardly dared to look timidly sideways at the healthy little creature whom she reluctantly held on her trembling knees. She had been brought up among people who had a stern abhorrence of the naked human body, and it made her look at this healthy, happy and now peacefully sleeping baby with revulsion and secret fear; she instinctively hid her own nakedness even from herself, and shrank from touching the little boy's soft, pink flesh as if it were a sin. She was afraid, and didn't know why. All her instincts told her to say no, but she did not want to respond so brusquely to the old man's kindly words, for she increasingly loved and revered him. She felt that she could not deny him anything. And his silence and the question in his waiting glance weighed so heavily on her that she could have cried out with a loud, wordless animal scream. She felt unreasonable dislike of the peacefully slumbering child; he had intruded into her one quiet, untroubled hour and destroyed her dreamy melancholy. But she felt weak and defenceless in the face of the calm old man's kindly wisdom. He was like a pale and lonely star above the dark depths of her life. Once again, as she did in answer to all his requests, she bowed her head in humble confusion.

He said no more, but set about beginning the picture. First he only sketched the outline, for Esther was still far too uneasy and bewildered to embody the meaning of his work. Her dreamy expression had entirely disappeared. There was something tense and desperate in her eyes as she avoided looking at the sleeping, naked infant on her lap, and fixed them instead in endless scrutiny on the walls full of pictures and ornaments to which she really felt indifferent. Her stiff hand showed that she was afraid she might have to bring herself to touch the little body. In addition, the weight on her knees was heavy, but she dared not move. However, the tension in her face showed more and more strongly what a painful effort she was making. In the end the painter himself began to have some inkling of her discomfort, although he ascribed it not to her inherited abhorrence of nakedness but to maidenly modesty, and he ended the sitting. The baby himself went on sleeping like a replete little animal, and did not notice when the painter carefully took him off the girl's lap and put him down on the bed in the next room, where he stayed until his mother, a sturdy Dutch seaman's wife brought to Antwerp for a while by chance, came to fetch him. But although Esther was free of the physical burden she felt greatly oppressed by the idea that she would now have to suffer the same alarm every day.

For the next few days she both came to the studio and left it again uneasily. Secretly, she hoped that the painter would give up this plan as well, and her decision to ask him to do so with a few calm words became compelling and overwhelming. Yet she could never quite bring herself do it; personal pride or a secret sense of shame kept the words back even as they came to her lips like birds ready to take flight. However, as she came back day after day, even though she was so restless, her shame gradually became an unconscious lie, for she had already come to terms with it, as you might come to terms with an unwelcome fact about yourself. She simply did not understand what had happened. Meanwhile the picture was making little progress, although the painter described it cautiously to her. In reality the frame of his canvas contained only the empty and unimportant lines of the figures, and a few fleeting attempts at choosing shades of colour. The old man was waiting for Esther to reconcile herself to his idea, and as his hope that she would verged on certainty he did not try to hurry matters along. For the time being, he made her sittings shorter, and talked a great deal of unimportant matters, deliberately ignoring the presence of the baby and Esther's uneasiness. He seemed more confident and cheerful than ever.

And this time his confidence was well-founded. One morning it was bright and warm, the rectangle of the window framed a light, translucent landscape—towers that were far away, yet the golden gleam on them made them look close; rooftops from which smoke rose in a leisurely fashion, curling up into the deep damask blue of the sky and losing itself there; white clouds very close, as if they were about to descend like downy fluttering birds into the darkly flowing sea of roofs. And the sun cast great handfuls of gold on everything, rays and dancing sparks, circles of light like little clinking coins, narrow strips of it like gleaming daggers, fluttering shapes without any real form that leapt nimbly over the floorboards as if they were bright little animals. This dappled, sparkling play of light had woken the baby from sleep as it tapped at his closed eyelids, until his eyes opened and he blinked and stared. He began moving restlessly on Esther's lap as she reluctantly held him. However, he was not trying to get away from her, only grabbing awkwardly with his clumsy little hands at the sparkling light dancing and playing around them, although he could not seize them, and his failure only made him try harder. His fat little fingers tried to move faster and faster. The sunny light showed the warm flow of blood shining rosily through them, and this simple game made the child's clumsy little body such a charming sight that it cast a spell even on Esther. Smiling with her superior knowledge at the baby's vain attempts to catch and hold the light, she watched his endless game without tiring, quite forgetting her reluctance to hold the innocent, helpless infant. For the first time she felt that there was true human life in the smooth little body—all she had felt before was his naked flesh and the dull satisfaction of his senses—and with childish curiosity of her own she followed all his movements. The old man watched in silence. If he spoke he feared he might revive her truculence and the shame she had forgotten, but his kindly lips wore the satisfied smile of a man who knows the world and its creatures. He saw nothing startling in this change, he had expected and counted on it, confident of the deep laws of nature that never fail. Once again he felt very close to one of those miracles of life that are always renewing themselves, a miracle that can suddenly use children to call forth the devoted kindness of women, and they then give it back to the children, so the miracle passes from being to being and never loses its own childhood but lives a double life, in itself and in those it encounters. And was this not the divine miracle of Mary herself, a child who would never become a woman, but would live on in her child? Was that miracle not reflected in reality, and did not every moment of burgeoning life have about it an ineffable radiance and the sound of what can never be understood?

The old man felt again, deeply, that proximity to the miraculous the idea of which, whether divine or earthly, had obsessed him for weeks. But he knew that he stood outside a dark, closed gate, from which he must humbly turn away again, merely leaving a reverent kiss on the forbidden threshold. He picked up a brush to work, and so chase away ideas that were already lost in clouded gloom. However, when he looked to see how close his copy came to reality, he was spellbound for a moment. He felt as if all his searching so far had been in a world hung about with veils, although he did not know it, and only now that they were removed did its power and extravagance burn before him. The picture he had wanted was coming to life. With shining eyes and clutching hands, the healthy, happy child turned to the light that poured its soft radiance over his naked body. And above that playful face was a second, tenderly bent over the child, and itself full of the radiance cast by that bright little body. Esther held her slender, childish hands on both sides of the baby to protect and avert all misfortune from him. And above her head was a fleeting light caught in her hair and seeming to shine out of it from within. Gentle movement united with moving light, unconsciousness joined dreaming memory, they all came together in a brief and beautiful image, airy and made of translucent colours, an image that could be shattered by a moment's abrupt movement.

The old man looked at the couple as if at a vision. The swift play of light seemed to have brought them together, and as if in distant dreams he thought of the Italian master's almost forgotten picture and its divine serenity. Once again he felt as if he heard the call of God. But this time he did not lose himself in dreams, he put all his strength into the moment. With vigorous strokes, he set down the play of the girl's childish hands, the gentle inclination of her bent head, her attitude no longer harsh. It was as if, although the moment was transitory, he wanted to preserve it for ever. He felt creative power in him like hot young blood. His whole life was in flux and flow, light and colour flowed into that moment, forming and holding his painting hand. And as he came closer to the secret of divine power and the unlimited abundance of life than ever before, he did not think about its signs and miracles, he lived them out by creating them himself.

The game did not last long. The child at last got tired of constantly snatching at the light, and Esther was surprised to see the old man suddenly working with feverish haste, his cheeks flushed. His face showed the same visionary light as in the days when he had talked to her about God and his many miracles, and she felt fervent awe in the presence of a mind that could lose itself so entirely in worlds of creation. And in that overwhelming feeling she lost the slight sense of shame she had felt, thinking that the painter had taken her by surprise at the moment when she was entirely fulfilled by the sight of the child. She saw only the abundance of life, and its sublime variety allowed her to feel again the awe that she had first known when the painter showed her pictures of distant, unknown people, cities as lovely as a dream, lush landscapes. The deprivations of her own life, the monotony of her intellectual experience took on colour from the sound of what was strange and the magnificence of what was distant. And a creative longing of her own burnt deep in her soul, like a hidden light burning in darkness.

That day was a turning point in the history of Esther and the picture. The shadows had fallen away from her. Now she walked fast, stepping lightly, to those hours in the studio that seemed to pass so quickly; they strung together a whole series of little incidents each of which was significant to her, for she did not know the true value of life and thought herself rich with the little copper coins of unimportant events. Imperceptibly, the figure of the old man retreated into the background of her mind by comparison with the baby's helpless little pink body. Her hatred had turned to a wild and almost greedy affection, such as girls often feel for small children and little animals. Her whole being was poured into watching and caressing him; unconsciously and in a passionate game, she was living out a woman's most sublime dream, the dream of motherhood. The purpose of her visits to the studio eluded her. She came, sat down in the big armchair with the healthy little baby, who soon recognized her and would laugh back at her, and began her ardent flirtation with him, quite forgetting that she was here for the sake of the picture, and that she had once felt this naked child was nothing but a nuisance. That time seemed as far away as one of the countless deceptive dreams that she used to spin in her long hours in the dark, dismal alley; their fabric dissolved at the first cautious breath of a wind of reality. Only in those hours at the studio did she now seem to live, not in the time she spent at home or the night into which she plunged to sleep. When her fingers held the baby's plump little hands, she felt that this was not an empty dream. And the smile for her in his big blue eyes was not a lie. It was life, and she drank it in with an avidity for abundance that was a rich, unconscious part of her heritage, and also a need to give of herself, a feminine longing before she was a woman yet. This game already had in it the seed of deeper longing and deeper joy. But it was still only a flirtatious dance of affection and admiration, playful charm and foolish dream. She cradled the baby like a child cuddling her doll, but she dreamt as women and mothers dream—sweetly, lovingly, as if in some boundless distant space.

The old man felt the change with all the fullness of his wise heart. He sensed that he was further from her now, but not stranger, and that he was not at the centre of her wishes but left to one side, like a pleasant memory. And he was glad of this change, much as he also loved Esther, for he saw young, strong, kind instincts in her which, he hoped, would do more than his own efforts to break through the defiance and reserve of the nature she had inherited. He knew that her love for him, an old man at the end of his days, was wasteful, although it could bring blessing and promise to her young life.

He owed wonderful hours to the love for the child that had awakened in Esther. Images of great beauty formed before him, all expressing a single idea and yet all different. Soon it was an affectionate game—his sketches showed Esther playing with the child, still a child herself in her unbounded delight, they showed flexible movements without harshness or passion, mild colours blending gently, the tender merging of tender forms. And then again there were moments of silence when the child had fallen asleep on her soft lap, and Esther's little hands watched over him like two hovering angels, when the tender joy of possession lit in her eyes, and a silent longing to wake the sleeping face with loving play. Then again there were seconds when the two pairs of eyes, hers and the baby's, were drawn to each other unconsciously, unintentionally, each seeking the other in loving devotion. Again, there were moments of charming confusion when the child's clumsy hands felt for the girl's breast, expecting to find his mother's milk there. Esther's cheeks would flush bashfully at that, but she felt no fear now, no reluctance, only a shy surge of emotion that turned to a happy smile.

These days were the creative hours that went into the picture. The painter made it out of a thousand touches of tenderness, a thousand loving, blissful, fearful, happy, ardent maternal glances. A great work full of serenity was coming into being. It was plain and simple—just a child playing and a girl's head gently bending down. But the colours were milder and clearer than he had ever painted colours before, and the forms stood out as sharply and distinctly as dark trees against the glow of an evening sky. It was as if there must be some inner light hidden in the picture, shedding that secret brightness, as if air blew in it more softly, caressingly and clearly than in any other earthly work. There was nothing supernatural about it, and yet it showed the mystical mind of the man who had created it. For the first time the old man felt that in his long and busy creative life he had always been painting, brushstroke after brushstroke, some being of which he really knew nothing. It was like the old folk tale of the magical imps who do their work in hiding, yet so industriously that people marvel in the morning to see all they did overnight. That was how the painter felt when, after moments of creative inspiration, he stepped back from the picture and looked critically at it. Once again the idea of a miracle knocked on the door of his heart, and this time he hardly hesitated to let it in. For this work seemed to him not only the flower of his entire achievement, but something more distant and sublime of which his humble work was not worthy, although it was also the crown of his artistic career. Then his cheerful creativity would die away and turn to a strange mood when he felt fear of his own work, no longer daring to see himself in it.

So he distanced himself from Esther, who now seemed to him only the means of expressing the earthly miracle that he had worked. He showed her all his old kindness, but once again his mind was full of the pious dreams that he had thought far away. The simple power of life suddenly seemed to him so wonderful. Who could give him answers? The Bible was old and sacred, but his heart was earthly and still bound to this life. Where could he ask whether the wings of God descended to this world? Were there signs of God still abroad today, or only the ordinary miracles of life?

The old man did not venture to wish for the answer, although he had seen strange things during his life. But he was no longer as sure of himself as in the old days when he believed in life and in God, and did not stop to wonder which of them was really true. Every evening he carefully covered up the picture, because once recently, on coming home to see silver moonlight resting on it like a blessing, he felt as if the Mother of God herself had shown him her face, and he could almost have thrown himself down in prayer before the work of his own hands.

Something else, however, happened at this time in Esther's life, nothing in itself strange or unlikely, but it affected the depths of her being like a rising storm and left her trembling in pain that she did not understand. She was experiencing the mystery of maturity, turning from a child into a woman. She was bewildered, since no one had taught her anything about it in advance; she had gone her own strange way alone between deep darkness and mystical light. Now longing awoke in her and did not know where to turn. The defiance that used to make her avoid playing with other children or speaking an unnecessary word burnt like a dark curse at this time. She did not feel the secret sweetness of the change in her, the promise of a seed not yet ready to come to life, only a dull, mysterious pain that she had to bear alone. In her ignorance, she saw the legends and miracles of which the old painter had spoken like lights leading her astray, while her dreams followed them through the most unlikely of possibilities. The story of the mild woman whose picture she had seen, the girl who became a mother after a wonderful Annunciation, suddenly struck her with almost joyful fear. She dared not believe it, because she had heard many other things that she did not understand. However, she thought that some miracle must be taking place inside her because she felt so different in every way, the world and everyone in it also suddenly seemed so different, deeper, stranger, full of secret urges. It all appeared to come together into an inner life trying to get out, then retreating again. There was some common factor at work;

she did not know where it lay, but it seemed to hold everything that had once been separate together. She herself felt a force that was trying to take her out into life, to other human beings, but it did not know where to turn, and left behind only that urgent, pressing, tormenting pain of unspent longing and unused power.

In these hours when she was overwhelmed by desperation and needed some kind of support to cling to, Esther tried something that she had thought impossible before. She spoke to her foster father. Until now she had instinctively avoided him, because she felt the distance between them. But now she was driven over that threshold. She told him all about it, and talked about the picture, she looked deep into herself to find something gleaned from those hours that could be useful to her. And the landlord, visibly pleased to hear of the change in her, patted her cheeks with rough kindness and listened. Sometimes he put in a word, but it was as casual and impersonal as the way he spat out tobacco. Then he told her, in his own clumsy fashion, what had just happened to her. Esther listened, but it was no use. He didn't know what else to say to her and didn't even try. Nothing seemed to touch him except outwardly, there was no real sympathy between them, and his words suggested an indifference that repelled her. She knew now what she had only guessed before—people like him could never understand her. They might live side by side, but they did not know each other; it was like living in a desert. And in fact she thought her foster father was the best of all those who went in and out of this dismal tavern, because he had a certain rough plainness about him that could turn to kindness.

However, this disappointment could not daunt the power of her longings, and they all streamed back towards the two living beings she knew who spanned the morning and evening of human life. She desperately counted the lonely night hours still separating her from morning, and then she counted the morning hours separating her from her visit to the painter. Her ardent longings showed in her face. And once out in the street she abandoned herself entirely to her passion like a swimmer plunging into a foaming torrent, and raced through the hurrying crowd, stopping only when, with flushed face and untidy hair, she reached the door of the house she longed to see. In this time of the change in her, she was overcome by an instinctive urge to make free, passionate gestures, and it gave her a wild and desirable beauty.

That greedy, almost desperate need for affection made her prefer the baby to the old man, in whose friendly kindness there was a serenity that rejected stormy passion. He knew nothing about the feminine change in Esther, but he guessed it from her demeanour, and her sudden ecstatic transports made him uneasy. Sensing the nature of the elemental urge driving her on, he did not try to rein it in. Nor did he lose his fatherly love for this lonely child, although his mind had gone back to contemplation of the abstract interplay of the secret forces of life. He was glad to see her, and tried to keep her with him. The picture was in fact finished, but he did not tell Esther so, not wishing to part her from the baby on whom she lavished such affection. Now and then he added a few brushstrokes, but they were minor details—the design of a fold, a slight shading in the background, a fleeting nuance added to the play of light. He dared not touch the real idea behind the picture any more, for the magic of reality had slowly retreated, and he thought the dual aspect of the painting conveyed the spiritual nature of the wonderful creativity that now, as the memory of his execution of it faded, seemed to him less and less like the work of earthly powers. Any further attempt at improvement, he thought, would be not only folly but a sin. And he made up his mind that after this work, in which his hand had clearly been guided, he would do no more paintings, for they could only be lesser works, but spend his days in prayer and in searching for a way to reach those heights whose golden evening glow had rested on him in these late hours of his life.

With the fine instinct that the orphaned and rejected harbour in their hearts, like a secret network of sensitive fibres encompassing everything said and unsaid, Esther sensed the slight distance that the old man who was so dear to her had placed between them, and his mild tenderness, which was still the same, almost distressed her. She felt that at this moment she needed his whole attention and the free abundance of his love so that she could tell him all that was in her heart, all that now troubled it, and ask for answers to the riddles around her. She waited for the right moment to let out the words to express her mental turmoil, but the waiting was endless and tired her out. So all her affection was bent on the child. Her love concentrated on that helpless little body; she would catch the baby up and smother him with warm kisses so impetuously, forgetting his vulnerability, that she hurt him and he began to cry. Then she was less fiercely loving, more protective and reassuring, but even her anxieties were a kind of ecstasy, just as her feelings were not truly maternal, but more of a surge of longing erotic instincts dimly sensed. A force was trying to emerge in her, and her ignorance led her to turn it on the child. She was living out a dream, in a painful dazed state; she clung convulsively to the baby because he had a warm, beating heart, like hers, because she could lavish all the tenderness in her on his silent lips, because with him, unconsciously longing for a human touch, she could clasp another living creature without fearing the shame that came over her if she said a single word to a stranger. She spent hours and hours like that, never tiring, and never realizing how she was giving herself away.

For her, all the life for which she longed so wildly was now contained in the child. These were dark times, growing even darker, but she never noticed. The citizens of Antwerp gathered in the evenings and talked of the old liberties and good King Charles, who had loved his land of Flanders so much, with regret and secret anger. There was unrest in the city. The Protestants were secretly uniting. Rabble who feared the daylight assembled, as ominous news arrived from Spain. Minor skirmishes and clashes with the soldiers became more frequent, and in this uneasy, hostile atmosphere the first flames of war and rebellion flared up. Prudent people began to look abroad, others consoled and reassured themselves as well as they could, but the whole country was in a state of fearful expectation, and it was reflected in all faces. At the tavern, the men sat together in corners talking in muted voices, while the landlord spoke of the horrors of war, and joked in his rough way, but no one felt like laughing. The carefree cheerfulness of easy-going folk was extinguished by fear and restless waiting.

Esther felt nothing of this world, neither its muted alarms nor its secret fevers. The child was contented as always, and laughed back at her in his own way—and so she noticed no change in her surroundings. Confused as she was, her life followed a single course. The darkness around her made her fantastic dreams seem real, and it was a reality so distant and strange that she was incapable of any sober, thoughtful understanding of the world. Her femininity, once awakened, cried out for a child, but she did not know the dark mystery involved. She only dreamt a thousand dreams of having a child herself, thinking of the simple marvels of biblical legends and the magical possibility conjured up by her lonely imagination. If anyone had explained this everyday miracle to her in simple words, she might perhaps have looked at the men passing her by with the bashful but considering gaze that was to be seen in the eyes of girls at that time. As it was, however, she never thought of men, only of the children playing in the street, and dreamt of the miracle that might, perhaps, give her a rosy, playful baby some day, a baby all her own who would be her whole happiness. So wild was her wish for one that she might even have given herself to the first comer, throwing aside all shame and fear, just for the sake of the happiness she longed for, but she knew nothing about the creative union of man and woman, and her instincts led her blindly astray. So she returned, again and again, to the other woman's baby. By now she loved him so deeply that he seemed like her own.

One day she came to visit the painter, who had noticed with secret uneasiness her extreme, almost unhealthily passionate love of the child. She arrived with a radiant face and eagerness sparkling in her eyes. The baby was not there as usual. That made her anxious, but she would not admit it, so she went up to the old man and asked him about the progress of his picture. As she put this question the blood rose to her face, for all at once she felt the silent reproach of the many hours when she had paid neither him nor his work any attention. Her neglect of this kindly man weighed on her conscience. But he did not seem to notice.

"It is finished, Esther," he said with a quiet smile. "It was finished long ago. I shall be delivering it tomorrow."

She turned pale, and felt a terrible presentiment that she dared not consider more closely. Very quietly and slowly she asked, "Then I can't come and see you any more?"

He put out both hands to her in the old, warm, compelling gesture that always captivated her. "As often as you like, my child. And the more often that is the happier I shall be. As you see, I am lonely here in this old room of mine, and when you are here it is bright and cheerful all day. Come to see me often, Esther, very often."

All her old love for the old man came welling up, as if to break down all barriers and pour itself out in words. How good and kind he was! Was he not real, and the baby only her own dream? At that moment she felt confident again, but other ideas still hung over that budding confidence like a storm cloud. And the thought of the child tormented her. She wanted to suppress her pain, she kept swallowing the words, but they came out at last in a wild, desperate cry. "What about the baby?"

The old man said nothing, but there was a harsh, almost unsparing expression on his face. Her neglect of him at this moment, when he had hoped to make her soul entirely his own, was like an angry arm warding him off. His voice was cold and indifferent as he said, "The baby has gone away."

He felt her glance hanging on his lips in wild desperation. But a dark force in him made him cruel. He added nothing to what he had said. At that moment he even hated the girl who could so ungratefully forget all the love he had given her, and for a second this kind and gentle man felt a desire to hurt her. But it was only a brief moment of weakness and denial, like a single ripple running away into the endless sea of his gentle kindness. Full of pity for what he saw in her eyes, he turned away.

She could not bear this silence. With a wild gesture, she flung herself on his breast and clung to him, sobbing and moaning. Torment had never burnt more fiercely in her than in the desperate words she cried out between her tears. "I want the baby back, my baby. I can't live without him, they've stolen my one small happiness from me. Why do you want to take the baby away from me? I know I've been unkind to you... Oh, please forgive me and let me have the baby back! Where is he? Tell me! Tell me! I want the baby back..."

The words died away into silent sobbing. Deeply shaken, the old man bent down to her as she clung to him, her convulsive weeping slowly dying down, and she sank lower and lower like a dying flower. Her long, dark hair had come loose, and he gently stroked it. "Be sensible, Esther, and don't cry. The baby has gone away, but—"

"It's not true, oh no, it can't be true!" she cried.

"It *is* true, Esther. His mother has left the country. Times are bad for foreigners and heretics here—and for the faithful and God-fearing as well. They have gone to France, or perhaps England. But why so despairing? Be sensible, Esther, wait a few days and you'll see, you will feel better again."

"I can't, I won't," she cried through more tears. "Why have they taken the baby away from me? He was all I had... I must have him back, I must, I must. He loved me, he was the only creature in the world who was mine, all mine... how am I to live now? Tell me where he is, oh, tell me..."

Her mingled sobs and lamentations became confused, desperate murmuring growing softer and more meaningless, and finally turning to hopeless weeping. Ideas shot like lightning through her tormented mind, she was unable to think clearly and calm down. All she thought and felt circled crazily, restlessly and with pitiless force around the one painful thought obsessing her. The endless silent sea of her questing love surged with loud, despairing pain, and her words flowed on, hot and confused, like blood running from a wound that would not close. The old man had tried to calm her distress with gentle words, but now, in despair, he could say nothing. The elemental force and dark fire of her passion seemed to him stronger than any way he knew of pacifying her. He waited and waited. Sometimes her torrent of feeling seemed to hesitate briefly and grow a little calmer, but again and again a sob set off words that were half a scream, half weeping. Her young soul, rich with love to give, was bleeding to death in her pain.

At last he was able to speak to Esther, but she wouldn't listen. Her eyes were fixed on a single image, and a single thought filled her heart. She stammered it all out, as if she were seeing hallucinations. "He had such a sweet laugh... he was mine, all mine for all those lovely days, I was his mother... and now I can't have him any more. If only I could see him again, just once... if I could only see him just once." And again her voice died away in helpless sobs. She had slowly slipped down from her resting place against the old man's breast, and was clinging to his knees with weary, shaking hands, crouching there surrounded by the flowing locks of her dark hair. As she stooped down, moving convulsively, her face hidden by her hair, she seemed to be crushed by pain and anger. Monotonously, her desperate mind tiring now, she babbled those words again and again. "Just to see him again... only once... if I could see him again just once!"

The old man bent over her.

"Esther?"

She did not move. Her lips went on babbling the same words, without meaning or intonation. He tried to raise her. When he took her arm it was powerless and limp like a broken branch, and fell straight back again. Only her lips kept stammering, "Just to see him again... see him again, oh, see him again just once..."

At that a strange idea came into his baffled mind as he tried to comfort her. He leant down close to her ear. "Esther? You *shall* see him again, not just once but as often as you like."

She started up as if woken from a dream. The words seemed to flow through all her limbs, for suddenly her body moved and straightened up. Her mind seemed to be slowly clearing. Her thoughts were not quite lucid yet, for instinctively she did not believe in so much happiness revealing itself after such pain. Uncertainly she looked up at the old man as if her senses were reeling. She did not entirely understand him, and waited for him to say more, because everything was so indistinct to her. However, he said nothing, but looked at her with a kindly promise in his eyes and nodded. Gently, he put his arm around her, as if afraid of hurting her. So it was not a dream or a lie spoken on impulse. Her heart beat fast in expectation. Willing as a child, she leant against him as he moved away, not knowing where he was going. But he led her only a few steps across the room to his easel. With a swift movement, he removed the cloth covering the picture.

At first Esther was motionless. Her heart stood still. But then, her glance avid, she ran up to the picture as if to snatch the dear, rosy, smiling baby out of his frame and bring him back to life, cradle him in her arms, caress him, feel the tenderness of his clumsy limbs and bring a smile to his comical little mouth. She did not stop to think that this was only a picture, a piece of painted canvas, only a dream of real life; in fact she did not think at all, she only felt, and her eyelids fluttered in blissful ecstasy. She stood close to the painting, never moving. Her fingers trembled and tingled, longing to feel the child's sweet softness again, her lips burnt to cover the little body with loving kisses again. A fever, but a blessed one, ran through her own body. Then warm tears came to her eyes, no longer angry and despairing, but happy as well as melancholy, the overflowing expression of many strange feelings that suddenly filled her heart and must come out. The convulsions that had shaken her died down, and an uncertain but mild mood of reconciliation enveloped her and gently, sweetly lulled her into a wonderful waking dream far from all reality.

The old man again felt a questioning awe in the midst of his delight. How miraculous was this work that could mysteriously inspire even the man who had created it himself, how unearthly was the sublimity that radiated from it! Was this not like the signs and images of the saints whom he honoured, and who could suddenly make the poor and oppressed forget their troubles and go home liberated and inspired by a miracle? And did not a sacred fire now burn in the eyes of the girl looking at her own portrait without curiosity or shame, in pure devotion to God? He felt that these strange paths must have some destination, there must be a will at work that was not blind like his own, but clear-sighted and master of all its wishes. These ideas rejoiced in his heart like a peal of bells, and he felt he had been touched by the grace of Heaven.

Carefully, he took Esther's hand and led her away from the picture. He did not speak, for he too felt warm tears coming to his eyes and did not want to show them. A warm radiance seemed to rest on her head as it did in the picture of the Madonna. It was as if something great beyond all words was in the room with them, rushing by on invisible wings. He looked into Esther's eyes. They were no longer tearfully defiant, but shadowed only by a gentle reflective bloom. Everything around them seemed to him brighter, milder, transfigured. God's sanctity, miraculously close, was revealing itself to him in all things.

They stood together like that for a long time. Then they began to talk as they used to do, but calmly and sensibly, like two human beings who now understood each other entirely and had no more to search for. Esther was quiet. The sight of the picture had moved her strangely, and made her happy because it restored the happiness of her dearest memory to her, because she had her baby back, but her feelings were far more solemn, deeper and more maternal than they had ever been in reality. For now the child was not just the outward appearance of her dream but part of her own soul. No one could take him away from her. He was all hers when she looked at the picture, and she could see it at any time. The old man, shaken by mystical portents, had willingly answered her desperate request. And now she could feel the same blessed abundance of life every day, her longings need no longer be timid and fearful, and the little childlike figure who to others was the Saviour of the world also, unwittingly, embodied a God of love and life to the lonely Jewish girl.

She visited the studio several more days running. But the painter was aware of his commission, which he had almost forgotten. The merchant came to look at the picture and he too, although he knew nothing about the secret miracles of its creation, was overwhelmed by the gentle figure of the Mother of God and the simple expression of an eternal symbol in its execution. He warmly shook hands with his friend, who, however, turned away his lavish praise with a modest, pious gesture, as if he were not standing in front of his own work. The two of them decided not to keep the altar deprived of this adornment any longer.

Next day the picture occupied the other wing of the altarpiece, and the first was no longer alone. And the pair of Madonnas, strangers but with a slight similarity, were a curious sight. They seemed like two sisters, one of them still confidently abandoning herself to the sweetness of life, while the other had already tasted the dark fruit of pain and knew a terror of times yet to come. But the same radiance hung over both their heads, as if stars of love shone above them, and they would take their path through life with its joy and pain under those stars.

Esther herself followed the picture to church, as if she found her own child there. Gradually the memory that the child was a stranger to her was dying away, and true maternal feelings were aroused in her, making her dream into reality. For hours on end she would lie prostrated before the painting, like a Christian before the image of the Saviour. But hers was another faith, and the deep voices of the bells called the congregation to devotions that she did not know. Priests whose words she could not understand sang, loud choral chanting swept like dark waves through the church, rising into the mystic twilight above the pews like a fragrant cloud. And men and women whose faith she hated surrounded her, their murmured prayers drowning out the quiet, loving words she spoke to her baby. However, she was unaware of any of that. Her heart was too bewildered to look around and take any notice of other people; she merely gave herself up to her one wish, to see her child every day, and thought of nothing else in the world. The stormy weather of her budding youth had died down, all her longings had gone away or had flowed into the one idea that drew her back to the picture again and again, as if it were a magical magnet that no other power could withstand. She had never been so happy as she was in those long hours in the church, sensing its solemnity and its secret pleasures without understanding them. She was hurt only when some stranger now and then knelt in front of the picture, looking adoringly up at the child who was hers, all hers. Then she was defiantly jealous, with anger in her heart that made her want to hit out and shed tears. At such moments her mind was increasingly troubled, and she could not distinguish between the real world and the world of her dreams. Only when she lay in front of the picture again did stillness return to her heart.

Spring passed on, the mild, warm weather in which the picture had been finished still held, and it seemed that after all her stormy suffering, summer too would give her the same great and solemn gift of quiet maternal love. The nights were warm and bright, but her fever had died away, and gentle, loving dreams came over Esther's mind. She seemed to be at peace, rocking to a rhythm of calm passion as the regular hours went by, and all that had been lost in the darkness now pointed her ahead along a bright path into the future.

At last the summer approached its climax, the Feast of St Mary, the greatest day in Flanders. Long processions decked out with pennants blowing in the breeze and billowing banners went through the golden harvest fields that were usually full of busy workers. The monstrance held above the seed corn in the priest's hands as he blessed it shone like the sun, and voices raised in prayer made a gentle sound, so that the sheaves in the fields shook and humbly bowed down. But high in the air clear bells rang in the distance, to be answered joyfully from church towers far away. It was a mighty sound, as if the earth itself were singing together with the woods and the roaring sea.

The glory of the day flowed back from the fertile land into the city and washed over its menacing walls. The noise of craftsmen at work died down, the day labourers' hoarse voices fell silent, only musicians playing fife and bagpipes went from street to street, and the clear silvery voices of dancing children joined the music-making. Silken robes trimmed with yellowing lace, kept waiting in wardrobes all the last year, saw the light of day again, men and women in their best clothes, talking cheerfully, set out for church. And in the cathedral, with its doors open to invite in the pious with clouds of blue incense and fragrant coolness, a springtime of scattered flowers bloomed, pictures and altars were adorned with lavish garlands made by careful hands. Thousands of candles cast magical light into the sweet-scented darkness where the organ roared, and singing, mysterious radiance and mystical twilight reached the heights and depths of the great building.

And then, suddenly a pious and God-fearing mood seemed to flow out into the streets. A procession of the devout formed; up by the main altar the priests raised the famous portrait of St Mary, which seemed to be surrounded by whispered rumours of many miracles, it was borne aloft on the shoulders of the pious, and a solemn procession began. The picture being carried along brought silence to the noisy street, for the crowd fell quiet as people bowed down, and a broad furrow of prayer followed the portrait until it was returned to the cool depths of the cathedral that received it like a fragrant grave.

That year, however, the pious festival was under a dark cloud. For weeks the country had been bearing a heavy burden. Gloomy and as yet unconfirmed news said that the old privileges were to be declared null and void. The freedom fighters known as the Beggars who opposed Spanish rule were making common cause with the Protestants. Dreadful rumours came from the countryside of Protestant divines preaching to crowds of thousands in open places outside the towns and cities, and giving Communion to the armed citizens. Spanish soldiers had been attacked, and churches were said to have been stormed to the sound of the singing of the Geneva Psalms. There was still no definite word of any of this, but the secret flickering of a coming conflagration was felt, and the armed resistance planned by the more thoughtful at secret meetings in their homes degenerated into wild violence and defiance among the many who had nothing to lose.

The festival day had brought the first wave of rioting to Antwerp in the shape of a rabble united in nothing but an instinct to join sudden uprisings. Sinister figures whom no one knew suddenly appeared in the taverns, cursing and uttering wild threats against Spaniards and clerics. Strange people of defiant and angry appearance who avoided the light of day emerged from nooks and crannies and disreputable alleys. There was more and more trouble. Now and then there were minor skirmishes. They did not spill over into a general movement, but were extinguished like sparks hissing out in isolation. The Prince of Orange still maintained strict discipline, and controlled the greedy, quarrelsome and ill-intentioned mob who were joining the Protestants only for the sake of profit.

The magnificence of the great procession merely provoked repressed instincts. For the first time coarse jokes mingled with the singing of the faithful, wild threats were uttered and scornful laughter. Some sang the text of the Beggars' song to a pious melody, a young fellow imitated the croaking voice of the preacher, to the delight of his companions, others greeted the portrait of the Virgin by sweeping off their hats with ostentatious gallantry as if to their lady love. The soldiers and the few faithful Catholics who had ventured to take part in the procession were powerless, and had to grit their teeth and watch this mockery as it became ever wilder. And now that the common people had tasted defiant power, they were becoming less and less amenable. Almost all of them were already armed. The dark impulse that had so far broken out only in curses and threats called for action. This menacing unrest lay over the city like a storm cloud on the feast day of St Mary and the days that followed.

Women and the more sober of the men had kept to their houses since the angry scenes had endangered the procession. The streets now belonged to the mob and the Protestants. Esther, too, had stayed at home for the last few days. But she knew nothing of all these dark events. She vaguely noticed that there were more and more people crowding into the tavern, that the shrill sound of whores' voices mingled with the agitated talk of quarrelling, cursing men, she saw distraught women, she saw figures secretly whispering together, but she felt such indifference to all these things that she did not even ask her foster father about them. She thought of nothing but the baby, the baby who, in her dreams, had long ago become her own. All memory paled beside this one image. The world was no longer so strange to her, but it had no value because it had nothing to give her; her loving devotion and youthful need of God were lost in her thoughts of the child. Only the single hour a day when she stole out to see the picture—it was both her God and her child—breathed real life into her. Otherwise she was like a woman lost in dreams, passing everything else by like a sleepwalker. Day after day, and even once on a long summer night heavy with warm fragrance, when she had fled the tavern and made sure she was shut up in the cathedral, she prostrated herself before the picture on her knees. Her ignorant soul had made a God of it.

And these days were difficult for her, because they kept her from her child. While festive crowds thronged the tall aisles on the Feast of St Mary, and surging organ music filled the nave, she had to turn back and leave the cathedral with the rest of the people crowding it, feeling humbled like a beggar woman because worshippers kept standing in front of the two pictures of St Mary in the chapel that day, and she feared she might be recognized. Sad and almost despairing, she went back, never noticing the sunlight of the day because she had been denied a sight of her child. Envy and anger came over her when she saw the crowds making pilgrimage to the altarpiece, piously coming through the tall porch of the cathedral into that fragrant blue darkness.

She was even sadder next day, when she was not allowed to go out into the streets, now so full of menacing figures. Her room, to which the noise of the tavern rose like a thick, ugly smoke, became intolerable to her. To her confused heart, a day when she could not see the baby in the picture was like a dark and gloomy sleepless night, a night of torment. She was not strong enough yet to bear deprivation. Late in the evening, when her foster father was sitting in the tavern with his guests, she very quietly went down the stairs. She tried the door, and breathed a sigh of relief; it was not locked. Softly, already feeling the mild fresh air that she had missed for a long time, she slipped through the door and hurried to the cathedral.

The streets through which she swiftly walked were dark and full of muffled noise. Single groups had come together from all sides, and news of the departure of the Prince of Orange had let violence loose. Threatening remarks, heard only occasionally and uttered at random in daytime, now sounded like shouts of command. Here and there drunks were bawling, and enthusiasts were singing rebel songs so loud that the windows echoed. Weapons were no longer hidden; hatchets and hooks, swords and stakes glinted in the flickering torchlight. Like a greedy torrent, hesitating only briefly before its foaming waves sweep away all barriers, these dark troops whom no one dared to resist gathered together.

Esther had taken no notice of this unruly crowd, although she once had to push aside a rough arm reaching for her as she slipped by when its owner tried to grab her headscarf. She never wondered why such madness had suddenly come into the rabble; she did not understand their shouting and cries. She simply overcame her fear and disgust, and quickened her pace until at last, breathless, she reached the tall cathedral deep in the shadow of the houses, white moonlit cloud hovering in the air above it.

Reassured, shivering only slightly, she came into the cathedral through a side door. It was dark in the tall, unlit aisles, with only a mysterious silvery light trembling around the dull glass of the windows. The pews were empty. No shadow moved through the wide, breathless expanses of the building, and the statues of the saints stood black and still before the altars. And like the gentle flickering of a glow-worm there came, from what seemed endless depths, the swaying light of the eternal flame above the chapels. All was quiet and sacred here, and the silent majesty of the place so impressed Esther that she muted her tapping footsteps. Carefully, she groped her way towards the chapel in the side aisle and then, trembling, knelt down in front of the picture in boundless quiet rejoicing. In the flowing darkness, it seemed to look down from dense, fragrant clouds, endlessly far away yet very close. And now she did not think any more. As always, the confused longings of her maturing girlish heart relaxed in fantastic dreams. Ardour seemed to stream from every fibre of her being and gather around her brow like an intoxicating cloud. These long hours of unconscious devotion, united with the longing for love, were like a sweet, gently numbing drug; they were a dark wellspring, the blessed fruit of the Hesperides containing and nourishing all divine life. For all bliss was present in her sweet, vague dreams, through which tremors of longing passed. Her agitated heart beat alone in the great silence of the empty church. A soft, bright radiance like misty silver came from the picture, as if shed by a light within, carrying her up from the cold stone of the steps to the mild warm region of light that she knew in dreams. It was a long time since she had thought of the baby as a stranger to her. She dreamt of the God in him and the God in every woman, the essence of her own body, warm with her blood. Vague yearning for the divine, questing ecstasy and the rise of maternal feelings in her spun the deceptive network of her life's dream between them. For her, there was brightness in the wide, oppressive darkness of the church, gentle music played in the awed silence that knew nothing of human language and the passing of the hours. Above her prostrated body, time went its inexorable way.

Something suddenly thudded against the door, shaking it. Then came a second and a third thud, so that she leapt up in alarm, staring into the dreadful darkness. Further thunderous crashing sounds shook the whole tall, proud building, and the isolated lamps rolled like fiery eyes in the dark. Someone was filing through the bolt of the door, now knocked half off its hinges, with a shrill sound like helpless screams in the empty space. The walls flung back the terrifying sounds in violent confusion. Men possessed by greedy rage were hammering at the door, and a roar of excited voices boomed through the hollow shell of the church as if the sea had broken its bounds to come roaring in, and its waves were now beating against the groaning walls of the house of God.

Esther listened, distraught, as if woken suddenly from sleep. But at last the door fell in with a crash. A dark torrent of humanity poured in, filling the mighty building with wild bawling and raging. More came, and more. Thousands of others seemed to be standing outside egging them on. Torches suddenly flared drunkenly up like clutching, greedy hands, and their mad, blood-red light fell on wild faces distorted by blind excitement, their swollen eyes popping as if with sinful desires. Only now did Esther vaguely sense the intentions of the dark rabble that she had already met on her way. The first axe-blows were already falling on the wood of the pulpit, pictures crashed to the floor, statues tipped over, curses and derisive cries swirled up out of this dark flood, above which the torches danced unsteadily as if alarmed by such crazy behaviour. In confusion, the torrent poured onto the high altar, looting and destroying, defiling and desecrating. Wafers of the Host fluttered to the floor like white flower petals, a lamp with the eternal flame in it, flung by a violent hand, rushed like a meteor through the dark. And more and more figures crowded in, with more and more torches burning. A picture caught fire, and the flame licked high like a coiling snake. Someone had laid hands on the organ, smashing its pipes, and their mad notes screamed shrilly for help in the dark. More figures appeared as if out of a wild, deranged dream. A fellow with a bloodstained face smeared his boots with holy oil, to the raucous jubilation of the others, ragged villains strutted about in richly embroidered episcopal vestments, a squealing whore had perched the golden circlet from a statue in her tousled, dirty hair. Thieves drank toasts in wine from the sacred vessels, and up by the high altar two men were fighting with bright knives for possession of a monstrance set with jewels. Prostitutes performed lascivious, drunken dances in front of the shrines, drunks spewed in the fonts of holy water. Angry men armed with flashing axes smashed anything within reach, whatever it was. The sounds rose to a chaotic thunder of noise and screaming voices; like a dense and repellent cloud of plague vapours, the crowd's raging reached to the black heights of the cathedral that looked darkly down on the leaping flames of torches, and seemed immovable, out of reach of this desperate derision.

Esther had hidden in the shadow of the altar in the side chapel, half fainting. It was as if all this must be a dream, and would suddenly disappear like a deceptive illusion. But already the first torches were storming into the side aisles. Figures shaking with fanatical passion as if intoxicated leapt over gratings or smashed them down, overturned the statues and pulled pictures off the shrines. Daggers flashed like fiery snakes in the flickering torchlight, angrily tearing into cupboards and pictures, which fell to the ground with their frames smashed. Closer and closer came the crowd with its smoking, unsteady lights. Esther, breathless, stayed where she was, retreating further into the dark. Her heart missed a beat with alarm and dreadful anticipation. She still did not know quite what was happening, and felt only fear, wild, uncontrollable fear. A few footsteps were coming closer, and then a sturdy, furious fellow broke down the grating with a blow.

She thought she had been seen. But next moment she saw the intruders' purpose, when a statue of the Madonna on the next altar crashed to the floor in pieces. A terrible new fear came to her—they would want to destroy her picture too, her child—and the fear became certainty when picture after picture was pulled down in the flickering torchlight to the sound of jubilant derision, to be torn and trampled underfoot. A terrible idea flashed through her head—they were going to murder the picture, and in her mind it had long ago become her own living child. In a second everything in her flared up as if bathed in dazzling light. One thought, multiplied a thousand times over, inflamed her heart in that single second. She must save the baby, *her* baby. Then dream and reality came together in her mind with desperate fervour. The destructive zealots were already making for the altar. An axe was raised in the air—and at that moment she lost all conscious power of thought and leapt in front of the picture, arms outstretched to protect it…

It was like a magic spell. The axe crashed to the floor from the now powerless hand holding it. The torch fell from the man's other hand and went out as it fell. The sight struck these noisy, frenzied people like lightning. They all fell silent, except for one in whose throat the gasping cry of "The Madonna! The Madonna!" died away.

The mob stood there white as chalk, trembling. A few dropped to their knees in prayer. They were all deeply shaken. The strange illusion was compelling. For them, there was no doubt that a miracle had happened, one of the kind often authenticated, told and retold—the Madonna, whose features were obviously those of the young mother in the picture, was protecting her own likeness. Pangs of conscience were aroused in them when they saw the girl's face, which seemed to them nothing short of the picture come to life. They had never been more devout that in that fleeting moment.

But others were already storming up. Torches illuminated the group standing there rigid and the girl pressing close to the altar, hardly moving herself. Noise flooded into the silence. At the back a woman's shrill voice cried, "Go on, go on, it's only the Jew girl from the tavern." And suddenly the spell was broken. In shame and rage, the humiliated rioters stormed on. A rough fist pushed Esther aside. She swayed. But she kept on her feet, she was fighting for the picture as if it really were her own warm life. Swinging a heavy silver candlestick, she hit out furiously at the iconoclasts with her old defiance; one of them fell, cursing, but another took his place. A dagger glinted like a short red lightning flash, and Esther stumbled and fell. Already the pieces of the splintered altar were raining down on her, but she felt no more pain. The picture of the Madonna and Child, and the picture of the Madonna of the Wounded Heart both fell under a single furious blow from an axe.

And the raving crowd stormed on; from church to church went the looters, filling the streets with terrible noise. A dreadful night fell over Antwerp. Terror and trembling made its way into houses with the news, and hearts beat in fear behind barred gates. But the flame of rebellion was waving like a banner over the whole country.

The old painter, too, shuddered with fear when he heard the news that the iconoclasts were abroad. His knees trembled, and he held a crucifix in his imploring hands to pray for the safety of his picture, the picture given him by the revelation of God's grace. For a whole wild, dark night dreadful ideas tormented him. And at first light of dawn he could not stay at home any longer.

Outside the cathedral, his last hope faded and fell like one of the overturned statues. The doors had been broken down, and rags and splinters showed where the iconoclasts had been like a bloody trail left behind them. He groped his laborious way through the dark to his picture. His hands went out to the shrine, but they met empty air, and sank wearily to his sides again. The faith in his breast that had sung its pious song in praise of God's grace for so many years suddenly flew away like a frightened swallow.

At last he pulled himself together and struck a light, which flared briefly from his tinder, illuminating a scene that made him stagger back. On the ground, among ruins, lay the Italian master's sweetly sad Madonna, the Madonna of the Wounded Heart, transfixed by a dagger thrust. But it was not the picture, it was the figure of the Madonna herself. Cold sweat stood out on his brow as the flame went out again. He thought this must be a bad dream. When he struck his tinder again, however, he recognized Esther lying there dead of her wound. And by a strange miracle she, who in life had been the embodiment of his own picture of the Virgin, revealed in death the features of the Italian master's Madonna and her bleeding, mortal injury.

Yes, it was a miracle, an obvious miracle. But the old man would not believe in any more miracles. At that hour, when he saw the girl who had brought mild light into the late days of his life lying there dead beside his smashed picture, a string broke in his soul that had so often played the music of faith. He denied the God he had revered for seventy years in a single minute. Could this be the work of God's wise, kind hand, giving so much blessed creativity and bringing splendour into being, only to snatch them back into darkness for no good purpose? This could not be a benign will, only a heartless game. It was a miracle of life and not of God, a coincidence like thousands of others that happen at random every day, coming together and then moving apart again. No more! Could good, pure souls mean so little to God that he threw them away in his casual game? For the first time he stood in a church and doubted God, because he had thought him good and kind, and now he could not understand the ways of his creator.

For a long time he looked down at the dead girl who had shed such gentle evening light over his old age. And when he saw the smile of bliss on her broken lips, he felt less savage and did God more justice. Humility came back into his kindly heart. Could he really ask who had performed this strange miracle, making the lonely Jewish girl honour the Madonna in her death? Could he judge whether it was the work of God or the work of life? Could he clothe love in words that he did not know, could he reject God because he did not understand his nature?

The old man shuddered. He felt poor and needy in that lonely hour. He felt that he had wandered alone between God and earthly life all these long years, trying to understand them as twofold when they were one and yet defied understanding. Had it not been like the work of some miraculous star watching over the tentative path of this young girl's soul—had not God and Love been at one in her and in all things?

Above the windows the first light of dawn was showing. But it did not bring light to him, for he did not want to see new days dawning in the life he had lived for so many years, touched by its miracles yet never really transfigured by them. And now, without fear, he felt close to the last miracle, the miracle that ceases to be dream and illusion, and is only the dark eternal truth.

IN
THE
SNOW

A SMALL MEDIEVAL German town close to the Polish border, with the sturdy solidity of fourteenth-century building: the colourful, lively picture that it usually presents has faded to a single impression of dazzling, shimmering white. Snow is piled high on the broad walls and weighs down on the tops of the towers, around which night has already cast veils of opaque grey mist.

Darkness is falling fast. The hurry and bustle of the streets, the activity of a crowd of busy people, is dying down to a continuous murmur of sound that seems to come from far away, broken only by the rhythmic, monotonous chime of evening bells. The day's business is over for the weary workers who are longing for sleep, lights become few and far between, and finally they all go out. The town lies there like a single mighty creature fast asleep.

Every sound has died away, even the trembling voice of the wind over the moors is only a gentle lullaby now, and you can hear the soft whisper of snowflakes dusting down on the surfaces where their wandering ends...

But suddenly a faint sound is heard.

It is like the distant, hasty beat of hoofs coming closer. The startled man in the guardhouse at the gate, drowsy with sleep, goes to the window in surprise to listen. And sure enough, a horseman is approaching at full gallop, making straight for the gate, and a minute later a brusque voice, hoarse from the cold, demands entrance. The gate is opened. A man steps through it, leading in a steaming horse which he immediately hands to the gatekeeper. He swiftly allays the man's doubts with a few words and a sizeable sum of money, and then, his confident and rapid strides showing that he knows the place, he crosses the deserted white market place, and goes down quiet streets and along alleys deep in snow, making for the far end of the little town.

Several small houses stand there, crowding close together as if they needed each other's support. They are all plain, unassuming, smoky and crooked, and they stand in eternal silence in these secluded streets. They might never have known cheerful festivities bubbling over with merriment, no cries of delight might ever have shaken those blank, hidden windows, no bright sunshine might ever have been reflected in their panes. Alone, like shy children intimidated by others, the houses press together in the narrow confines of the Jewish quarter.

The stranger stops outside one of these houses, the largest and relatively speaking the finest. It belongs to the richest man in the little community, and also serves as a synagogue.

Bright light filters through the crack between the drawn curtains, and voices are raised in religious song inside the lighted room. This is the peaceful celebration of Chanukah, a festival of rejoicing in memory of the victory of the Maccabaeans, a day that reminds these exiled people, reduced to servitude by Fate, of their former great power. It is one of the few happy days that life and the law will allow them. But the song sounds melancholy, yearning, and the bright metal of the voices singing it has rusted with all the thousands of tears that have been shed. Out in the lonely street, the singing echoes like a hopeless lament, and is blown away on the wind.

The stranger stands outside the house for some time, inactive, lost in thought and dreams, and tears rise in his throat as he instinctively joins in the ancient, sacred melodies that flow from deep within his heart. His soul is full of profound devotion.

Then he pulls himself together. His steps faltering now, he goes to the closed doorway and brings the knocker down heavily, with a dull thud that shakes the door.

The vibration is felt through the entire building as the sound echoes on.

At once the singing in the room above stops dead, as if at an agreed signal. The people inside have turned pale and are looking at one another in alarm. Their festive mood has instantly evaporated. Dreams of the victorious power of such men as Judas Maccabaeus, by whose side they were all standing in spirit a moment ago, have fled; the bright vision of Israel that they saw before their eyes has gone, they are poor, trembling, helpless Jews again. Reality has asserted itself.

There is a terrible silence. The trembling hand of the prayer leader has sunk to his prayer book, the pale lips of his congregation will not obey them. A dreadful sense of foreboding has fallen on the room, seizing all throats in an iron grip.

They well know why.

Some while ago they heard an ominous word, a new and terrible word, but they were aware of its murderous meaning for their own people. The Flagellants were abroad in Germany, wild, fanatically religious men who flailed their own bodies with scourges in Bacchanalian orgies of lust and delight, deranged and drunken hordes who had already slaughtered and tortured thousands of Jews, intending to deprive them of what they held most holy, their age-old belief in the Father. That was their worst fear. With blind, stoical patience they had accepted exile, beatings, robbery, enslavement; they had all known late-night raids with burning and looting, and they shuddered to think of living in such times.

Then, only a few days earlier, rumours had begun spreading that one company of Flagellants was on its way to their own part of the country, which so far had known them only by hearsay, and it was said to be not far off. Perhaps the Flagellants have already arrived?

Terrible fear has seized on them all, making their hearts falter. They already see those forces, greedy for blood, men with faces flushed by wine, brandishing blazing torches and breaking violently into their homes. Already the stifled cries of their women ring in their ears, crying out for help as they pay the price of the murderers' wild lust; they already feel the flashing weapons strike. It is like a clear and vivid dream.

The stranger listens for sounds in the room above, and when no one lets him in he knocks again. Once more the dull echo of his knock resounds through the silence and distress inside the building.

By now the master of the house, the prayer leader, whose flowing white beard and great age give him the look of a patriarch, has been the first to recover some composure. He quietly murmurs, "God's will be done," and then bends down to his granddaughter. She is a pretty girl and, in her fear resembles a deer turning its great, pleading eyes on the huntsman. "Look out and see who's there, Lea."

All eyes are on the girl's face as she goes timidly to the window, and draws back the curtain with pale, trembling fingers. Then comes a cry from the depths of her heart. "Thank God, it's only one man."

"Praise the Lord." It is a sound like a sigh of relief on all sides. Now movement returns to the still figures who had been oppressed by the dreadful nightmare. Separate groups form, some standing in silent prayer, others talking in frightened, uncertain voices, discussing the unexpected arrival of the stranger, who is now being let in through the front gate.

The whole room is full of the hot, stuffy aroma of logs burning and a large crowd of people, all of them gathered around the richly laid festive table on which the sign and symbol of this holy evening stands, the seven-branched candlestick. The candles shine with a dull light in the smouldering vapours. The women wear dresses adorned with jewellery, the men voluminous robes with white prayer bands. There is a sense of deep solemnity in the crowded room, a solemnity such as only genuine piety can bring.

Now the stranger's quick footsteps are coming up the steps, and he enters the room.

At the same time a sharp gust of biting wind blows into the warm room through the open door. Icy cold streams in with the snow-scented air, chilling everyone. The draught puts out the flickering candles on the candlestick; only one of them still wavers unsteadily as it dies down. Suddenly the room is full of a heavy, oppressive twilight, as if cold night might suddenly fall within these walls. All at once the peace and comfort are gone. Everyone feels that the extinguishing of the sacred candles is a bad omen, and superstition makes them shiver again. But no one dares to say a word.

A tall, black-bearded man, who can hardly be more than thirty years old, stands at the door. He quickly divests himself of the scarves and coats in which he had been muffled up against the cold, and as soon as his face is revealed in the faint light of that last little flickering candle flame, Lea runs to him and embraces him.

This is Josua, her fiancé from the neighbouring town.

The others also crowd eagerly around him, greeting him happily, only to fall silent next moment, for he frees himself from his fiancée's arms with a grave, sad expression, and the weight of his terrible knowledge has dug deep furrows on his brow. All eyes are anxiously turned on him, and he cannot defend himself and what he has to say from the raging torrent of his own emotions. He takes the girl's hands as she stands beside him, and quietly forces himself to utter the fateful news.

"The Flagellants are here."

The eyes that had been turned questioningly to him stare, fixed on his face, and he feels the pulse of the hands he is holding falter suddenly. The prayer leader clutches the edge of the heavy table, his fingers trembling, so that the crystal glasses begin to sing softly, sending quavering notes through the air. Fear digs its claws into desperate hearts again, draining the last drops of blood from the frightened, devastated faces staring at the bearer of the news.

The last candle flickers once more and goes out.

Only the lamp hanging from the ceiling now casts a faint light on the dismayed, distraught people; the news has struck them like a thunderbolt.

One voice softly murmurs the resigned phrase with which Fate has made them familiar. "It is God's will."

But the others still cannot grasp it.

However, the newcomer is continuing, his words brusque and disconnected, as if he could hardly bear to hear them himself.

"They're coming—many of them—hundreds. And crowds of people with them—blood on their hands—they've murdered thousands—all our people in the East. They've been in my town already…"

He is interrupted by a woman's dreadful scream. Her floods of tears cannot soften its force. Still young, only recently married, she falls to the floor in front of him.

"They're there? Oh, my parents, my brothers and sisters! Has any harm come to them?"

He bends down to her, and there is grief in his voice as he tells her quietly, making it sound like a consolation, "They can feel no human harm any more."

And once again all is still, perfectly still. The awesome spectre of the fear of death is in the room with them, making them tremble. There is no one present here who did not have a loved one in that town, someone who is now dead.

At this the prayer leader, tears running into his silver beard and unable to control his shaking voice, begins to chant, disjointedly, the ancient, solemn prayer for the dead. They all join in. They are not even aware that they are singing, their minds are not on the words and melody that they utter mechanically; each is thinking only of his dear ones. And the chant grows ever stronger, they breathe more and more deeply, it is increasingly difficult for them to suppress their rising feelings. The words become confused until at last they are all sobbing in wild, uncomprehending sorrow. Infinite pain, a pain beyond words, has brought them all together like brothers.

Deep silence descends. But now and then a great sob can no longer be suppressed. And then comes the heavy, numbing voice of the messenger telling his tale again.

"They are all at rest with the Lord. Not one of them escaped, only I, through the providence of God..."

"Praise be to his name," murmurs the whole circle with instinctive piety. In the mouths of these broken, trembling people, the words sound like a worn-out formula.

"I came home late from a journey, and the Jewish quarter was already full of looters. I wasn't recognized, I could have run for it—but I had to go in, I couldn't help going to my place, my own people, I was among them as they fell under flailing fists. Suddenly a man came riding my way, struck out at me—but he missed, swaying in the saddle. Then all at once the will to live took hold of me, that strange chain that binds us to our misery—passion gave me strength and courage. I pulled him off his horse, mounted it, and rode away on it myself through the dark night, here to you. I've been riding for a day and a night."

He stops for a moment. Then he says, in a firmer voice, "But enough of all that now! First of all, what shall we do?"

The answer comes from all sides.

"Escape!"—"We must get away!"—"Over the border to Poland!"

It is the one way they all know to help themselves, age-old and shameful, yet the only way for the weaker to oppose the strong. No one dreams of physical resistance. Can a Jew defend himself or fight back? As they see it, the idea is ridiculous, unimaginable; they are not living in the time of the Maccabaeans now, they are enslaved again. The Egyptians are back, stamping the mark of eternal weakness and servitude on the people. Even the torrent of the passing years over many centuries cannot wash it away.

Flight, then.

One man did suggest, timidly, that they might appeal to the other citizens of the town for protection, but a scornful smile was all the answer he got. Again and again, their fate has always brought the oppressed back to the necessity of relying on themselves and on their God. No third party could be trusted.

They discussed the practical details. Men who had regarded making money as their sole aim in life, who saw wealth as the peak of human happiness and power, now agreed that they must not shrink from any sacrifice if it could speed their flight. All possessions must be converted into cash, however unfavourable the rate of exchange. There were carts and teams of horses to be bought, the most essential protection from the cold to be found. All at once the fear of death had obliterated what was supposed to be the salient quality of their race, just as their individual characters had been forged together into a single will. In all the pale, weary faces, their thoughts were working towards one aim.

And when morning lit its blazing torches, it had all been discussed and decided. With the flexibility of their people, used to wandering through the world, they adjusted to their sad situation, and their final decisions and arrangements ended in another prayer.

Then each of them went to do his part of the work.

And many sighs died away in the soft singing of the snowflakes, which had already built high walls towering up in the shimmering whiteness of the streets.

The great gates of the town closed with a hollow clang behind the last of the fugitives' carts.

The moon shone only faintly in the sky, but it turned the myriad flakes whirling in their lively dance to silver as they clung to clothes, fluttered around the nostrils of the snorting horses, and crunched under wheels making their way with difficulty through the dense snowdrifts.

Quiet voices whispered in the carts. Women exchanged reminiscences of their home town, which still seemed so close in its security and self-confidence. They spoke in soft, musical and melancholy tones. Children had a thousand things to ask in their clear voices, although their questions grew quieter and less frequent, and finally gave way to regular breathing. The men's voices struck a deeper note as they anxiously discussed the future and murmured quiet prayers. They all pressed close to one another, out of their awareness that they belonged together and instinctive fear of the cold. It blew through all the gaps and cracks in the carts with its icy breath, freezing the drivers' fingers.

The leading cart came to a halt.

Immediately the whole line of carts following behind it stopped too. Pale faces peered out from the tarpaulin covers of these moving tents, wondering what had caused the delay. The patriarch had climbed out of the first cart, and all the others followed his example, understanding the reason for this halt.

They were not far from the town yet; through the falling white flakes you could still, if indistinctly, make out the tower rising from the broad plain as if were a menacing hand, with a light shining from its spire like a jewel on its ringed finger.

Everything here was smooth and white, like the still surface of a lake, broken only by a few small, regular mounds surmounted by fenced-in trees here and there. They knew that this was where their dear ones lay in quiet, everlasting beds, rejected, alone and far from home, like all their kind.

Now the deep silence is broken by quiet sobbing, and although they are so used to suffering hot tears run down their rigid faces, freezing into droplets of bright ice on the snow.

As they contemplate this deep and silent peace, their mortal fears are gone, forgotten. Suddenly, eyes heavy with tears, they all feel an infinite, wild longing for this eternal, quiet peace in the "good place" with their loved ones. So much of their childhood sleeps under this white blanket, so many good memories, so much happiness that they will never know again. Everyone senses it; everyone longs to be in the "good place".

But time is short, and they must go on.

They climb back into the carts, huddling close to each other, for although they did not feel the biting cold while they were out in the open, the icy frost now steals over their shaking, shivering bodies again, making them grit their teeth. And in the darkness of the carts their eyes express unspeakable fear and endless sorrow.

Their thoughts, however, keep going back the way they have come, along the path of broad furrows left by the horse-drawn carts in the snow, back to the "good place", the place of their desires.

It is past midnight now, and the carts have travelled a long way from the town. They are in the middle of the great plain which lies flooded by bright moonlight, while white, drifting veils seem to hover over it, the shimmering reflections of the snow. The strong horses trudge laboriously through the thick snow, which clings tenaciously, and the carts jolt slowly, almost imperceptibly on, as if they might stop at any moment.

The cold is terrible, like icy knives cutting into limbs that have already lost much of their mobility. And gradually a strong wind rises as well, singing wild songs and howling around the carts. As if with greedy hands reaching out for prey, it tears at the covers of the carts which are constantly shaking loose, and frozen fingers find it hard to fasten them back in place more firmly.

The storm sings louder and louder, and in its song the quiet voices of the men murmuring prayers die away. It is an effort for their frozen lips to form the words. In the shrill whistling of the wind the hopeless sobs of the women, fearful for the future, also fall silent, and so does the persistent crying of children woken from their weariness by the cold.

Creaking, the wheels roll through the snow.

In the cart that brings up the rear, Lea presses close to her fiancé, who is telling her of the terrible things he has seen in a sad, toneless voice. He puts his strong arm firmly around her slender, girlish waist as if to protect her from the assault of the cold and from all pain. She looks at him gratefully, and a few tender, longing words are exchanged through the sounds of wailing and the storm, making them both forget death and danger.

Suddenly an abrupt jolt makes them all sway.

Then the cart stops.

Indistinctly, through the roaring of the storm, they hear loud shouts from the teams of horse-drawn carts in front, the crack of whips, the murmuring of agitated voices. The sounds will not die down. They leave the cart and hurry forward through the biting cold to the place where one horse in a team has fallen, carrying the other down with it. Around the two horses stand men who want to help but can do nothing; the wind blows them about like puppets with no will of their own, the snowflakes blind their eyes, and their hands are frozen, with no strength left in them. Their fingers lie side by side like stiff pieces of wood. And there is no help anywhere in sight, only the plain that runs on and on, a smooth expanse, proudly aware of its vast extent as it loses itself in the dim light from the snow and in the unheeding storm that swallows up their cries.

Once again the full, sad awareness of their situation comes home to them. Death reaches out for them once more in a new and terrible form as they stand together, helpless and defenceless against the irresistible, invincible forces of nature, facing the pitiless weapon of the frost.

Again and again the storm trumpets their doom in their ears. You must die here—you must die here.

And their fear of death turns to hopeless resignation.

No one has spoken the thought out loud, but it came to them all at the same time. Clumsily, stiff-limbed, they climb back into the carts and huddle close together again, waiting to die.

They no longer hope for any help.

They press close, all with their own loved ones, to be with one another in death. Outside, their constant companion the storm sings a song of death, and the flakes build a huge, shining coffin around the carts.

Death comes slowly. The icy, biting cold penetrates every corner of the carts and all their pores, like poison seizing on limb after limb, gently, but never doubting that it will prevail.

The minutes slowly run away, as if giving death time to complete its great work of release. Long and heavy hours pass, carrying these desperate souls away into eternity.

The storm wind sings cheerfully, laughing in wild derision at this everyday drama, and the heedless moon sheds its silver light over life and death.

There is deep silence in the last cart of all. Several of those in it are dead already, others are under the spell of hallucinations brought on by the bitter cold to make death seem kinder. But they are all still and lifeless, only their thoughts still darting in confusion, like sudden hot flashes of lightning.

Josua holds his fiancée with cold hands. She is dead already, although he does not know it.

He dreams.

He is sitting with her in that room with its warm fragrance, the seven candles in the golden candlestick are burning, they are all sitting together as they once used to. The glowing light of the happy festival rests on smiling faces speaking friendly words and prayers. And others, long dead, come in through the doorway, among them his dead parents, but that no longer surprises him. They kiss tenderly, they exchange familiar words. More and more approach, Jews in the bleached garments of their forefathers' time, and now come the heroes, Judas Maccabaeus and all the others; they all sit down together to talk and make merry. More come, and still more. The room is full of figures, his eyes are tiring with the sight of so many, changing more and more quickly, giving way to one another, his ear echoes to the confusion of sounds. There is a hammering and droning in his pulse, hotter and hotter—

And suddenly it is over. All is quiet now.

By this time the sun has risen, and the snowflakes, still falling, shine like diamonds. The sun makes the broad mounds that have risen overnight, covered over and over with snow, gleam as if they were jewels.

It is a strong, joyful sun that has suddenly begun to shine, almost a springtime sun. And sure enough, spring is not far away. Soon it will be bringing buds and green leaves back again, and will lift the white shrouds from the grave of the poor, lost, frozen Jews who have never known true spring in their lives.

THE BURIED CANDELABRUM

I N THE CIRCUS MAXIMUS, on a fine June day in the year 455, a combat between two tall Heruli and a sounder of Hyrcanian boar had reached its sanguinary close when, in the third hour of the afternoon, disquiet spread among the thousands of onlookers. At first it was only those seated near the imperial box who noticed that something was amiss. A horseman, dusty and travel-stained by a long ride, descended the stairway with its statues on either side, and approached the bedizened dais where Maximus lolled, surrounded by courtiers. The Emperor listened to the tidings, sprang to his feet, and—disregarding the convention which forbade him to leave while the games were in progress—hastened out, followed by his train. The senatorial benches likewise and those of the other dignitaries quickly emptied. The cause must be grave indeed for such a breach of etiquette. Naturally the common folk grew uneasy.

Attempts were made to distract the attention of the crowd. Trumpet blasts announced a new "turn". The grid rose. A roar issued from the dark interior as a black-maned lion was goaded into the arena to encounter the short swords of a troop of gladiators. In vain, for the show had lost interest. Waves of alarm, crowned by a spume of anxious and excited faces, spread irresistibly from tier to tier. Quitting their places, the plebs gathered in knots and pointed to the empty seats of the mighty; they questioned one another eagerly; catcalls were heard; the amusement had ceased to amuse; and at length (how or where started no one knew) a rumour ran through the vast amphitheatre, a name of ill-omen, "The Vandals!"—"The Vandals!"

Genseric and his men, the dreaded pirates of the Mediterranean, had landed at Portus, to attack the heart of the Empire. Vast numbers of them were already marching along the Via Portuensis. "Vandals, Vandals." The whisper became a shout, and changed itself into the still more terrible word, "Barbarians, barbarians." Hundreds screamed it; thousands screamed it, in the huge circus. Panic-stricken, disorderly, the crowds raced along the stone courses toward the exits, driven by fear like leaves before the wind. Janitors, marshals, and soldiers of the watch forsook their posts, fighting through the press with fists, staves, and swords; women and children were trampled underfoot; the outlets were funnels, each containing a mass of shrieking humanity. Within a few minutes the enormous edifice of stone and marble was empty, save for the corpses of those who had been struck down, or trampled to death. The gigantic oval, still glowing beneath the summer sun, was vacated, save for the lion, whose antagonists (death-defying gladiators though they were) had also fled. Puzzled and forsaken, the black-maned king of beasts once more roared his challenge into the void.

The Vandals were approaching. Messenger after messenger spurred into the imperial city, each bringing worse news than the last. The barbarians had landed from a fleet of a hundred sailing ships and galleys, a lightly equipped and swiftly moving multitude. Cavalry as well as infantry, for white-robed Berbers and Numidians, riders from the nomadic tribes of Northern Africa, were speeding along the road to the capital in advance of their Teutonic allies. On the morrow, or the next day, the whole invading force, fired by the lust for plunder, would assail the doomed town. The Roman army (captives and mercenaries) was far away, fighting near Ravenna; and the walls of Rome had never been repaired since Alaric breached them. No one even dreamed of defence. The minority, who had property to lose as well as life, made ready to escape, loading their valuables into mule-carts, for they hoped to get away with at least some of their possessions. Their hopes were vain. The long-suffering populace rose in wrath against those who had lorded it over them in time of peace, and now tried to flee in time of war.

When Maximus, the Emperor, set forth from the palace with such baggage as he had time to get together, curses were volleyed at him and were soon reinforced by deadlier missiles—stones. Growing fiercer, the mob assailed the cowardly deserter, and made an end of him with bludgeons and hatchets. The warders followed the customary routine, and closed the gates at nightfall. Alas, the shutting of the gates served only to prison fear within the city. Like a pestilential vapour, forebodings of a terrible fate hovered over the silent and shadowed houses, while darkness fell like a pall upon the once glorious but now decadent and trembling Rome. Yet the stars shone as usual, serenely indifferent to human woes, and the crescent moon sank as tranquilly as if no barbarian invasion threatened. Sleepless and desperate, the Romans awaited the coming of the Vandals, as a man about to be executed lays his head on the block awaiting the fall of an axe already poised for the stroke.

Slowly, surely, purposefully, victoriously, the main force of the Vandals advanced along the deserted road leading from Portus to Rome. The blond, long-haired Teutons marched in good order, century by century, while in front of them, wheeling and curvetting, rode their dark-skinned auxiliaries from the desert, mounted on thoroughbreds, bare-footed and stirrupless. In the midst of his army was Genseric, King of the Vandals. From the saddle he smiled good-humouredly at his warriors. Now middle-aged, inured to battle from earliest youth, he had learned from his spies that there was no likelihood of serious resistance; that his forces were on their way, not to a strenuous fight, but to a week or two of easy and pleasurable looting.

In truth, no Roman stood to arms. Not until the King reached the gate of the city, did anyone attempt to stay his progress. Here there appeared Pope Leo, first of the Leos, Leo the Great, in full pontificals, attended by the senior clergy. Leo hoped to repeat the success of three years earlier, when he had persuaded Attila, King of the Huns, to depart from Italy without sacking Rome. At sight of the imposing greybeard, the club-footed Genseric politely dismounted and limped to meet the Holy Father. But he did not kiss the hand of the priest who wore the Fisherman's ring, nor make obeisance, for, being an Arian, he looked upon the Pope as a heretic and a usurper. Coldly and unresponsively he listened to the Latin oration, in which Leo begged the Vandal monarch to spare the Holy City. Through an interpreter he replied that, being himself a Christian as well as a soldier, he did not propose to burn and destroy Rome—though Rome herself, ambitious and greedy for power, had razed thousands of cities to the ground. In his magnanimity he would spare the possessions of the Church and the bodies of the women, and would merely have the place looted "sine ferro et igne", in accordance with the right of the stronger to work his will upon the vanquished. "But," he said menacingly, as his equerry held the stirrup for him to remount, "you will do well to hearken to my counsel, and open the gates to me without more ado."

His orders were obeyed. Not a spear was pointed, not a sword brandished. Within the hour, Rome was at the mercy of the Vandals. But the victorious raiders did not fling themselves lawlessly upon the defenceless town. They marched in quietly, restrained by Genseric's iron hand, these tall, upstanding, flaxen-haired warriors, striding along the Via Triumphalis, staring curiously at the marble statues, whose mute lips seemed to promise such an abundance of loot. His goal was the Palatinum, the imperial residence. He ignored the rows of waiting senators, who had timidly assembled to do him reverence, and he did not even accept a banquet, or so much as glance at the splendid gifts which some of the wealthier citizens had brought to appease him. No, what the stern soldier had in mind was how best, most swiftly, and most methodically to get possession of the riches of the capital. Poring over a map, he allotted a century to each district, making the centurions responsible for the good conduct of their men. There was to be no indiscriminate and lawless looting. Genseric had in view a systematic spoliation of Rome. The gates were closed and guarded, the breaches in the walls were manned, that not an ingot or a coin should be removed. Then his men commandeered boats, carts, and beasts of burden, pressing thousands of slaves into the service, to make sure that as speedily as possible the treasures of imperial Rome should be removed to the pirates' lair on the southern coast of the Mediterranean. The work of plunder was carried out methodically, coldly, and noiselessly. For thirteen days the quivering city was disarticulated and stripped bare.

Parties of Vandal warriors went from house to house, from temple to temple, each detachment led by a nobleman and accompanied by a clerk. They seized whatever was valuable and transportable; gold and silver chalices, ingots, coins, jewels, necklaces from the Amber Coast, furs from Transylvania, malachite from Pontus, swords from Persia. Deft workmen were constrained to remove mosaics from the walls of the temples and porphyry slabs from the peristyles of the mansions. All was done according to plan, with the utmost care. With the aid of windlasses, the bronze chariot-teams were taken down from the triumphal arches; the interior of the temple of Jupiter Capitolinus was cleared of its valuables; and slaves were sent onto the roof to remove the gilt tiles one by one.

As for the bronze pillars, which were too large to take away intact without the sacrifice of much time and trouble, Genseric had them knocked to pieces or sawn in sunder, that he might ship the metal in fragments. Street after street, house after house, was cleared by these locusts; and when the plunderers had done with the habitations of the living, they turned to break open the tumuli, the abiding-places of the dead. Out of the stone sarcophagi they took the jewelled combs which had been thrust into the now mouldering hair of dead noblewomen; they tore golden anklets and bracelets from skeletons; silver mirrors too, they found, and signet-rings which had been interred with the corpses; they impounded even the obols which, in accordance with ancient custom, had been placed in the mouths of the deceased to pay Charon the ferryman for the voyage across the Styx.

As had been arranged by the King, the booty was piled in orderly heaps. The golden-winged Nike was prostrate between a gem-studded casket containing the bones of a saint and an ivory dice-box that had belonged to a lady of rank. Silver ingots lay upon purple garments, and precious glassware adjoined fragments of base metal. Each article thought worth taking to Carthage was recorded by the clerk on one of his parchments, not only to keep tally, but to give this wholesale theft a veneer of legality. Followed by his notables, Genseric hobbled through the medley, poking at various objects with his stick, scrutinizing the jewels, well pleased, and distributing praise. He was delighted as he watched the heavily freighted carts and the boats deep in the water leave the capital. But no house in the city was fired and there was no bloodshed. Quietly and in regular succession, as in a mine, the loaded wagons and boats went from the town to the harbour and came back empty from Portus to Rome. Never within the memory of man had there been so great a plundering effected in thirteen days as in this bloodless Vandal sack of Rome.

For thirteen days no voice was raised above a whisper in the myriad-housed city, nor did anyone laugh. The lutes were silent in the dwelling-rooms, and the chanting was stilled in the churches. The only noises were made by the hammers and crowbars of the devastators, the wains that creaked under their load, the oxen that grunted as they tugged, the mules that tightened the traces, the drivers as they cracked their whips. Sometimes, indeed, a neglected cur would whine for food, which his master was too busy or too anxious to provide; or the sound of a trumpet would come from the wall, where the guard was being relieved. But in the houses men, women, and children held their breath. Rome, which had conquered the world, lay prostrate at a conqueror's feet; and when, at night, the breeze blew through the deserted streets, the sound was like the groans of a wounded man who feels his lifeblood flowing from his veins.

On the thirteenth evening of the Vandals' plunder-raid, the Jews of the Roman community were assembled in the house of Moses Abtalion, on the left bank of the Tiber, where the yellow river curves slothfully like an overfed serpent. Abtalion was a "small man" among his co-religionists, nor was he learned in the Law, being only a middle-aged craftsman whose hands were stained by his occupation as dyer; but they had chosen his house for a meeting-place because his workshop on the ground floor was more roomy than the attic chambers in which most of them dwelt. Since the coming of Genseric and his hordes, they had assembled day after day, wearing their white shrouds, to pray in the gloomy shuttered shops, stubborn and almost stupefied, amid rolls of carpet, bales of brightly coloured cloth, and well-filled barrels of oil and wine. So far, the Vandals had not troubled them. Twice or thrice, a century, accompanied by noblemen and clerks, marched through the Jewish quarter, which was low-lying, so that its narrow streets showed abundant traces of repeated inundations, and walls and flagstones sweated damp. One disdainful glance sufficed to convince the treasure-hunters that they would waste their pains here. No peristyles paved with marble, no triclinia glittering with gold, no bronze statues or costly vases. The Vandals did not tarry, but went elsewhere in search of spoil.

Nevertheless the hearts of the Roman Jews were heavy. Generation after generation, ever since the Diaspora, these exiles from the Holy Land had found that disaster to the country of their adoption betokened disaster to them also. When fortune smiled, the Gentiles forgot them or paid them little heed. The princes wore sumptuous clothing and gave themselves up to their craze for architecture and display; while the coarser lusts of the mob were satisfied with the chase and gambling and the unceasing round of gladiatorial shows. But always, when trouble came, the cry was "Blame the Jews". It was unlucky for the Jews when the Gentiles among whom they lived sustained a defeat; bad for them when a town was sacked; bad for them when a pestilence broke out. No matter what evil should befall, it would be laid to their charge. To rebel against this injustice was futile, for they were few and weak, no longer men of war as their valiant forefathers had been. Their only resource was prayer.

Throughout this fortnight when Rome was being despoiled by the Vandals, the Jews, therefore, prayed evening after evening, and on into the small hours. What else could a righteous man do, in an unrighteous and violent world where might was held to be right, than turn away from earth and look to Jehovah for aid?

These barbarian invasions had been going on for decades. From the north and the south, from the east and the west they came, fair-haired and dark, speaking divers tongues, but robbers without exception. Hardly was one conquest finished when the next began, for the invaders trod on one another's heels. The ungodly were at war throughout the world, and continued to harry the pious. Jerusalem had fallen, Babylon and Alexandria; now it was Rome's turn. Where the Chosen People sought rest, unrest came; where they desired peace, they were afflicted by war. Who could escape his destiny? In this tormented world, refuge, tranquillity, and consolation could be found only in prayer. Yes, prayer dispelled alarm with words of promise, appeased terror through the chanting of litanies, enabled the heavy-hearted to wing their way Godward. Hence it was meet to pray in time of trouble, and better still to pray when gathered together, for God's good gifts came most abundantly to those who sought them in common.

So the Jews of the Roman confraternity had assembled to pray. The pious murmur flowed from their bearded mouths gently and unceasingly, just as outside the windows the current of the Tiber rippled gently and unceasingly past the planking of the levee—eating away the bank wherever it was undefended. The men did not look at one another, and yet their rounded shoulders moved in unison, since the time was set by the familiar words of the psalms they were intoning, the psalms which their fathers and forefathers had intoned hundreds and thousands of times before them. So automatic was it that they scarcely realized their lips were moving, hardly understood the significance of the words they uttered. The despairful and prayerful monotone issued, as it were, from a trance, from an obscure land of dreams.

Then they came to themselves with a jerk, straightening their bent backs, for the door-knocker had been violently sounded.

Even in good times the Jews of the Diaspora were wont to be alarmed by any sudden or unexpected happening. How could good come of it when a stranger demanded admittance in the middle of the night? The murmur ceased, as if cut with shears, so that the plashing of the river sounded louder than before. They listened, their throats tense with alarm. Again the knocker thundered, and an impatient fist banged on the door.

"Coming," answered Abtalion, rising and scuttling forth into the entry. The flame of the wax candle, which was stuck to the table by some of its own meltings, flickered as the craftsman threw open the workshop door while the hearts of all those present throbbed under stress of fear.

They recovered, however, on recognizing the new arrival. It was Hyrcanus ben Hillel, master of the imperial mint, a man of whom the community was proud, since he was the only Jew who had the right to cross the threshold of the palace. By special favour of the court he was allowed to live beyond Trastevere, and might even wear the coloured robes reserved for Romans of distinction; but now his raiment was torn, and his face besoiled.

They crowded round him, eager to hear his tidings, all the more because his expression showed that they were evil.

Hyrcanus ben Hillel drew a deep breath and struggled vainly to speak. At length he managed to pant:

"Ruin has befallen us, the greatest of disasters. They have found it; they have seized it."

"Found what, Hyrcanus?"—"Seized what?"—A similar cry came from every mouth.

"The Candelabrum, the Menorah. When the barbarians entered the city, I hid it beneath the garbage in the kitchen. Purposely I left the other holy things in the treasury: the Table of Shewbread, the Silver Trumpets, Aaron's Rod, and the Altar of

Incense. Too many of the servants in the palace knew about our treasures, and it would have courted a search had I hidden them all. One thing only did I hope to save from among the temple furniture—Moses' Seven-Branched Candlestick, the Lampstand from Solomon's House, the Menorah. The rogues had taken what I had left for them to see, the room was stripped bare, they had ceased hunting and were about to leave, and I was glad at heart in the conviction that we had saved the Candelabrum, at least. But one of the slaves (a murrain seize him) had watched me hiding it, and betrayed the hiding-place—in the hope of a reward which would enable him to buy his freedom. He showed them, and they discovered it. Now everything is gone which once stood in the Holy of Holies, in the House of Solomon: the Altar and the Vessels and the Mitre of the Priest and the Menorah. This very evening the Vandals are carrying off the Candelabrum to their ships."

For a moment, silence followed. Then came a wailing chorus:

"The Lampstand... Woe, and yet again woe... The Menorah... God's Seven-Branched Candlestick... Woe, woe... The Lampstand from God's Altar... the Menorah."

The Jews staggered like drunken men; they beat their breasts; they held their hips and screamed as though in pain; as if struck blind, the reverend elders lamented.

"Silence!" commanded a powerful voice, and the distraught men did as they were bid. He who spoke was the senior member of the community, the oldest and the wisest, the most learned in the Law, Rabbi Eliezer, whom they called Kab ve Nake, which being interpreted means "the pure and clear". Nigh upon eighty years of age was he, with a huge snow-white beard. Seamed was his visage by the painful ploughshare of unrelenting thought; but the eyes beneath the bushy brows were bright as ever, and full of kindness. He raised his hand, the skin being yellowed like parchment with the tale of his years, and waved it as if to dispel the clamour and make room for the thoughtful words he was about to utter.

"Silence!" he repeated. "Children scream in alarm. Grown men consider what is to be done. Let us resume our seats and hold counsel together. The mind is more active when the body is at rest."

Shamefacedly the men sat down on stools and benches. Rabbi Eliezer talked to them, in low tones, almost as if communing with himself.

"Indeed we have suffered a terrible misfortune. Long since, the holy furnishings of the Tabernacle were taken away from us, to be kept in the Emperor's treasury, and none of us save Hyrcanus ben Hillel was permitted to set eyes on them. Still, we knew they had been in safekeeping since the days of Titus. In the imperial treasury, they were at least close at hand. These Roman aliens seemed more congenial to us when we remembered that the sacred emblems which had wandered for a thousand years—had been in Jerusalem, then in Babylon, had come back thence to Zion—were at rest in the capital of the Empire where we abode, we who had been despoiled of them. No longer were we allowed to lay bread on the Table of the Lord, but of this Table we thought as often as we broke bread. We could not kindle the lamps on the Lampstand; but whenever we lighted a lamp we remembered the Menorah, which stood untended and dark in the house of the stranger. The holy furniture of the Tabernacle was ours no longer, but we were more or less at ease since it was well guarded. Now the wanderings of the Candelabrum are to begin again. It is not, as we had hoped would happen some day, returning to the home of our fathers, but going elsewhere, and who can say whither? Still, let us not complain. Lament is unavailing. Let us bethink ourselves."

The men listened, wordless, with bowed heads. Eliezer, stroking his beard from time to time, went on, again as if talking to himself:

"The Candelabrum is of pure gold, and often have I wondered why God commanded it should be made of such costly metal. Why did he enjoin upon Moses to make it so heavy, of a talent of pure gold, seven-branched, with its knops and its flowers, all of beaten gold? Often I have pondered whether being so valuable did not endanger the Menorah, for wealth attracts evil, and precious things are a lure to robbers. But now I am aware that I was thinking vain thoughts, and that what God commands has a sense and a purpose which pass our shallow understanding. It has been revealed to me that because they were so precious have these holy things been preserved through the ages. Had they been of base metal, and unadorned, the robbers would have destroyed them unheeding, to make of them chains or swords. Instead they preserved the precious things as precious, though unaware of their holiness. Thus one robber steals them from another, but none venture to destroy them; each remove is but a stage in the journey back to God.

"Let us reflect a while. What can barbarians know of the Menorah? Only what they see for themselves, that it is made of gold. If we could appeal to their cupidity, could offer twice or thrice the value of the gold, perhaps we could buy it back. We Jews are no fighters. Sacrifice alone is our strength. We must send messengers to the dispersed communities of our people, asking them to join forces and purses with us for the redemption of the sacred Candelabrum. This year we must double or triple what we usually contribute for the Temple, stripping the clothes from our backs and the rings from our fingers. We must buy the Menorah, even if we have to pay seven times its weight in pure gold."

He was interrupted by a sigh; from Hyrcanus ben Hillel, who looked up, sad-eyed, and said softly:

"No use, Rabbi; I've tried that in vain. It was my first thought. I betook myself to their valuers and clerks, but they were rude and harsh. Then I forced my way into Genseric's presence and offered to redeem the Lampstand with a great sum. He was wroth, would scarcely listen to my words, and shuffled impatiently with his feet. Thereupon, beside myself, I wrestled with him in speech, assuring him (fool that I was) that the Menorah had once stood in Solomon's Temple, and had been brought back by Titus as the most splendid object with which to grace a triumph. The barbarian monarch laughed scornfully, saying:

"'I do not need your money. So much gold have I seized here in Rome that I can pave my stables with it, and have my horses' hoofs set with jewels. If the Seven-Branched Candlestick once stood in King Solomon's Temple, it is not for sale to you or to any other. Titus, you say, had it carried before him here in Rome when celebrating his triumph after the conquest of Jerusalem? Well, it shall be carried before me when I celebrate my triumph in Carthage after the conquest of Rome. If the Menorah served your God, it shall now serve the true God. I have spoken. Go!'"

"You should not have gone, Hyrcanus ben Hillel," protested the assembled Jews. "You should have been firmer."

"Do you think I gave way so readily? I flung myself on the floor in front of him and embraced his knees. But his heart was as hard as were his iron-shod shoes. He kicked me away as contemptuously, as mercilessly, as he would have kicked a stone. At a sign from him, his menials beat me with staves and thrust me forth. Barely did I escape with life, and not with a whole skin."

Only now did they understand why Hyrcanus ben Hillel's raiment was torn and bedraggled, why his face was bruised and besoiled, and why there was clotted blood on his brow. Voices were stilled. In the silence they could hear from afar the rattle of the carts in which the plunder was being driven away through the night. Then, reverberating from one end of the city to the other, came trumpet blasts from the departing Vandals. Profound silence followed, while the same thought struck one and all:

"The sack of Rome is finished. The Menorah is lost to us for ever."

Rabbi Eliezer raised his head wearily, and asked:

"Tonight the barbarians remove it?"

"Yes, tonight. They are taking the Menorah in a wagon, which is being driven along the Via Portuensis while we sit here. Those trumpets must have been the signal for the rearguard to assemble. Tomorrow morning the Lampstand will be shipped."

Eliezer bowed his head once more and seemed to fall into a doze. For a few minutes he was absent-minded, paying no heed to his companions' perturbed glances. At length he looked up and said tranquilly:

"Tonight? Well and good. Then we must go with it."

They gazed at him in astonishment. But the old man repeated, firmly:

"Yes, we must go with it. Our duty is clear. Recall what is prescribed for us in Holy Writ. When the Ark of the Covenant was borne before us, we had to follow; only when the Ark rested, could we rest. If the insignia of God wander, we must wander likewise."

"But, Rabbi, how can we cross the sea? We have no ships."

"Let us make for the coast. It is but one night's march."

Hyrcanus rose to his feet, saying:

"As always, Rabbi Eliezer's words are wise. We must go with the Menorah. 'Tis but another stage of our unending journey. When the Ark of the Covenant moves onward, and the Candelabrum, we must follow, the whole congregation of the Chosen."

Came a plaintive voice from a corner of the room. It was Simeon the carpenter, a hunchback, who trembled with fear.

"But what if the Vandals should seize us? Hundreds, already, have they carried into bondage. They will beat us, will slay us, will sell our children as slaves—and nothing will be gained."

"Silence, poltroon!" rejoined another. "Control your fears. If any one of us is seized, he is seized. If any one of us should be killed, he will die for the holy emblem. We must all go, and we will."

"Yes, all, all," they cried in chorus.

Rabbi Eliezer waved his hand to arrest the clamour. Again he closed his eyes, as usual when he wanted to reflect. After a while he resumed:

"Simeon is right. You do ill to revile him as a coward and a weakling. He is right. We should be foolish to venture the lives of the whole confraternity among these nocturnal marauders. Is not life the greatest gift of God, who does not wish the least of his creatures to throw it away? Simeon is right, the barbarians would lay hands on our children, to make bondmen and bondwomen of them across the sea. Neither our young men nor our boys shall go forth with us into the night. But we who are old are useless to ourselves and to others. They will not make slaves of us, who cannot pull lustily in their galleys, who have hardly strength to dig our own graves, and whom even death can rob of little. It is for us to go with the furniture of the Tabernacle. Let those only make ready whose age is above threescore years and ten."

At the word, the old, those whose beards were white, severed themselves from the rest of the company. There were ten, and when Eliezer, "the pure and clear", joined them, the number was made up to eleven. "The Fathers of our People," thought the younger men, looking at them reverently, the veterans of a generation most of whom had passed away. Rabbi Eliezer detached himself from them once more, to mingle with the young and the middle-aged. He spake:

"We, the elders, are going, and you need not be troubled about our fate. But stay, while I consider. One who is yet a boy must go with us, to bear witness to those of the next generation and that which will follow. We shall not long survive, our light burns low, our course is nearly run, our voices will soon be hushed. Needful is it that one should live on for many years, one who will have set eyes upon the Lampstand from the Altar of the Lord, that in tribe after tribe and in generation after generation knowledge shall endure concerning the most sacred of our treasures, which shall not be lost for ever, but shall move onward upon its eternal pilgrimage. A child, a little boy, too young to understand what he is doing, must accompany us that he may testify in days to come."

There was silence for a space, while each of his auditors thought of a son whom he dreaded to send forth into the dangers of that night. But Abtalion the dyer did not hesitate long.

"I will fetch Benjamin, my grandson. He is seven, having lived as many years as there are branches on the Menorah. Is not that a sign? Meanwhile prepare for the journey, making free of such victuals as my poor house can offer."

He departed. The elders seated themselves at the table, and the younger men served them with wine and food. Before breaking bread, the Rabbi uttered the prayer which their forefathers had repeated thrice every day. Thrice, now, in the thin voices of old age, the others said after Eliezer the heartfelt petition:

"Be merciful, O Lord, unto thy people Israel; in thy lovingkindness restore thy sacred emblem to Zion and bring back to Jerusalem the service of the sacrifice."

Having said this prayer three times, the elders made ready to depart. Calmly and deliberately, as though performing a sacred task, they took off their shrouds and made them into a bundle with their praying-shawls and their phylacteries. The younger men, meanwhile, brought bread and fruit for the journey, and strong staves for support. Each of the intending travellers then wrote upon parchment directions as to the disposal of his property should he fail to return, and these documents were duly witnessed.

Abtalion the dyer, after removing his shoes, mounted the wooden staircase as silently as possible, but he was stout and solidly built, so the treads groaned beneath his weight. Cautiously he lifted the latch and opened the door that led into the living-room. Since they were poor folk, this was for the joint use of the head of the family and his wife, their son and daughter-in-law, their daughters, and their grandchildren. The shutters were closed, but between the chinks the silver moonbeams made their way mistily into the crowded apartment. While walking on tiptoe Abtalion could see that, for all his precautions, his wife and his son's wife had awakened, and were staring at him in alarm.

"What's the matter?" asked one of them.

Abtalion made no reply. Gropingly he went to the left corner at the back, where Benjamin slept. The grandfather leaned solicitously over the pallet. The little boy was sound asleep, but his fists were clenched and his features twitched. He must be having a nightmare. Abtalion stroked his disordered hair, to wake him up; but he slept on, quieted by the caress. The little fists relaxed, so did the lips; the sleeper smiled and stretched his arms contentedly. Abtalion was remorseful at the thought of having to waken the youngster from what were now pleasant dreams. But, having no choice, he shook the child. Benjamin awoke, terror-stricken. A Jewish child in exile soon learned to dread the unexpected. His father was startled when an unheralded visitor knocked loudly at the door; the elders were startled when a new edict was read in the streets of Rome; they were alarmed when an emperor died and a new one took his place. Every child of the Jewish quarter had come to anticipate evil as the outcome of change. Before he knew his letters and could spell out the shorter words of Scripture, the Hebrew youngster had learned this much—to dread everyone and everything on earth.

Confusedly little Benjamin stared at the nocturnal visitor, and was about to scream when Abtalion clapped a hand upon the opened mouth. Then, recognizing his grandfather, the child was appeased. Abtalion bent low, and whispered:

"Gather up your clothing and your shoes, and come with me. Quietly. No one must hear."

The boy sprang out of bed, reassured and proud. Secrets between him and Grandfather. That was fine. He asked no questions, but fumbled for the necessary garments and footgear.

They were creeping to the door, when the boy's mother raised her head from the pillow. She sobbed as she asked:

"Where are you taking Benjamin?"

"Peace," answered Abtalion menacingly. "It is not fitting for a woman to question me."

He closed the door behind him. All the women in the upstairs room were awake now. Through the thin door came a buzz of chattering mingled with sobs. As the eleven old men and the youngster emerged into the street, it was obvious that tidings of their strange and perilous mission had soaked through the walls. The alley was on the alert. Fears and plaints came from every house. But the elders did not look up at the windows nor yet at the house-doors on either side. Silently and resolutely they set forth. It was close on midnight.

Great was their surprise to find the city gate unguarded. The tucket they had heard had assembled the last of the Vandals. These were now marching westward along the Via Portuensis; but the Romans, behind barred doors, did not yet venture to believe that their troubles were over. Thus the road leading to the harbour was deserted; no wains or packhorses, not a man or a shadow; nothing to be seen but the white milestones shimmering in the moonlight. The pilgrims, therefore, strode unchallenged through the open gate.

"Let us hasten," said Hyrcanus ben Hillel. "The carts freighted with plunder must be far on the road to Portus. Perhaps they had already started before the trumpets were sounded. We will speed in pursuit."

They put their best foot foremost, marching three abreast. In the front rank were Abtalion on the left, Eliezer on the right, and between the septuagenarian and the octogenarian tripped along the seven-year-old boy, a little frightened by this adventure, sleepy too, but kept awake by excitement. In three more ranks followed the rest of the elders, each gripping his bundle in the left hand, holding his staff in the right; heads all bowed, as if they were bearing an invisible coffin on their shoulders. The haze of the Campagna enveloped them. No refreshing breeze dispelled the marshy vapour, which hung heavily athwart the plain with its reek of decaying vegetation, and gave a greenish tinge to the waning moon. It was uncanny, on so suffocating a night, to be striding towards insecurity, past the scattered burial mounds looking in the half-light like dead animals on either side of the way, and past the pillaged houses, emptied of their inhabitants, with unshuttered windows as if staring at the strange spectacle of the hoary pilgrims. For a long while, however, there was no hint of danger. The road slumbered like the countryside through which it led, its white surface beneath the moonlit mist recalling that of a frozen river. Except for the open windows of deserted houses there was nothing to show that the barbarians had gone by, until, down a side-track to the left, the wanderers sighted a Roman villa in flames. No farm this; but a patrician's country mansion. The roof-tree had already fallen in; the coils of smoke that rose above where it had been were tinged red by the fires that still raged amid the walls; and to each of the eleven old men came the unspoken thought:

"It is as if I were looking upon the pillar of cloud and the pillar of fire which went before the Tabernacle of the Lord when our forefathers followed the Ark of the Covenant, even as I and my companions now follow the Menorah."

Between Grandfather Abtalion and Rabbi Eliezer, trotted the boy, panting, in his eagerness not to be a drag on his elders. He was silent because the others said not a word, but his little heart fluttered against his ribs. He was afraid, now that the excitement of novelty was passing; mortally afraid because he could not guess why they had dragged him out of bed at such an hour, afraid because he did not know where the old men were taking him; most afraid of all because never before had he been in the open country after dark, and beneath the open sky. He was familiar with night in the alleys of the Jewish quarter; but there the blackness of the sky was but a narrow strip in which two or three stars twinkled. No reason to dread that ribbon of sky, which familiarity had robbed of its terrors. He knew it best as he glimpsed it between the slats, which broke it up into tiny fragments, too small to be alarming; while he listened, before he fell asleep, to the prayers of the men, the coughing of the sick, the shuffling feet of those who went by in the alley, the caterwauling on the roof, the crackling of the logs as they burned on the hearth. On the right was Mother, on the left Rachel; he was safe, warm, cosy; never alone.

But here the night was threatening, huge, and void. How tiny felt the little boy beneath the vast expanse of heaven. Had not the old men been with him to protect him, he would have burst into tears, would have tried to crawl into some hiding-place where he could escape from the huge dome which marched with him as he marched, always the same, always oppressive.

Happily there was room in his breast for pride as well as fear; pride because the elders in whose presence Mother dared not raise her voice, and before whom the children quaked—because these great and wise men had chosen him, little Benjamin, to accompany them upon their quest. What did it mean? What could it mean? Child though he was, he felt sure that something tremendous must account for this procession through the night. Most eager, therefore, was he to show himself worthy of their choice, trying to take manly strides with his little legs, and refusing to admit even to himself that he was afraid. But the test of his courage and endurance lasted too long. He grew more and more tired, frightened of the very shadows of himself and his companions; alarmed by the sound of their footsteps upon the paved road. Now, when a bat, blundering through the night, almost touched his forehead, he shuddered and screamed at the black, unknown horror. Gripping Abtalion's hand, he cried:

"Grandfather, Grandfather, where are we going?"

Without even turning to look at the lad, his grandfather growled:

"Hold your tongue, and don't drag back. Little boys must be seen and not heard."

The youngster shrank, as if from a blow, ashamed at having given vent to his terror. In thought he scolded himself: "Of course, I ought not to have asked." Still, he could not restrain his sobs.

But Rabbi Eliezer, the pure and clear, looked reproachfully at Abtalion over the little one's head, saying:

"Nay, friend, it is you who are to blame. How natural that the child should ask that question! What could he do but wonder at our taking him from his bed and bringing him forth with us into the night? Moreover, why should he not learn the object of our pilgrimage? We bring him with us because he is of our blood, and therefore partaker in our destinies. Surely he will continue to sustain our sorrows long after we have been laid to rest? He is to live on, bearing witness to those of a coming time as the last member of our Roman community to see the Lampstand from the Table of the Lord. Why should you wish him to remain in ignorance? We have brought him with us to watch and to know, and to give tidings of this night in days to come."

Abtalion made no answer, feeling justly reproved. Rabbi Eliezer tenderly stroked Benjamin's hair, and said encouragingly:

"Ask, child, ask freely, and I shall answer with the same freedom. Better to ask than to be ignorant. Only through asking can we gain knowledge, and only through knowledge can we win our way to righteousness."

The boy was elated that the sage whom all the community revered should talk to him as an equal. He would gladly have kissed the Rabbi's hand, yet was too timid. His lips trembled, but he uttered no sound. Rabbi Eliezer—whose wisdom was not only the wisdom of books, since he had also the wisdom of those who know the human heart—understood, despite the darkness, all that Benjamin thought and felt. He sympathized with their little companion's impatience to know the whither and the why of this strange expedition, so he fondled the hand which lay as light and tremulous as a butterfly in his own withered palm.

"I will tell you where we are going, and will hide nothing. There is naught wrongful in our purpose, though it must be hidden from those whom ere long we shall join. God, who looks down on us from heaven, knows and approves. He knows the beginning as clearly as we know it ourselves; and he knows what we cannot know, the end."

While speaking thus to the child, Rabbi Eliezer did not slacken his pace. The others quickened their steps for a moment, to draw nearer, and hearken to his words of wisdom.

"We walk along an ancient road, my child, on which our fathers and forefathers walked in days of yore. In ages past we were a nation of wanderers, as we have become once more, and as we are perhaps destined to remain until the end of time. Not like the other peoples have we lands of our own, where we can grow and harvest our crops. We move continually from place to place; and when we die, our graves are dug in foreign soil. Yet scattered though we are, flung like weeds into the furrows from north to south and from east to west, we have remained one people, united as is no other, held together by our God and our faith in him. Invisible is the tie which binds us, the invisible God. I know, child, that this passeth your understanding, for at your tender age you can grasp only the life of the senses, which perceive nothing but the corporeal, that which can be seen, touched, or tasted, like earth and wood and stone and brass. For that very reason the Gentiles, being children in mind, have made unto themselves gods of wood and stone and metal. We alone, we of the Chosen People, have no such tangible and visible gods (which we call idols), but an invisible God whom we know with an understanding that is above the senses. All our afflictions have come from this urge which drives us into the suprasensual, which makes us perpetual seekers for the invisible. But stronger is he who relies upon the invisible rather than on the visible and the palpable, since the latter perisheth, whereas the former endureth for ever. Spirit is in the end stronger than force. Therefore, and therefore alone, little Benjamin, have we lived on through the ages, outlasting time because we are pledged to the timeless, and only because we have been loyal to the invisible God has the invisible God kept faith with us.

"Child, these words of mine will be too deep for you. Often and often we elders are troubled because the God and the Justice in whom we believe are not visible in this our world. Still, even though you cannot now understand me, be not therefore troubled, but go on listening."

"I listen, Rabbi," murmured the boy, bashful but ecstatic.

"Filled with this faith in the invisible, our fathers and forefathers moved on through the world. To convince themselves of their own belief in this invisible God who never disclosed himself to their eyes and of whom no image may be graven, our ancestors made them a sign. For narrow is our understanding; the infinite is beyond our comprehension. Only from time to time does a shadow of the divine cast itself into our life here below. Fitfully and feebly a light from God's invisible countenance illumines our darkness. Hence, that we may be ever reminded of our duty to serve the invisible, which is justice and eternity and grace, we made the furniture of the Tabernacle, where God was unceasingly worshipped—made a Lampstand, called the Menorah, whose seven lamps burned unceasingly; and an altar whereon the shewbread was perpetually renewed. Misunderstand me not. These were not representations of the divine essence, such as the heathen impiously fashion. The holy emblems testified to our eternally watchful faith; and whithersoever we wandered through the world, the furnishings of the Holy Place wandered with us. Enclosed in the Ark of the Covenant, they were safeguarded in a Tabernacle, which our forefathers, homeless as are we this night, bore with them on their shoulders. When the Tabernacle with its sacred furniture rested, we likewise rested; when it was moved onward, we followed. Resting or journeying, by day or by night, for thousands of years we Jews thronged round this Holy of Holies; and as long as we preserve our sense of its sanctity, so long, even though dispersed among the heathen, shall we remain a united people.

"Now listen. Among the furnishings of the Holy Place were the Altar of the Shewbread, which also bore the fruits of the earth in due season; the Vessels from which clouds of incense rose to heaven; and the Tables of Stone whereon God had written his Commandments. But the most conspicuous of all the furniture was a Lampstand whose lamps burned unceasingly to throw light on the Altar in the Holy of Holies. For God loves the light which he kindled; and we made this Lampstand in gratitude for the light which he bestowed on us to gladden our eyes. Of pure gold, of beaten work, was the Lampstand cunningly fashioned. Seven-branched was it, having a central stem and three branches on each side, every one with a bowl made like unto an almond with a knop and a flower, all beaten work of pure gold. When the seven lamps were lighted, each light rose above its golden flower, and our hearts rejoiced to see. When it burned before us on the Sabbath, our souls became temples of devotion. No other symbol on earth, therefore, is so dear to us as this Seven-Branched Lampstand, and wherever you find a Jew who continues to cherish his faith in the Holy One of Israel, no matter under which of the winds of heaven his house stands, you will find in that house a model of the Menorah lifting its seven branches in prayer."

"Why seven?" the boy ventured to ask.

"Ask, and you shall be answered, child. To ask reverently is the beginning of wisdom. Seven is the most holy of numbers, for there were Seven Days of Creation, the crowning wonder being the creation of man in God's own image. What miracle can be greater than that we should find ourselves in this world, be aware of it and love it, and know something of its Creator? By making light in the firmament of heaven, God enabled our eyes to see and our spirit to know. That is why, with its seven branches, the Lampstand praises both lights, the outer and the inner. For God has given us also an inner light in Holy Writ; and just as we see outwardly with our eyes, so does Scripture enable us to see inwardly by the light of the understanding. What flame is to the senses, that is Scripture to the soul; for in Scripture all is recounted, explained, and enjoined: God's doings, and the deeds of our fathers; what is allowed to us and what forbidden; the creative spirit and the regulative law. In a twofold way God, through his light, enables us to contemplate the world: from without by the senses, and from within by the spirit; and thanks to the divine illumination we can even achieve self-knowledge. Do you understand me, child?"

"No," gasped the little boy, too proud to feign.

"Of course not," said Rabbi Eliezer gently. "These things are too deep for a mind so young. Understanding will come with the years. For this present, bear in mind what you can understand of all I have told you. The most sacred things of those we had as emblems on our wanderings, the only things remaining to us from our early days, were the Five Books of Moses and the Seven-Branched Lampstand, the Torah and the Menorah. Bear those words in mind."

"The Torah and the Menorah," repeated Benjamin solemnly, clenching his fists as if to aid his memory.

"Now listen further. There came a time, long, long ago, when we grew weary of wandering. Man craves for the earth, even as the earth craves for man. After forty years in the wilderness, we entered the Promised Land, as Moses had foretold, and we took possession of it. We ploughed and sowed and harvested, planted vineyards and tamed beasts, tilled fruitful fields which we surrounded with hedges and hurdles, being glad at heart that we no longer sojourned among strangers to be unto them a scorn and a hissing. We believed that our wanderings were finished for ever and a day, being foolhardy enough to declare that the land was our very own—whereas to no man is land given, but only lent for a season. Always are mortals prone to forget that having is not holding, and finding is not keeping. He who feels the ground firm beneath his feet builds him a house, fancying that thus he roots himself as firmly as do the trees. Therefore we built houses and cities; and since each of us had a home of his own, it was meet that we should wish our Lord and Protector likewise to have an abiding-place among us, a House of God which should be greater and more splendid than any human habitation. Thus it came to pass during the years when we were settled at peace in the Land of Promise that there ruled over us a king who was wealthy and wise, known as Solomon—"

"Praised be his name," interposed Abtalion gently.

"Praised be his name," echoed the others, without slackening in their stride.

"—who built a house upon Mount Moriah, where aforetime Jacob, dreaming, saw a ladder set up on the earth, and the top of it reached to heaven; and behold the angels of God ascending and descending on it. Wherefore on awaking Jacob said: 'Holy is this place, and holy shall it be to all the peoples of the earth.' And here Solomon built the Temple of the Lord, of stone and cedar wood and finely wrought brass. When our forefathers looked upon its walls they felt assured that God would dwell perpetually in our midst, and give us peace to the end of time. Even as we rested in our homes, so did the Tabernacle rest in the House of God, and within the Tabernacle the Ark of the Covenant, which we had borne with us for so long. By day and by night burned unceasingly before the Altar the seven flames of the Menorah, for this and all that was sacred to us were enshrined in the Holy of Holies; and God himself, though invisible as he shall be while time endures, rested peaceably in the land of our forefathers, in the Temple of Jerusalem."

"May my eyes behold it once again," came the voices in a litany.

"But listen further, my child. Whatever man possesses is entrusted to him only as a loan, and his happiness is unstable as a shadow. Not for ever, as we fancied, was our peace established, for a fierce people came from the east and forced a way into our town, even as the robbers whom you have seen forced a way into the city of the Gentiles among whom we have sojourned. What they could seize, they seized; what was portable, they carried away; what they could destroy, they destroyed. But our invisible goods they could not take from us—God's word and God's eternal presence. The Menorah, however, the holy Lampstand, they took from the Table of the Lord and carried it away; not because it was holy (since these sons of Belial knew naught of holiness), but because it was made of gold, and robbers love gold. Likewise they took the Altar and the Vessels, and drove our whole people into captivity in Babylon—"

"Babylon? What is Babylon? Where is Babylon?"

"Ask freely, child, and with God's will you shall be answered. Babylon was a great city, big as Rome, lying nearly as far to the east of Jerusalem as Rome lies to the west. Look you, we have walked for three hours since leaving the gate of Rome, and already we ache with weariness, but that march was a hundred times as long. Think, then, how far to the east the Menorah was taken by the robbers, and we driven with it into captivity. Mark this, also, that to God distance is nothing. To man it is otherwise; but perhaps the meaning of our unending pilgrimage is that what is sacred to us grows more sacred with distance, and our hearts are humbled by affliction. However that may be, when God saw that his Word was still holy to us in exile, that we stood the test, he softened the heart of one of the kings of that alien people. Aware that we had been wronged, he let our forefathers return to the Promised Land, giving back to them the Lampstand and the furniture of the Tabernacle. Then did our forefathers leave Chaldea and make their way home to Jerusalem across deserts, mountains, and thickets. From the ends of the earth they returned to the place which they had never ceased to cherish in their memories. We rebuilt the Temple on Mount Moriah; again the seven lamps of the Seven-Branched Lampstand flamed before God's Altar, and our hearts flamed with exultation. Now mark this, Benjamin, that you may grasp the meaning of our pilgrimage which begins tonight. No other thing made by the hands of men is so holy, so ancient, and so travelled hither and thither, as this Seven-Branched Menorah, which is the most precious pledge of the unity and purity of the Chosen People. Always when our lot is saddened the lamps of the Menorah are extinguished."

Rabbi Eliezer paused. At this the boy looked up, his eyes flaming like the lamps of the sacred emblem, eager with expectation that the story should be continued. The Rabbi smiled as he noticed this impatience, and stroked the lad's hair, saying:

"Have no fear, little one. The tale is not ended. Our destiny marches on. I could talk to you for years and fail to recount a thousandth part of all that has happened to us and all that awaits us. Listen then, since you are a good listener, to what befell after our return to Jerusalem from Babylon. Once more we thought that the Temple had been established for ever. But once more enemies came, across the sea this time, from the land where we now sojourn as strangers. A famous general led them, son of an Emperor, and himself in due time to be Emperor; Titus was he called—"

"Accursed be his name," intoned the elders.

"—who breached our walls and destroyed the Temple. Impiously he entered the Holy of Holies and snatched the Lampstand from the Altar. He plundered the Lord's House, and had the sacred furnishings carried before him when he celebrated his triumph upon his return to Rome. The foolish populace rejoiced, thinking that Titus had conquered our God, and that this was one of the captives who marched before him in fetters. So proud of his victory was the miscreant, that he had an arch built to commemorate it, with graven images that showed forth how he had ravaged the House of God."

"Rabbi," asked the boy, "tell me, is that the arch decorated with so many stone images? The arch in the great square, the arch which Father said I must never, never go through?"

"That's the one, child. Never go through it, but pass by without looking, for this memorial of Titus's triumph is likewise the memorial of one of the most sorrowful days in our history. No Jew may walk beneath the Arch of Titus, on which are graven images to show how the Romans mocked what was and always will be holy to us. Remember unfailingly—"

The old man broke off, for Hyrcanus ben Hillel had sprung forward from the rear to lay a hand upon his lips. The others were terrified by this irreverent freedom, but Hyrcanus silently pointed forward. Yes, there was something partially disclosed by the fog-bedimmed moon—a dark shape that seemed to wriggle along the white road like a huge caterpillar. Now, when the elders halted and listened, they could hear the creaking of heavily laden carts. Above these or beside them there flashed spears which looked like blades of grass that shine in the dew of morning—the lances of the Numidian rearguard escorting the spoil.

They kept good watch, the lancers, for a number of them wheeled their horses, to gallop back with levelled weapons and uttering shrill cries. Their burnouses streamed in the breeze, so that it seemed as if their chargers were winged. Involuntarily the eleven old men drew together in a bunch, the child in their midst. The lancers did not tarry until the steel points were close to the suspect pursuers; then they drew rein so suddenly that their mounts reared. Even in the faint light, the cavalrymen could see that these were no warriors, designing to recapture the booty, but peaceful whitebeards, infirm and old, each with staff and scrip. Thus in Numidia, too, did pious elders make pilgrimage from shrine to shrine. The fierce lancers, suspicions allayed, laughed encouragingly, showing white teeth. The leader whistled, once more the troop wheeled, and thundered down the road after the carts they were convoying, while the old men stood and trembled, hardly able to believe they were to be left unharmed.

Rabbi Eliezer, the pure and clear, was the first to regain composure. Gently he tapped the little boy's cheek.

"You're a brave lad, Benjamin," he said, leaning forward over the youngster. "I was holding your hand, and it did not shake. Shall I go on with my story? You have not yet heard whither we are going, or why we did not seek our beds as usual."

"Please go on, Rabbi," answered the boy, eagerly.

"I told you, you will remember, how Titus (accursed be his name), having laid impious hands on our holy treasures, carried them off to Rome and, in the vanity of his triumph, made a display of them all over the city. Thereafter, however, the Emperors of Rome put the Menorah and the other sacred objects from Solomon's Temple for safe-keeping in what they called the Temple of Peace—a foolish name, for when has peace ever lasted in our contentious world? Nor would Jehovah permit the furniture of the Tabernacle which had adorned his own Holy House in Zion to remain in a heathen temple, so one night he sent a fire to consume that building with all its contents, save only our Lampstand and other treasures which were rescued from the devouring flames, to show once again that neither fire nor distance nor the hand of a robber has power over the Menorah. This was a sign, a warning from God, that the Romans should restore the sacred emblems to their own sacred place, where they would be honoured, not because they were made of gold, but because they were holy. But when did such fools understand a sign, or when did men's stubborn hearts bow before the light of reason?"

Having paused to sigh, Rabbi Eliezer resumed:

"Thus the Gentiles took the Lampstand and put it away in one of the Emperor's other houses; and because it remained there in safe-keeping for years and for decades, they believed it to be theirs for all eternity. Nevertheless it is untrue to say that there is honour among thieves. What one robber has stolen will be taken from him forcibly by another. Just as Rome sacked Jerusalem, so has Carthage sacked Rome. Even as the Romans plundered us, they themselves have been plundered, and as they defiled our sacred places, so have their sacred places been defiled. But the robbers have also taken away what was ours, the Menorah, the emblem which used to stand on God's Altar in King Solomon's

House. Those wains which drive westward through the darkness are carrying to the coast that which is dearest to us in the world. Tomorrow the barbarians will put the Lampstand on one of their ships, to sail away with it into foreign parts, where it will be beyond the reach of our longing eyes. Never again will the Lampstand shed its beams upon us who are old and near to death. Nevertheless as those who have loved anyone when alive escort the body upon its last journey to the tomb, thus testifying their affection, so today do we escort the Menorah upon the first stage of its journey into foreign parts. What we are losing is the holiest of our treasures. Do you understand, now, little one, the meaning of our mournful pilgrimage?"

The child walked on with hanging head, and made no answer. He seemed to be thinking things over.

"Never forget this, Benjamin. We have brought you with us as witness, that in days to come, when we are beneath the sod, you may bear testimony to the way in which we were loyal to the sacred emblem, and may teach others to remain faithful. You will fortify them in the faith which sustains us, the faith that the Menorah will one day return from its wanderings in the darkness, and, as of old, will with its seven flames shed a glorious light upon the Table of the Lord. We awoke you from your slumbers that your heart might also awaken, and that you will be able to tell those of a later generation what befell this night. Store up everything in your mind that you may console others by telling them how your own eyes have seen the Menorah which has moved onward for thousands of years among strangers, even as our people have wandered. Firmly do I believe that it will never perish so long as we remain alive as God's Chosen People faithful to the Law."

Still Benjamin answered not a word. Rabbi Eliezer, the pure and clear, sensed the resistance which must underlie this stubborn silence. He leaned forward, therefore, over the little boy, and asked, gently as was his manner: "Have you understood me?"

The child was froward. "No," he said curtly. "I don't understand, Rabbi. For if... if the Menorah is so dear to us and so holy... why do we let them take it away from us?"

Heaving a sigh, the old man said: "There is reason in your question, my boy. Why do we let them take it away from us? Why don't we resist? When you are older, you will learn that in this world, alas, might is right, and that the righteous man can seldom prevail. Men of violence establish their will upon earth, which is a place where piety and righteousness have little power. God has taught us to suffer injustice, not trying to establish the right with the strong hand."

Rabbi Eliezer said these words as he marched forward with bowed head. Thereupon Benjamin snatched away his hand and stopped short. Bluntly, almost masterfully, did the boy, in his excitement, apostrophize Eliezer:

"But God? Why does he permit this robbery? Why does not he help us? You told me that he is a just God and almighty. Why does he favour the robbers instead of the righteous?"

Except for Eliezer, the old men were outraged by these words. They all stopped in their stride, feeling as if their hearts had ceased to beat. Like the blast of a trumpet the little boy's defiance had been hurled into the night, as if he were declaring war against God. Ashamed of his grandson, Abtalion shouted:

"Silence! Blaspheme not!"

But the Rabbi cut him short:

"Be you silent, rather. Why should you find fault with the innocent child? His unsophisticated heart has but blurted out a question which, in truth, we ask ourselves daily and hourly, you and I and the rest of us; a question which the wisest of our people have asked since the beginning of time. From of old the Jewish sages and prophets have inquired why Jehovah should deal so harshly with us among the nations, seeing that we serve him more fervently than any others. Why should he thrust us beneath the feet of our enemies that they may trample us into the dust, we who were the first to know God and to praise him in his unfathomable ways? Why does he destroy what we build; why does he frustrate our dearest hopes? Why does he drive us forth into exile whenever we think we have found rest; why does he incite the heathen to rage against us ever more furiously? Why does he visit us with supreme affliction, we whom he made his Chosen People, we whom he first initiated into his mysteries? Far be it from me to deceive this simple child. If his question be blasphemous, then I myself am a blasphemer every day of my life. Look you, I acknowledge it to you all. I also am froward. I also continually arraign God. Day after day do I, now eighty years of age, ask the question which has just been asked by a seven-year-old boy. Why should God visit upon us more than upon all others such unceasing tribulations? Why does he allow us to be despoiled, helping those who plunder us to gain their ends? Often and often do I beat my breast in shame, but never can I stifle these urgent questionings. I should not be a Jew, I should not be a human being, if these meditations did not torment me day after day, these blasphemies as you call them which will continue to trouble me for as long as I draw breath."

The rest of the elders were astounded, nay, horrified. Never had any of them seen Kab ve Nake, the pure and clear, so greatly moved. This arraignment must have surged up from depths which were ordinarily concealed. They could scarcely recognize him as he stood there quaking with emotion and distress, and shamefacedly turning his head away from the child who looked up at him with wonder. Speedily, however, Rabbi Eliezer mastered his emotion, and, bending once more over the little boy, he said appeasingly:

"Forgive me for speaking to these others, and to one who stands over us all, instead of answering your question. In the simplicity of your heart, little one, you ask me why God should permit this crime against us and against himself. In my own simplicity I answered you, as frankly as I could: 'I do not know.' We do not know God's plans; we cannot read his thoughts; and his ways are past finding out. But ever and again, when I arraign him in the madness of my suffering and in the extremity of our general distress, I try to console myself with the assurance that perhaps, after all, there is some meaning in the afflictions with which he visits us, and that maybe each of us is atoning for a wrong. No man can say who hath committed it. Perhaps Solomon the Wise was unwise when he builded the Temple at Jerusalem, as if God were a man coveting a habitation here on earth and among one of its peoples. It may have been sinful of Solomon to adorn the Holy House as he did, as though gold were more than piety and marble more than inward stability. May not we Jews have departed from God's will by desiring, like the other nations, to have house and home of our own, saying 'This land is ours' and speaking of 'our Temple' and 'our God' even as a man saith 'my hand' and 'my hair'? Perhaps that was why he had the Temple destroyed, and tore us away from our homes, that we might cease to turn our affections towards things visible and tangible, and remain faithful in the spiritual field alone to him the unattainable and the invisible. Maybe this is our true path, that we shall be ever afoot, looking sorrowfully back and yearningly forward, perpetually craving for repose, and never able to find rest. For the only road of holiness is that pursued by those who do not know their destination, but continue to march on steadfastly, as we march onward this night through darkness and danger, not knowing our goal."

The boy listened attentively, but Rabbi Eliezer was drawing to a close:

"Ask no more questions, Benjamin, for your questions exceed my capacity to answer. Wait patiently. Some day, perhaps, God will answer you out of your own heart."

The old man was silent, and silent likewise were the other elders. They stood motionless in the middle of the road; the silence of the night enwrapped them, while they felt as if they were standing in that outer darkness which lies beyond the realm of time.

Then one of them trembled and raised his hand. Seized with anxiety, he signed to the others to listen. Yes, through the stillness came a murmur. It was as if someone had gently plucked the strings of a harp; an obscure tone, but gradually swelling like the wind blowing out of the obscurity that hid the sea. Quickly, quickly, it rose to a roar, for now the wind raged, tossing the branches of the trees, making the bushes rustle loudly, while the dust whirled up from the road. The very stars in the sky seemed to tremble. The old men, knowing that God often spoke out of the storm, wondered if they were about to hear his voice in answer. Each looked timidly on the ground. Unthinkingly they joined hands, clasping one another for joint support in face of the threatening terror, and each could feel the alarmed throbbing of another's pulses.

But nothing happened. The flurry-scurry of the brief whirlwind subsided as rapidly as it had arisen; the rustle in the bushes and the grass ceased. Nothing happened. No voice spake; no sound broke the renewed and intimidating stillness. When they ventured to raise their eyes from the ground, they perceived that, in the east, an opaline light was showing on the horizon. The flurry of wind had been nothing more than that which usually precedes the dawn. Nothing more? We take it lightly, but is it not a daily miracle that day should tread upon the heels of night? As they stood there, still disquieted, the crimson in the eastern sky strengthened and spread, while the outlines of surrounding objects began to detach themselves from the gloom. Yes, the night was finished, the night of their pilgrimage.

"Dawn cometh," murmured Abtalion. "Let us pray."

The eleven old men drew together. Benjamin stood apart, being too young to share in this ritual, though he looked on with interest and excitement. The elders withdrew the praying-shawls from their scrips to wrap them round head and shoulders. Their phylacteries, too, they strapped on, round the forehead and the left hand and wrist which lie nearest the heart. Then they turned eastward, towards Jerusalem, and prayed, expressing thanks to God who created the world and enumerating the eighteen attributes of his perfection. Intoning and murmuring, they swayed their bodies forward and backward in time with the words. The boy found many of these words too difficult to understand, but he saw the ardour with which the worshippers waved their bodies in the exaltation of the prayer as, shortly before, the grass had waved in God's wind. After the solemn "Amen", they made obeisance one and all. Then, having taken off the praying-shawls and the phylacteries, they put them back in their scrips and made ready to resume their march. They looked older, now, these old men, in the pitiless light of dawn; the furrows on their faces seemed deeper, the shadows beneath their eyes and at the corners of their mouths were darker. As if newly arisen from their own deathbeds, accompanied by the child who, though tired, was fresh and vigorous in comparison, they wearily proceeded upon the last stage of their journey.

*

Bright and limpid was the Italian morning when the eleven old men and the little boy reached the harbour of Portus where the yellow waters of the Tiber mingled sluggishly with the sea. Only a few of the Vandals' ships were still in the roads, and one after another was on its way to the offing, pennants flying gaily at the mastheads and holds full of loot. At length only one remained at anchor close to the shore, greedily swallowing the contents of the overloaded wagons, the remnants of the plunder from Rome. One cart after another drove onto the jetty, and slaves took load after load across the gangplank, carrying the burden on head or shoulders. Swiftly they bore chests packed with gold and amphorae filled to the neck with wine or oil. But hasten as they might, they were not quick enough for the impatient captain, who signed to the overseer to speed the embarkation with the lash. Now the last of the wains was being unloaded, the one which the pilgrims had been following throughout the night because it contained the Menorah. To begin with, its contents had been hidden by straw and sacking, but the old men shook with excitement as these wrappings were removed. Now had come the decisive moment, now or never must God work a miracle.

Benjamin's eyes were elsewhere. This was the first time he had seen the sea, which filled him with amazement. Like an enormous blue mirror it looked, arching to the sharp line of the horizon where sea passed into sky. Even larger it appeared to him than the dome of night with which he had so recently made acquaintance, the starry expanse of heaven. Spellbound he watched the play of the waves on the shore, chasing one another up the beach, breaking into foam, receding and continually reforming. How lovely was this sportive movement, such as he had never dreamed of in the dull, dark alley where he had been brought up. He threw out his chest, tiny though this chest was, vigorously breathing in the air which had a tang he had never before experienced, determined to make the fresh sea-breeze invigorate his timid Jewish blood and fill it with a new joy. He longed to go close to the edge of the troubled waters, to stretch out his slender arms and embrace the wide and wonderful prospect. As he looked at the beautiful blue waters sparkling in the early sunshine, he was thrilled by a new sense of happiness. How splendid and free and untroubled was everything here. The wheeling gulls reminded him of the white-winged angels of whom he had been told; gloriously white, too, were the sails of the ships, sails bellied by the wind. Then, when he closed his eyes for a moment and threw his head back, opening his mouth wide to inhale more of the salt-tasting air, there suddenly occurred to him the first words of Scripture he had been taught: "In the beginning God created the heaven and the earth." Never before had the name of God, mentioned so often by Rabbi Eliezer during the night walk, been full, as now, of meaning and form.

Then a loud cry startled him. The eleven elders screamed as with one voice, and instantly he ran to join them. The sackcloth had just been removed to uncover the contents of the last wagon, and as the Berber slaves bent to lift a silver image of Juno, a statue weighing several hundredweight, one of them who was standing in the cart kicked the Menorah out of his way. The Seven-Branched Lampstand fell from the wagon onto the ground. That was why the old men had uttered their cry of terror and wrath, to see the sacred emblem—on which Moses' eyes had rested, which had been blessed by Aaron, which had stood upon the Altar of the Lord in the House of Solomon—desecrated by falling into the dung from the team of oxen, defiled by dirt and dust. The slaves looked round inquisitively, wondering why the onlookers had screamed so dolorously. They could not understand why the foolish greybeards had yelled with horror, seizing one another by the arms to make a living chain of distress. No one had done them any harm. But the overseer, who would not suffer any pause in the work, lashed the toilers' naked backs with his whip, so once more subserviently they buried their arms in the straw of the load, this time to disengage a sculptured slab of porphyry, followed by another huge statue which, sustaining it by a pole and a rope round the head and the feet, they bore across the gangplank as they might have carried a slaughtered enemy. Speedily they emptied the wagon. Only the Lampstand, eternal symbol, still lay disregarded where it had fallen, half hidden by one of the wheels. The old men, still clasping one another's hands, were united also in the hope that the robbers, whom the overseer continued to speed at their task, would in their haste overlook the Menorah. Might it not be God's will, at the last moment, to save this precious object for his devoted worshippers?

But now one of the slaves caught sight of it, stooped, and lifted it onto his shoulders. Brightly it gleamed in the sunshine, so that the brightness of the morning grew yet more bright. This was the first time in their long lives that any of the elders save Hyrcanus ben Hillel had set eyes upon the lost treasure; and how lamentable that it should be only at a moment when the beloved object was again passing into the hands of the Gentiles, about to voyage into a foreign, a far-away land. The Berber slave was a big, strong, broad-shouldered man, but the golden Menorah was heavy, and he needed both hands to steady his burden as he walked across the swaying plank. Five steps, four steps, and it would have vanished for ever from their eyes. As if drawn by a mysterious force, the eleven elders, still clasped together, moved forward to the gangplank, their eyes blinded with tears, mumbling incoherently as spittle dribbled from their mouths. Drunken with sorrow they stumbled forward, hoping to be allowed to implant at least a pious kiss upon the holy emblem. One only among them, Rabbi Eliezer, though suffering no less than his brethren, remained clear-headed. He gripped Benjamin's hand, so firmly that the little boy found it hard to repress a cry of pain.

"Look, look well. You will be the last Jew alive to set eyes upon what was our most precious possession. You will bear witness how they took it away from us, how they stole it."

The child could hardly understand what the Rabbi meant; but sympathy with the old men's manifest agony surged up within him, and he felt that an unrighteous deed was being done. Anger, the uncontrollable fury of a child, boiled over. Without realizing what he was about, this seven-year-old boy snatched his hand away from Eliezer's and rushed after the Berber, who was at this moment crossing the gangplank, and who, strong though he was, tottered beneath the weight. This alien, this Gentile, should not take away the Lampstand. Benjamin flung himself upon the mighty porter, trying to snatch away his burden.

The slave, heavily laden, was staggered by the unexpected shock. It was only a little child who hung upon his arm; but, losing his balance upon the narrow plank, he fell beneath his burden, both of them on the quayside. The child fell with him. Furiously the Berber struck with all his strength at Benjamin's right arm. Feeling the pain, which was intense, Benjamin yelled at the top of his little voice, but his cry was drowned in the general hubbub. All who saw what had happened were shouting and yelling: the Jewish elders horror-stricken at the sight of the Menorah being once more rolled in the mud, and the Vandals on the ship shouting with wrath. The enraged overseer rushed up to flog the Jewish elders away with his whip. Meanwhile the slave, greatly incensed, had risen to his feet. Delivering a hearty kick (fortunately he was unshod) at the groaning child, he shouldered his burden once more and hastily but triumphantly bore it along the gangplank into the ship.

The elders paid no heed to the youngster. Not one of them noticed the writhing little body on the ground, since they had eyes only for the Menorah as it was carried on board, its seven lamps pointing upward as if in appeal to heaven. Shudderingly they watched how, as soon as the Berber had crossed the plank, other hands carelessly relieved him of his burden and threw it upon a pile of the general spoils. The boatswain sounded his whistle, the moorings were cast off, and from between decks, where the galley-slaves were chained to their benches, at the word of command forty oars took the water, one-two, one-two. Instantly the galley responded, and moved away from the quay. Foam curled on either side of the prow; noiselessly it departed, except for the plashing of the oars; as it crossed the bar it began to pitch and toss upon the waves as if it were breathing and alive; pursuing the fleet, the other galleys and the sailing ships, it steered southward towards Carthage.

The eleven old men stared after the vanishing galley. Again they had clasped hands, again they were trembling, a live chain of horror and distress. Without holding counsel together, without mutually confiding their secret thoughts, they had all hoped for a miracle. But the galley had hoisted sail, was running before a favourable wind, and as she grew smaller and smaller, so did their hopes even of a miracle decline, to be submerged at last in the huge ocean of despair. Now the vessel on which their gaze was fixed seemed no larger than a seagull, until at length, their eyes wet with tears, they could discern no further trace of her on the forsaken surface of the waters. They must abandon hope. Once again the Menorah had wandered off into the void, unresting as ever, utterly lost to the Chosen People.

At length, ceasing to look southward in the direction of Carthage, they bethought them of Benjamin, who lay where he had been struck down, groaning with the pain of his broken arm. Having gently raised the bruised and bleeding form, they laid him on a litter. They were all ashamed at having left it to this little boy to make a bold attempt at recovering the Lampstand; and Abtalion had good reason to dread what the women of his household would say when he brought back his grandson thus crippled. But Rabbi Eliezer, the pure and clear, consoled them, saying:

"Do not bewail what has happened, nor pity the lad. He has come well out of it. Recall the words of Holy Writ, how, upon the threshing-floor, Uzzah put forth his hand to the Ark of God, and took hold of it; for the oxen shook it. And the anger of the Lord was kindled against Uzzah; and God smote him there for his error; and there he died by the Ark of God—for God does not wish that things which are most holy shall be lightly touched by human hands. But he spared this child, who has suffered no more than a broken arm instead of being smitten to death. Perhaps there is a blessing in this hurt, and a calling."

The Rabbi bent low over the weeping boy.

"Be not wroth because of your pain, but accept it thankfully. Indeed it is a boon and our common heritage. Only through suffering doth our people thrive, and naught but distress can give us creative energy. A great thing hath happened to you, for you have touched a most holy emblem, without worse hurt than a broken arm when you might well have lost your life. Maybe you are set apart by this pain, and a sublime meaning is hidden in your destiny."

The boy looked up at Rabbi Eliezer, strengthened and full of faith. In his pride at having such words addressed to him by the sage, he almost forgot the pain. Not another groan passed his lips through the long hours during which they carried him home.

For decades after the sack of Rome by the Vandals there was continual unrest in the Western Empire—more than usually happens in seven generations. For twenty years there was a rapid succession of emperors: from Avitus, Majorian, Libius Severus, and Anthemius, each of them slaying or driving out his predecessor; through another Teuton invasion of Italy from the north and a plundering of Rome; to the brief day of the last emperors of the West, Glycerius, Julius Nepos, and Romulus Augustulus. Another Teuton, Odoacer, King of the Heruli, took Rome, overthrew the Western Empire in 476, took the title of King of Italy, and reigned until he in turn was overthrown by Theodoric, King of the Goths. These Gothic invaders fancied that their kingdom, established by mighty warriors, would endure for ever; but it too passed in a generation while other barbarians continued to come down from the north, and in Byzantium the Eastern Empire, the only successor of Rome, stood firm. It seemed as if there were to be no peace in the thousand-year-old city beside the Tiber since the Menorah had been carried away through the Porta Portuensis.

The eleven old men who had followed the Menorah upon its journey from Rome to Portus had long since passed away in due course of nature; so, likewise, had their children, and their children's children had grown old: but still there lived on Benjamin, Abtalion's grandson, who had witnessed the Vandal raid. The boy had become a stripling, the stripling had grown to manhood, and was now exceedingly old. Seven of his sons had died before him, and of his grandchildren one had been smitten to death when, during the reign of Theodoric, the mob burned the synagogue.

Benjamin lived on, with a withered arm, the outcome of a badly set fracture. He lived on as a forest giant may survive the storms that lay low the trees on either side. He saw emperors reign and perish, kingdoms rise and fall; but death spared him, and his name was honoured, almost holy, among all the Jewish exiles. Benjamin Marnefesh did they call him, because of his withered arm, the name meaning "one whom God has sorely tried". He was venerated as the last survivor of those who had set eyes upon Moses' Lampstand, the Menorah from Solomon's Temple which, its lamps unlighted, was buried in the Vandals' treasure house.

When Jewish merchants came to Rome from Leghorn and Genoa and Salerno, from Mainz and Treves, or from the Levant, they made it their first business to call on Benjamin Marnefesh, that they might see with their own eyes the man who had himself seen the holy emblem on which the eyes of Moses and of Solomon had rested. They made obeisance before him as one of the chosen of the Lord; with a thrill of terror they contemplated his withered arm; and with their own fingers they ventured to touch the fingers which had actually touched the Menorah. Though everyone knew the story (since in those days news spread by word of mouth as readily as it now spreads in print), they all begged him to tell them his memories of that wonderful night. With unfailing patience, old Benjamin would recount the expedition the twelve of them had made on the fateful occasion; and his huge white beard seemed to glisten as he repeated the words that had been spoken by the long-dead Rabbi Eliezer, the pure and clear.

"Nor need we of the Chosen People despair," he would conclude. "The wanderings of the sacred emblem are not yet finished. The Lampstand shall return to Jerusalem, shall not for ever be separated from those who reverence it. Once again shall our nation come together around it."

When his visitors left him, it was with gladdened hearts; and one and all they prayed that he might live many years yet, he, the consoler, the witness, the last of those who had seen the Menorah.

Thus Benjamin, the sorely tried, the child of that night hallowed by ancient memories, lived to be seventy, to be eighty, to be eighty-five, to be eighty-seven. His shoulders were bowed beneath the weight of his years, his vision was dimmed, and often he was tired out long before the day was done. Yet none of the Jews of the Roman community would believe that death could strike him down, seeing that his life bore witness to so great a happening. It was unthinkable that the eyes of him who had seen the Lampstand of the Lord could be closed in death before they had seen the return of the Seven-Branched Menorah, and they cherished his survival as a token of God's favour. His presence must grace every festival, and he must join in every religious service. When he walked the streets of the Jewish quarter, the oldest bowed before old Benjamin, everyone whom he passed blessed his footsteps, and wherever the faithful assembled in sorrow or rejoicing he must be seated in the first place.

Thus did the Jews of the Roman congregation do honour as usual to Benjamin Marnefesh when, as custom prescribed, they assembled at the cemetery on the saddest day of the year, the Black Fast, the ninth of Ab, the day of the destruction of the Temple, the gloomy day on which their forefathers had been made homeless and had been dispersed among all the lands of the earth. They could not meet in the synagogue, which had recently been destroyed by the populace, and it therefore seemed meet to them that they should draw near to their dead on this day of supreme affliction—outside the city, at the place where their fathers were interred in alien soil, they would come together to bemoan their own severance from the Promised

Land. They sat among the tombs, some of them on gravestones already broken. They knew themselves to be inheritors of their forefathers' grief, as they read the names and the praises of the deceased. Upon many of the tombstones, emblems had been chiselled: crossed hands for one who had been a member of the priesthood; or the vessels of the Levites, or the lion of the tribe of Judah, or the star of David. One of the upright gravestones had a sculptured image of the Seven-Branched Lampstand, the Menorah, to show that the man buried beneath it had been a sage and a light among the people of Israel. Before this tombstone, with his eyes fixed on it, sat Benjamin Marnefesh amid his companions—all of them with torn raiment and ashes scattered upon their heads, all bent like weeping willows over the black waters of their sorrow.

It was late in the afternoon, and the sun was sinking behind the pines and the cypresses. Brightly coloured butterflies fluttered round the crouching Jews as they might have fluttered round decaying tree-stumps; dragonflies with iridescent wings settled unheeded upon their drooping shoulders; and in the lush grass beetles crawled over their shoes. The brilliant foliage trembled in the breeze, but, glorious as was the evening, the mourners did not raise their eyes, and their hearts were full of sorrow. Again and again they deplored the sad fate of their people in its dispersal. They neither ate nor drank; they did not look at the glories which surrounded them; they only continued to intone lamentations about the destruction of the Temple and the fall of Jerusalem. Though every word they uttered was familiar, they continued their litany to intensify their pain and lacerate their hearts the more. Their only wish, on this day of affliction, the day of the Black Fast, was to intensify their sense of suffering, to become ever more keenly aware of the woes of the Chosen People in which their dead forefathers had participated. They recounted one to another all the tribulations which had befallen the Jews throughout the ages. Even as now in Rome, so everywhere that a Jewish community existed, there crouched on this day and at this hour Hebrews in torn raiment and with ashes on their heads. Among the tombs they lamented, from end to end of the civilized world, uttering the same plaints. Everywhere they reminded one another that the daughters of Zion were fallen and had become a mockery among the nations. They knew that these universal lamentations of the faithful remained their firmest tie.

As they sat and lamented, they did not notice how the sunlight grew more and more golden, while the dark stems of the pines and the cypresses were glowing red, as if illumined from within. They failed to realize that the ninth of Ab, the day of the great mourning, was drawing to its close, and that the hour of evening prayer had come. It was at this moment that the rusty iron hinges of the cemetery gates creaked loudly. The mourners heard it. They knew that someone had entered, but did not rise. The stranger, without a word, stood silent, aware that the hour of prayer had come. Then the leader of the community perceived the newcomer, and greeted him, saying:

"Receive our blessing. Peace be with you, O Jew."

"A blessing upon all here," answered the stranger.

The leader spoke again, asking: "Whence come you, and to what community do you belong?"

"The community to which I belonged no longer exists. I fled hither from Carthage by ship. Great things have happened there. Justinian, Emperor of the East, sent from Byzantium an army to attack the Vandals. Belisarius, his general, took the city by storm. That nest of pirates has fallen. The King of the Vandals is a prisoner, and his realm has been destroyed. Belisarius has seized all that the robbers have got together during the last hundred years, and is taking it to Byzantium. The war is over."

The Jews received this tidings mutely and indifferently, without rising. What was Byzantium to them, and what was Carthage? Edom and Amalek, ever at odds. The heathen were always making war against one another, war without purpose. Sometimes one side conquered, sometimes the other; but never did righteousness prevail. What did such things matter to the Chosen People? What did they care for Carthage, for Rome, or for Byzantium? Only one town was of any concern to them—Jerusalem.

One member alone of the Roman community, Benjamin Marnefesh, the sorely tried, raised his head with interest, to inquire:

"What has happened to the Lampstand?"

"No harm has come to it, but Belisarius has carried it away with the other trophies. With the rest of his plunder, he is taking it to Byzantium."

Now, in turn, the others were alarmed. They grasped the meaning of Benjamin's question. Once again the Menorah was on its wanderings, from foreign land to foreign land. The stranger's news was like an incendiary torch flung into the dark edifice of their mourning. They sprang to their feet, strode across the tombs, surrounded the man from Carthage, sobbing and weeping:

"Woe! To Byzantium!... Again across the seas!... To another foreign country!... Once more they have carried it off in triumph as did Titus, the accursed... Always to some other land of the Gentiles and never back to Jerusalem... Woe, woe hath befallen us!"

It was as if a branding-iron had been thrust into an old wound. The same unrest, the same fear seized them all. When the furnishings of the Holy of Holies wandered, they too would have to wander; to go anew among strangers; to seek a fresh home which would be no home. Thus had it happened ever since the Temple had been destroyed. Again and again there had been a new phase of the Diaspora. The old pain and the new seized them in a wild medley. They wept, they sobbed, they lamented; and the little birds which had been sitting peacefully upon the tombstones flew away in alarm.

One only among the assembled Jews, Benjamin, the old, old man, had remained seated upon a moss-grown tombstone, silent while the others shouted and wept. Unconsciously, he had clasped his hands. As if in a dream he sat there, smiling as he looked at the tombstone on which was graven the likeness of the Menorah. There appeared upon his furrowed countenance, encircled with white locks, something of the expression he had had as a child of seven long, long ago. The wrinkles seemed to vanish; the lips grew supple again, while the smile, one could have fancied, spread all over his body as if, bowed forward though he was, he was smiling from within.

At length one of the others grew aware of his expression, and was ashamed of himself for having lost control. Pulling himself together, he looked reverently at Benjamin, and nudged his nearest neighbour, with a nod of direction. One after the other, they silenced their lamentations, and looked breathlessly at the old man, whose smile hung like a white cloud over the darkness of their pain. Soon they were all as quiet as the dead among whose graves they were standing.

The silence made Benjamin aware that they were staring at him. Laboriously, being very frail, he arose from the tombstone on which he was sitting. Suddenly he appeared to radiate power such as he had never before possessed, as he stood there with his silvern locks flowing down across his forehead from beneath his small silk cap. Never had his fellow-believers felt so strongly as at this hour that Marnefesh, the sorely tried man, was a man with a mission. Benjamin began to speak, and his words sounded like a prayer:

"At length I know why God has spared me till this hour. Again and again I have asked myself why I, having grown useless from age, continue to break bread; why death should pass me by, since I am a weary do-nothing of an old man to whom eternal silence would be welcome. I had lost courage and trust, as I watched the excess of affliction with which our people has been visited. Now I understand that there is still a task for me to perform. I saw the beginning, and I am summoned to see the end."

The others listened attentively to these obscure words. After a pause, one of them, the leader of the community, asked in low tones: "What do you propose to do?"

"I believe that God has vouchsafed me life and vision for so long that I may once again set eyes on the Menorah. I must betake myself to Byzantium. Perhaps that which as a child I was unable to achieve will be possible to me in extreme old age."

His hearers trembled with excitement and impatience. Incredible was the thought that a decrepit man of eighty-seven would be able to win back the Lampstand from the mightiest emperor on earth; and yet there was fascination in the dream of this miracle. One of them ventured to ask:

"How could you endure so long a journey? A three weeks' voyage across tempestuous seas. I fear it would be too much for you."

"A man is always granted strength when he has a holy task to perform. When the eleven elders took me with them eighty years ago from Rome to Portus they did so doubtingly, being afraid that the walk would be beyond my strength; yet I kept pace with them to the end. It is needful, however, since I have a withered arm, that someone shall go with me as helper, a vigorous man and young, that he may bear witness to later generations even as I have borne witness to yours."

He glanced around the circle, letting his eyes rest on one of the young men after another, as if appraising them. Each trembled at this probationary glance, which seemed to pierce him to the soul. Every one of them longed to be chosen, but none would thrust himself forward. They waited eagerly for the decision. But Benjamin hung his head and murmured:

"No, I will not choose. You must cast lots. God will disclose to me the right companion."

The men drew together, cut grasses from the burial mounds, breaking off one much shorter than the others. He who drew the short blade was to go. The lot fell upon Jehoiakim ben Gamaliel, a man of twenty, tall and powerful, a blacksmith by trade, but unpopular. He was not learned in the Law and was of passionate disposition. His hands were stained with blood. At Smyrna, in a brawl, he had slain a Syrian, and had fled to Rome lest the constables should lay hands on him. Ill-pleased, the others silently wondered why the choice had thus fallen upon a man who was savage and mutinous instead of upon one who was reverent and pious. But when Jehoiakim drew the short blade of grass, Benjamin barely glanced at him and said:

"Make ready. We sail tomorrow evening."

The whole of the day which followed this ninth of Ab, the Jews of the Roman community were busily at work. Not a man among them plied his ordinary trade. All contributed the money they could spare; those who were poor borrowed upon whatever valuables they owned; the women gave their gold and silver buckles and such jewels as they possessed. Without exception they were sure that

Benjamin Marnefesh was destined to liberate the Menorah from its new captivity, and persuade Emperor Justinian, like King Cyrus of old, to send the people of Israel and the furnishings of the Temple back to Jerusalem. They wrote letters to the communities of the East, in Smyrna, Crete, Salonika, Tarsus, Nicaea, and Trebizond, asking them to send emissaries to Byzantium and to collect funds on behalf of the holy deed of liberation. They exhorted the brethren in Byzantium and Galata to accept Benjamin Marnefesh, the sorely tried, as a man chosen by the Lord for a sublime mission and to smooth his path for him. The women got ready wraps and cloaks and cushions for the journey; and also food prepared as the Law directs, that the lips of the pious need not be contaminated by unclean victuals on the voyage. Although the Jews in Rome were forbidden to drive in a cart or to ride on horseback, they secretly provided a vehicle outside the gates, that the old man might reach the harbour without the fatigue of a long walk.

To their surprise, however, Benjamin refused to enter this vehicle. Eighty years before, he had gone on foot from Rome to Portus, completing the march betwixt midnight and morning. He would do the same now, said the determined octogenarian. A foolhardy undertaking, thought his co-religionists to begin with, for a man almost decrepit to attempt so long a march. But they were amazed to see the way in which he stepped out, being as it were transfigured by his vocation. The tidings from Carthage had instilled new energy into his ageing limbs, and invigorated his senile blood. His voice, which for years had been the thin pipe of a very old man, was now deep-toned and masterful as, almost wrathfully, he refused to be coddled. They contemplated him with respectful admiration.

All through the night the Jewish men of Rome accompanied Benjamin Marnefesh upon the road which their ancestors had trod to accompany the Lampstand of the Lord. Privily, under cover of darkness, they had brought with them a litter to carry the old man should his strength give out. But Benjamin led the way lustily. In silence he marched, his mind filled with memories of long ago. At each milestone, at each turn of the road, he recalled more and more clearly those far-distant hours of his childhood. He remembered everything plainly, the voices of those who had generations ago been buried; and he recapitulated the words that had been spoken on that momentous journey. There on the left had risen the pillar of fire from the burning house; this was the milestone opposite which his companions' hearts had failed them when the Numidian lancers were charging down upon them. He recalled each one of his questions, and each one of Rabbi Eliezer's answers. When he reached the place where, at dawning, the elders had prayed at the roadside, he donned, as before, his praying-shawl and his phylacteries, and, turning to the east, intoned the very prayer which fathers and forefathers were accustomed to say morning after morning—the prayer which, handed down from generation to generation, children and grandchildren and great-grandchildren would continue to utter.

His companions wondered. Why should he speak the morning prayer at this hour? As yet there was no hint of dawn in the sky. Why, then, should so pious a man utter the morning prayer at this untimely instant? Contrary to all custom and tradition it was, a defiance of the prescriptions of the Law. Still, however strange a freak it seemed, they watched him reverently. What he, the chosen of the Almighty, did could not be wrong. If, when day had not yet dawned, he chose to thank God for the gift of light, he must have good reason for what he was doing.

Having said his prayer, old Benjamin refolded his praying-shawl, put away his phylacteries, and marched on lustily, as if his act of piety had refreshed him. When they reached Portus, day had begun. He gazed long out to sea, thinking of himself as a child when he had glimpsed the sea for the first time, watching the play of the waves on the shore and gazing out towards the horizon. "The same sea as of old, deep and unfathomable as God's thoughts," he piously reflected. Rejoicing, as before, in the brightness of the sky, he gave his blessing to each of his companions, convinced that he was taking leave of them for ever; then, accompanied by Jehoiakim, he went on board the ship. Like their fathers and grandfathers eighty years before, the Jews now watched with interest and excitement as the ship hoisted her sails and made for the offing. They knew they had set eyes upon the sorely tried Benjamin for the last time, and when the sails vanished in the distance they became aware of a keen sense of loss.

Steadily the merchant vessel proceeded on her course. The waves rose high, and dark clouds gathered in the west. The seamen were exceedingly anxious about the weather. But though once or twice they had baffling winds and rough water which was most uneasy for landsmen, they reached Byzantium safely three days after the arrival of Belisarius's fleet with the spoils of Carthage.

After the fall of the Western Empire and the consequent decline of Rome, Byzantium had become the sole mistress of the occidental civilized world. The streets of the capital were thronged with lively crowds, for it was years since there had been promise of so glorious a spectacle in a town which loved festivals and games far more than it loved God or righteousness. In the circus, Belisarius, conqueror of the Vandals, was to parade his victorious army and display his booty before the Basileus, the Master of the World. Enormous crowds packed the streets, which were gaily decorated with flags; the vast hippodrome was filled to bursting; and the fretful populace, tired of waiting, murmured in its impatience. The gorgeous imperial tribune, the cathisma, remained untenanted. When the Basileus arrived, he would come through the underground passage which connected the dais with his palace; but he was long in coming, and the expectant sightseers grew querulous.

At length a blast of trumpets heralded the great man's approach. The first to appear were the members of the imperial guard, tall soldiers resplendent in red uniforms and with flashing swords; next there rustled in, clad in silken garments, the chief dignitaries of the court, with the priests and the eunuchs; last of all, borne in brightly coloured litters, each with a canopy, came Justinian, the Basileus, the autocrat, wearing a golden crown that looked like a saint's halo, and Empress Theodora, glittering with jewels. As the ruling pair entered the imperial box, a roar of acclamation rose from all the tiers of the huge assembly. Forgotten now was the terrible fight which had broken out in the hippodrome only three years before between the Green and the Blue factions of the circus, when the Greens had proclaimed a rival emperor and thirty thousand had been slain by the imperial forces under Belisarius. Popular memories are short, and the victorious cause is readily acclaimed as the just one. Intoxicated by the display, overwhelmed by the frenzy of their own enthusiasm, the countless spectators shouted and howled and applauded in a hundred tongues, while the stone circles of the hippodrome echoed to their voices. It was a whole city, a whole world, which now adulated its rulers: Justinian, the grandson of a Macedonian peasant; and Theodora, the lovely actress who, before her marriage, had danced totally nude in this same arena, and had sold her favours to any casual lover who could pay a sufficient fee. These escapades, these disgraces, were forgotten, as every shame is wiped away by victory and every deed of violence is excused by a subsequent triumph.

But on the highest tiers, mute above the vociferating crowds, stood spectators of marble, hundreds upon hundreds of the statues of Hellas. From their peaceful temples they had been torn away, the images of the Gods; from Palmyra and Cos, from Corinth and Athens; from triumphal arches and from pedestals they had been snatched, white and shining in their glorious nudity. Unaffected by transient passions, immersed in the perpetual dream of their own beauty, they were dumb and unparticipating, motionless, utterly aloof from human turmoil. With eyes that were sculptured but unseeing, they stared steadfastly across the agitated hippodrome toward the blue waters of the Bosporus.

Now there came another flourish of trumpets, to announce that Belisarius's triumphal procession had reached the outer gates of the hippodrome. The portals were thrown open, and once more the spectators shouted thunderous acclamations. Here they were, the iron cohorts of Belisarius, the men who, under their famous commander, had re-established imperial rule in Northern Africa, conquering all Justinian's enemies, freeing Byzantium from its anxieties, and ensuring for the pleasure-loving crowds an unchecked supply of bread and circuses. Even louder were the shouts of applause at the appearance of the booty, the spoils of Carthage, to which there seemed to be no end. Behold the triumphal cars which the Vandals had seized long, long ago; next, sustained by a framework of poles borne on men's shoulders, came a bejewelled throne; this was followed by the altars of unknown gods, and by lovely statues, the work of artists who had doubtless been famous in other times and other lands; then chests filled to the brim with gold and chalices and vases and silken garments. The vast abundance of plunder which the Vandal pirates had got together from the ends of the earth had now been won by Belisarius for its rightful owner, Emperor Justinian. What could his loyal subjects do but shout themselves hoarse at the sight of so much wealth assembled from all lands for the enrichment of their own mighty ruler?

Amid such splendours, the jubilant onlookers scarcely noticed the coming of a few articles which seemed insignificant when compared with what had gone before; a small table of which the wood had been covered by plates of hammered gold, two silver trumpets, and a seven-branched lampstand. No cheers greeted these seemingly trifling utensils. But on one of the topmost tiers was an old, old man who groaned as, with his left hand, he grasped Jehoiakim's arm. After fourscore years, Benjamin Marnefesh again set eyes upon what he had seen only once before, as a child of seven—the sacred Candelabrum from Solomon's House, the Menorah which his little hand had grasped for a moment, with the result that ever since he had had a withered arm. Happy and glorious sight; the holy emblem was unchanged, uninjured. Invincible did the eternal Lampstand march through the eternity of days, and had now taken a long stride nearer home. The sense of God's grace in granting him another sight of the Menorah was overwhelming. Unable to contain himself, he shouted: "Ours, ours, ours for all eternity!"

But none marked his cry, not even those nearest to him. For at this moment the whole assembly was roaring with excitement. Belisarius, the victorious general, had entered the arena. Far behind the triumphal cars, far behind the vast wealth of spoil, he marched in the simple uniform he had worn on active service. But the populace knew him in an instant, shouting his name so loudly, so exultantly, that Justinian was jealous, and had a wry face when the commander-in-chief made obeisance before the Emperor.

A silence ensued, tense with expectation, and no less striking than the previous uproar. Gelimer, the last King of the Vandals in

Africa, mockingly clad in a purple robe, led in behind Belisarius the conqueror, now stood before the Emperor. Slaves tore off the purple garment, and the vanquished monarch prostrated himself. For a moment the myriads of onlookers held their breath, staring at the Basileus's hand. Would he grant grace or give the sign for immediate execution? Would he raise his finger or lower it? Look, Justinian lifted a forefinger, Gelimer's life was to be spared, and the crowd cheered approval. One only among the spectators disregarded this incident. Benjamin could think of nothing but the Menorah, which was slowly being carried round the arena. When, at length, the sacred emblem vanished through the exit, the old man's senses reeled.

"Lead me forth."

Jehoiakim grumbled. A young man, pleasure-loving, he wanted to see the rest of the show. But old Benjamin's bony hand gripped his arm impatiently.

"Lead me forth! Lead me forth!"

As if struck blind, the aged and sorely tried Benjamin Marnefesh groped his way across the town, leaning on Jehoiakim's arm, with the Menorah in imagination ever before his eyes, as he impatiently urged his guide not to tarry, but to bring him quickly to the Jewish quarter of the town. Benjamin had grown anxious lest the feeble flame of his life should flicker out prematurely, before he had had time to fulfil his mission and rescue the Lampstand.

Meanwhile in the synagogue at Pera the community had for hours and hours been awaiting their exalted guest. Just as in Rome the Jews were allowed to dwell only on the farther side of the Tiber, so in Byzantium were they restricted to the farther side of the Golden Horn. Here, as everywhere, to be held aloof was their destiny;

but in this aloofness there also lay the secret of their survival as a distinct people.

The synagogue was small and was therefore overcrowded and stuffy. Packed into it were not only the Jews of Byzantium, but others of the congregation assembled from far and from near. From Nicaea and Trebizond, from Odessa and Smyrna, from various towns in Thrace, from every Jewish community within reach, envoys had arrived to take part in the proceedings. Long since had news come that Belisarius had stormed the Vandals' stronghold, and was bringing back to Byzantium, with numerous other treasures, the Seven-Branched Lampstand. To all the coasts of the Mediterranean had the tidings spread, so that there was not a Jew in the Byzantine Empire who had not been made aware of it. Though scattered like chaff over the threshing-floors of the world, and many of them more at home in Gentile tongues than in their own Hebrew, the members of this dispersed people retained a common interest in the holy emblem, suffering on this account common sorrows and hoping for common joys; and though they were sometimes at enmity with one another or mutually forgetful, their hearts beat in unison when danger threatened. Again and again persecution and injustice reforged the chain out of which their unity had been fashioned, so that the strength of these bonds was perpetually renewed; and the more savage the bludgeonings of Fate, the more firmly were the Jews of the Diaspora recemented into the one Chosen People. Thus the rumour that the Menorah, the Lampstand of the Temple, the Light of the Jewish nation, had once more been liberated from duress, and was wandering as of old from Babylon and from Rome across lands and seas, had aroused every Jew as if the thing had happened to his own self. In the streets and in the houses they conversed eagerly about the matter, asking their rabbis and their sages to interpret Scripture and explain the significance of these wanderings. Why had the sacred emblem started on its travels once more? Were they to hope or were they to despair? Was there to be a fresh persecution, or were the old ones to come to an end? Would they be driven from their homes to roam no man knew whither, unresting as of old now that the Menorah was again on the move? Or did the deliverance of the Lampstand betoken their own deliverance likewise? Was the Diaspora at length to come to an end? Were they to regather in their ancient home, in the Land of Promise? Terrible was their impatience. Messengers hastened from place to place to learn what was happening to the Menorah, and intense was the disappointment of the Jews when finally they were informed that, as had happened half a thousand years before in Rome, so now was the Seven-Branched Candlestick to be borne in a triumph at Byzantium beneath the contemptuous eyes of a Gentile emperor.

By this intelligence they had been profoundly moved; but excitement rose to fever-heat when the letter from the Roman community arrived informing them that Benjamin Marnefesh, the man sorely tried, the man who in early childhood had been the last to set eyes upon the Menorah when the Vandals sacked Rome, was on his way to Byzantium. To begin with, amazement was their predominant feeling. For years and for decades every Jew, however far from Rome, had known about the wonderful deed of the seven-year-old boy who, when the Vandals were carrying off the Lampstand, had tried to snatch it from the robbers, and had been struck down with a broken arm. Mothers told their children about Benjamin Marnefesh, whom God's own hand had touched; and Jews learned in the Law told their pupils. This brave exploit of a little boy had become a pious legend like those in Holy Writ, like the tale of David's slaying of Goliath and many others. At eventide, in Jewish houses, the heroic deed was related over and over again by the mothers and the elders of the people, among the stories of Ruth and Samson and Haman and Esther.

Now had come the astounding, the almost incredible news that this legendary child still lived. Old though he was, Benjamin Marnefesh, the last witness, was on his way to Byzantium. This must be a sign from the Almighty. Not without reason could Jehovah have spared him far beyond the allotted span. Was it not likely that he had been preserved for a special mission, that he was to take the sacred emblem back to Jerusalem, and to lead his co-religionists thither as well? The more they talked the matter over among themselves, the less were they inclined to doubt. Faith in the coming of a saviour, a redeemer, was eternal in the blood of this outcast people, ready to blossom at the first warm breath of hope. Now it sprouted mightily and fructified in their hearts. In the towns and the villages the Gentiles among whom the Jews dwelt were mightily puzzled at the aspect of their Hebrew neighbours, who had changed betwixt night and morning. Those who, as a rule, were timid and cringing, ever in expectation of a curse or a blow, were now cheerful and ready to dance for joy. Misers who counted every crumb were buying rich apparel; men who were usually slow to speak stood up in the marketplace to preach and to prophesy; women heavy with child slipped off joyfully to gossip about the news with their neighbours; while the children waved flags and sported garlands. Those who were most powerfully impressed by the report began to make ready for the journey, selling their possessions to buy mules and carts that there should not be a moment's delay when the summons came to set out for Jerusalem. Surely they must travel when the Menorah was travelling; and was it not true that the herald who had once before accompanied the Lampstand for a space when it left Rome, was again on the way? What signs and wonders such as this had there been among the Jews during the latter generations of the Dispersion?

Thus every congregation which received the news in time had appointed an envoy to be on hand when the Menorah should reach Byzantium, and to take part in the deliberations of the Byzantine brethren. All who were thus chosen thrilled with happiness and blessed God's name. How wonderful it seemed to them in their petty and obscure lives of daily need and hourly peril that they, inconspicuous traders or common craftsmen, should be privileged to participate in such marvellous events and to set eyes upon the man whom the Almighty had spared to so great an age for the deed of deliverance. They bought or borrowed sumptuous raiment, as if they had been invited to a great banquet; during the days before departure they fasted and bathed and prayed diligently, that they might be clean of body and pure at heart when they started on their mission; and when they left their homes, the community turned out in force to accompany them for the first stage of the journey. Wherever there were Jewish confraternities on the road to Byzantium, they were proud to entertain the envoys and pressed money upon them for the redemption of the Candelabrum. With all the pomp of a mighty monarch's ambassador did these men of little account, the representatives of a poor and powerless people, proceed on their way; and when they encountered one another, joining forces for the rest of the journey, they eagerly discussed what would happen, excitement growing as they spoke. Naturally, as this fervour grew, each of them reacted on the other, and thus they became increasingly confident that they were about to witness a miracle and that the long-prophesied turn in the fortunes of their nation was to occur.

Behold them assembled, a motley crowd of ardent talkers holding lively converse in the synagogue at Pera. Now the boy whom they had sent to keep watch ran up panting, and waving a white cloth as he came, in token that Benjamin Marnefesh, the expected guest, had come across from Byzantium in a boat. Those who were seated sprang to their feet; those who had been talking most volubly were struck dumb with excitement; and one of them, an exceedingly old man, fell in a faint, being struck down by his emotions. None of the company, not even the leader of the community, ventured to go and meet the new arrival. Holding their breath they stood to await his coming; and when Benjamin, led by Jehoiakim, an imposing figure with his white beard and flashing eyes, drew near to the house, he seemed to them a patriarchal figure, the true lord and master of miracles. Their repressed enthusiasm broke forth.

"Blessed be thy coming! Blessed by thy name!" they shouted to him. In a trice they surrounded him, kissing the hem of his garment while the tears ran down their withered cheeks. They jostled one another to get near him, each of them piously wishing to touch the arm which had been broken in the attempt to rescue the Lord's Lampstand. The leader of the community had to intervene for the visitor's protection lest, in the frenzy of their greeting, they should overturn him and trample him beneath their feet.

Benjamin was alarmed at the exuberance of their welcome. What did they want? What did they expect of him? Anxiety overcame him when he realized the intensity of their anticipations. Gently yet urgently he protested.

"Do not look for so much from me or entertain such exalted ideas which I myself do not harbour. I can work no miracles. Be content with patient hope. It is sinful to ask for a miracle as if its performance were a certainty."

They hung their heads, disconcerted that Benjamin had read their secret thoughts; and they were ashamed of their impetuosity. Discreetly they drew aside, so that their leader could conduct Benjamin to the seat prepared for him, well stuffed with cushions, and raised above the seats of the others. But once more Benjamin protested, saying:

"No, far be it from me to sit above any of you. Not for me to be exalted, who am, perhaps, the lowliest of your company. I am nothing more than a very old man to whom God has left little strength. I came merely to see what would happen to the Menorah, and to take counsel with you. Do not expect me to work a miracle."

They complied with his wishes, and he sat among them, the only patient member of an impatient assembly. The leader of the community rose to give him formal greeting:

"Peace be unto you. Blessed be your coming and blessed your going. Our hearts are glad to see you."

The others maintained a solemn silence. In low tones, the leader resumed:

"From our brethren in Rome we received letters heralding your arrival, and we have done everything in our power. We have collected money from house to house and from place to place to help in the redemption of the Menorah. We have prepared a gift in the hope of softening the Emperor's heart. We are ready to bestow on him the most precious of our possessions, a stone from Solomon's Temple which our forefathers saved when the Temple was destroyed, and this we propose to offer Justinian. At this moment his most cherished purpose is to build a House of God more splendid than there has ever been in the world before, and from all lands and all cities he is collecting the most splendid and most sacred materials to this end. These things we have done willingly and joyfully. But we were terrified when we heard that our Roman brethren wanted us to gain access for you to the Emperor, that you might beg him to restore the sacred Lampstand. We were mightily alarmed, for Justinian, who rules over this land, regards us with disfavour. He is intolerant of all those who differ from him in the smallest particle, whether they be Christians of another sect than his own or heathens or Jews; and perhaps it will not be long before he expels us from his empire. Never has he admitted any member of our community to audience; and it was, therefore, bowed with shame that I came to tell you how impossible it would be for us to fulfil the request of our brethren in Rome—that no Jew would be admitted to the presence of Emperor Justinian."

The leader of the community, who had spoken timidly and deprecatingly, was silent. All present hung their heads. How was the miracle to take place? What change in the situation could be effected if the Emperor were to close his ears to the words of God's messenger, were to harden his heart? But now, when the leader spoke once more, his voice was firmer and clearer:

"Yet magical and comforting is it to learn again and ever again that to God nothing is impossible. When, heavy of heart, I entered this house, there came up to me a member of our community, Zechariah the goldsmith, a pious and just man, who informed me that the wish of our Roman brethren would be fulfilled. While we were aimlessly talking and striving, he set quietly to work, and what had seemed impossible to the wisest among us he was able to achieve by secret means. Speak, Zechariah, and make known what you have done."

From one of the back rows there stood up hesitatingly a small, slender, hunchbacked man, shy because so many eyes were turned on him. He lowered his head to hide his blushes for, a lonely craftsman, used only to his own company, he was little accustomed to conversation. He cleared his throat several times, and, when he began to speak, his voice was as small as a child's.

"No occasion to praise me, Rabbi," he murmured; "not mine the merit. God made things easy for me. For thirty years the treasurer has been well disposed towards me; for thirty years I have been one of his journeymen; and when, three years ago, the mob rose against the Emperor and plundered the mansions of the nobles, I hid him and his wife and child in my house for several days until the danger was past. I felt sure, therefore, that he would do anything I asked him, all the more since I had never asked him anything before. But when I knew that Benjamin was on the way, I ventured to put a request, and he went to tell Justinian that a great and private message was on the way across the sea. By God's grace this moved the Emperor, who wants to see our messenger from Rome. Tomorrow he will give audience to Benjamin and our leader, in the imperial reception room."

Shyly and quietly Zechariah resumed his seat. There was an amazed and reverent silence. Assuredly this was the miracle for which they had been waiting. Never before had it been known that a Jew should be received in audience by the unapproachable Emperor. They trembled, open-eyed, while the conviction that God's grace had been vouchsafed to them presided over their solemn silence. But Benjamin groaned like a sorely wounded man, saying:

"O God, O God! What burdens art thou laying on me? My heart is feeble and I cannot speak a word of the Greek tongue. How can I present myself before the Emperor, and why should I do so more than another? I was sent here only to bear testimony, to look upon the Menorah, not to seize it or get possession of it. Do not choose me. Let another speak. I am too old, I am too weak."

They were all horrified. A miracle had been vouchsafed, and now he who had been chosen to perform it was unwilling. But while they were still wondering what they could do to overcome their visitor's timidity, Zechariah again rose slowly to his feet. When he now spoke it was in a firmer voice than before. The man had grown resolute.

"No, Benjamin, you must go to the audience, and you only. A little thing it was that I did, but I would not have ventured to do it for any other than you. This much do I know, that if any one of us can do so it is you that will bring the Menorah to its resting-place."

Benjamin stared at the speaker.

"How can you tell?"

Zechariah repeated firmly: "I know, and I have long known. Only you, if anyone, can bring the Menorah to its resting-place."

Benjamin's heart was shaken by this definite assurance. He looked full at Zechariah, who was himself looking encouragingly at Benjamin, and smiling as he did so. Suddenly it seemed to Benjamin as if Zechariah's features were familiar, and in Zechariah's eyes there was also a light of recognition, for his smile broadened, and he spoke with reinforced confidence:

"Recall that night eighty years ago. Do you remember one of the old men of your company, Hyrcanus ben Hillel by name?"

Now it was Benjamin's turn to smile.

"How could I fail to remember him? I remember every word and every happening of that blessed night as if it had been yesterday."

Zechariah went on: "I am his great-grandson. Goldsmiths have we been for generations. When an emperor or a king has gold and gems, and has need of a cunning craftsman or an appraiser, he chooses one of our race. Hyrcanus ben Hillel, at Rome, kept watch over the Menorah in its imprisonment; and all of his family ever since, no matter in what place, have been awaiting the hour when the Lampstand might come into their charge in some other treasury, for where there are treasures, there are we as valuers and jewellers. My father's father said to my father and my father reported it to me that, after the night on which your arm was broken, Rabbi Eliezer, the pure and clear, proclaimed of you what you yourself could not yet know, being but a little child, that there must be some great meaning in your deed and in your suffering. 'If anyone,' said the Rabbi, 'then this little boy will redeem the Menorah.'"

All trembled. Benjamin looked down. Greatly moved, he said:

"No one has ever been kinder to me than was Rabbi Eliezer that night, and his words are sacred to me. Forgive me my cowardice. Once, long ago, when I was a child, I was courageous; but time and old age have dashed my spirits. I must implore you not to expect a miracle from me. If you ask me to go to the man who now holds the Lampstand in his grip, I will do my best, for woe unto him who should refrain from a pious endeavour. Truth to tell, I am not one of those who have the gift of eloquence, but perhaps God will put words into my mouth."

Benjamin's voice was low and diffident, so that it was plain he felt the burden of the task which had been imposed on him. Still more softly, he said:

"Forgive me if I leave you now. I am an old man, wearied by the journey and by the excitement of this day. With your permission, I will seek repose."

Respectfully they made way for him. One only of the company, the impetuous Jehoiakim, his companion, could not refrain from questioning old Benjamin, on the way to the appointed quarters:

"What will you say to the Emperor tomorrow?"

The old man did not look up, but murmured as if to himself:

"I do not know, nor do I want to know or to think about the matter. In myself there is no power. What I have to say must be given to me, by the Almighty."

Long that night the Jews sat together in Pera. Not one of them could sleep, or had any inclination to seek his couch, so they talked unceasingly, holding counsel. Never had they felt so near the realm of miracles. What if the Diaspora were really drawing to a close; if an end were about to come to the cruel distresses of life among the Gentiles, the everlasting persecutions, in which the Chosen People was trodden underfoot, afraid day after day and night after night of what the next hour would bring forth? What if this old man who had sat among them in the flesh were in very truth the Messiah, one of those mighty of speech such as had lived aforetime among their people, able to touch the hearts of kings and move them to righteousness? What unthinkable happiness, what incredible grace, to be able to bring home the sacred emblem, to rebuild the Temple and to live within its shadow. Like men drunken with wine they talked the matter over throughout the long night, their confidence growing all the while. They had forgotten the old man's warning that they were not to expect a miracle from him. Had they not, as pious Jews, learned from Holy Writ to look always for God's miracles? How could they go on living at all, the outcast and the oppressed, unless in perpetual expectation of this redemption? Interminable seemed the night, and they could no longer restrain their expectations. Again and again they glanced at the hourglass, thinking that its orifice must have become clogged. Again and again one of them went to the window to look for the first glimmer of dawn upon the darkened sea, and for the flames of coming day which would be appropriate to the flames that were burning in their hearts.

It was difficult for the leader to control his usually docile brethren. One and all they wanted, on the coming day, to accompany Benjamin to Byzantium, where they would stand outside the palace, while he, within, conversed with the ruler of the world. They wished to be close to him while this miracle was being worked. The leader had sternly to remind them how dangerous it would be for them to assemble in striking numbers in front of the imperial palace, for the populace was ever hostile to the Jews, upon whom suspicion would easily fall. Only by using threats could he induce them to stay in the synagogue at Pera, where, unseen by their enemies, they could pray to the invisible God, while Benjamin was received in audience by the great ruler. They prayed, therefore, and fasted throughout the day. So earnestly did they pray that it seemed as if all the homesickness of all the Jews of the world must be concentrated within the heart of each one of them. Of nothing else could they think than of their hopes that this miracle would be performed, and that, by God's grace, the curse of having to live among the Gentiles would be removed for ever from the Chosen People.

Noon was the appointed hour, and a few minutes before noon Benjamin accompanied by the leader of the community entered the colonnades of the square in front of Justinian's palace. Behind them came Jehoiakim, young and vigorous, bearing on his shoulders a heavy burden, which was carefully wrapped. Slowly, quietly, grave of mien, the two old men, plainly dressed in dark robes, made their way through the bronze portals of the reception room, behind which was the ornate throne-room of the Byzantine

Emperor. They were, however, kept waiting a long time in the ante-room, for such was the custom at Byzantium, where envoys and suitors were to be taught by this expedient how exceptional was the privilege of being vouchsafed a glimpse of the countenance of the mightiest man on earth. An hour and a second and a third passed, but no one offered either of the old men a stool or a chair. Unfeelingly they were left to stand upon the cold marble. There streamed by in busy idleness an endless train of courtiers, fat eunuchs, guardsmen, and fantastically dressed menials; but no one troubled about the Jews, no one looked at them or spoke to them; while from the walls the impassive mosaics stared down upon them, while from the pillared cupola the lavish gold decorations mingled their splendours with those of the sunlight. Benjamin and the leader of the community stood patiently in silence. Being old men of an oppressed race, they had learned to wait. Too long an experience had they had of the weary hours to trouble about the passing of one or two more. Only Jehoiakim, young and impatient, looked inquisitively at everyone who passed through, irritably counting the fragments of the mosaic, hoping thus to while away the time.

At length, when the sun was manifestly declining, the praepositus sacri cubiculi approached them and initiated them into the practices enjoined by the ritual of the Court upon anyone who was granted the privilege of looking upon the Emperor's countenance.

"As soon as the door opens," he said, "you must, with lowered heads, advance twenty paces to the place where a white vein is inserted into the coloured marble slabs on the floor; but no farther, lest your breath should mingle with that of His Majesty the Emperor. Before you venture to raise your eyes to look upon the autocrat, you must prostrate yourself three times, arms and legs outspread upon the floor. Then only may you draw near to the porphyry steps of the throne, to kiss the hem of the Basileus's purple robe."

"No," interposed Jehoiakim, hotly though in low tones. "Only before God Almighty may we prostrate ourselves in that fashion, not before any mortal. I will not do it."

"Silence," answered Benjamin severely. "Why should I not kiss the earth? Did not God create it? Even if it were wrong to prostrate oneself before a mortal, still we may do wrong in a sacred cause."

At this moment the ivory-inlaid door leading into the throne-room opened. There emerged a Caucasian embassy which had come to pay homage to the Emperor. The door closed noiselessly behind them, and the aliens stood dumbfounded in their fur caps and their silken robes. Their faces were distorted with anxiety. Obviously Justinian had given them a rough reception, because they had offered him an alliance in the name of their people instead of making complete submission. Jehoiakim was staring at the strangers curiously, and taking note of their unusual attire, when the praepositus ordered him to take his burden on his shoulders and instructed the old men to do exactly what he had told them. Then he smote on the door gently with his golden staff, which produced a faint, ringing note. It was opened silently from within, and thereupon the three visitors, joined by an interpreter at a sign from the praepositus, entered the spacious throne-room of the Emperor of Byzantium, the room known as the consistorium.

To right and left from the door to the middle of the huge apartment was ranged on each side a line of soldiers, and it was between these two lines that they had to advance. Each man stood to attention, dressed in a red uniform, sword strapped to his hips, wearing a gilded helmet decorated with a huge red horsetail, holding a long lance in his right hand, and having slung behind his shoulders a formidable battle-axe. As stiff and straight they stood as a wall of stone, all of the same height, and behind them, likewise as if turned to stone, stood the leaders of the cohorts, holding banners. Slowly the three visitors and the interpreter advanced between these walls of impassive figures, whose eyes were as motionless as their bodies, none seeming to notice the newcomers. In silence they reached the farther side of the room where doubtless (though they did not dare to raise their eyes) the Emperor was awaiting them. But when the praepositus, who preceded them with his golden staff uplifted, came to a halt, and, as was now permitted, they could raise their eyes towards the Emperor's throne, lo, there was no throne to be seen and no Emperor, but only a silken curtain stretched across the hall and cutting the outlook. Motionless they stood there, staring at this coloured, arresting partition.

Once more the master of the ceremonies raised his staff. Thereupon the curtain parted in the middle and was drawn back to either side by unseen cords. Now, at the top of three porphyry steps, there was seen in the background the bejewelled throne on which sat the Basileus beneath a golden canopy. Stiffly he sat, looking more like a graven image than a human being, a corpulent and powerfully built man whose forehead vanished beneath the glittering crown which haloed his head. No less statue-like were the guardsmen, wearing white tunics, golden helmets, and golden chains round their necks, who formed a double circle round the monarch, while in front of these stood, equally statuesque, the Court dignitaries, the senators, wearing mantles of purple silk. They seemed neither to breathe nor to see; and it was plain that they were thus drilled into motionlessness and sightlessness that any stranger who thus for the first time glimpsed the ruler of the world should himself be petrified with veneration.

In fact both the leader of the Jewish confraternity and Jehoiakim felt as if blinded, like one unexpectedly thrust from darkness into strong sunlight. Only Benjamin, by far the oldest man in the room, looked steadily and imperturbably at Justinian. During his one lifetime, ten emperors and rulers of Rome had mounted the throne and then passed away. He knew well, therefore, that, for all their costly insignia and invaluable crowns, emperors did not really differ from ordinary mortals who eat and drink, attend to the calls of nature, possess women, and die at last like anyone else. His soul was unshaken. Firmly he raised his eyes to look into the eyes of the mighty Emperor, from whom he had come to beg a favour.

At this moment, from behind, he was warningly touched on the shoulder by the golden staff, and was thus reminded of what custom prescribed. Difficult as it was for one whose limbs were stiffened by extreme old age, he flung himself upon the cold marble of the flooring, hands and feet outstretched. Thrice he pressed his forehead against the flooring, while his huge white beard rustled against the unfeeling stone. Then he arose, assisted by Jehoiakim, with lowered head advanced to the steps, and kissed the hem of the Emperor's purple robe.

The Basileus did not move, did not so much as flicker an eyelid. Sternly he looked, as it were, through the old man. It seemed to be indifferent to him, the Emperor, what might happen at his feet, and what worm might dare to touch the hem of his garment.

But the three, at a sign from the master of the ceremonies, had drawn back a little, and stood in a row, with the interpreter at a pace to the front to serve as their mouthpiece. Once more the praepositus raised his staff, and the interpreter began to speak. This man, he said, was a Jew, commissioned by the other members of his fraternity in Rome to bring the Emperor of the world thanks and congratulations for having avenged Rome upon the robbers and having freed seas and lands from these wicked pirates. Inasmuch as all the Jews in the world, who were His Majesty's faithful subjects, had learned that the Basileus, in his wisdom, had determined to build a new House of God in honour of sacred wisdom, Hagia Sophia, which was to be more splendid and more costly than any other temple yet built by the hands of man, they had, poor though they were, done their utmost to contribute a fragment to the sanctification of this edifice. Insignificant was their gift, in contrast with His Majesty's splendours, but still it was the greatest and most sacred object which had been preserved by them from ancient days. Their forefathers, when driven out of Jerusalem, had carried with them a stone from the Temple of Solomon. This they had brought with them today, hoping that it might be inserted among the foundations of the new House of God, that the latter might contain a fragment from King Solomon's Holy House, and be a blessing to the Holy House about to be built by Justinian.

Upon a sign from the praepositus, Jehoiakim carried the heavy stone to place it among the gifts which the Caucasian envoys had heaped up to the left of the throne; furs, Indian ivory, and embroidered cashmeres. But Justinian looked neither at the interpreter nor at the gift brought by the Jewish visitors. Bored and weary he stared into vacancy, and said, with a drowsy irritability mingled with contempt:

"Ask them what they want."

In flowery metaphors the interpreter explained that among the magnificent spoils brought back from Carthage by Belisarius there was a trifle which happened to be peculiarly dear to the Jewish people. The Seven-Branched Lampstand which the Vandals had stolen from Rome and taken to Carthage had originally come from Solomon's Temple, built by the Jews in ancient days as the

House of God. Therefore the Jews implored the Emperor to spare them this Lampstand, being ready to redeem it by paying twice its weight in gold, or, if need be, ten times its weight. There would not be a Jewish house or a Jewish hut anywhere in the world where the inmates would not daily pray for the health and welfare of the most gracious of all the Emperors and for his long reign.

The eyes of the Basileus did not soften. Spitefully he answered:

"I do not wish those who are not Christians to pray for me. But ask them to explain more fully what concern they have with this Lampstand, and what they propose to do with it."

The interpreter looked at Benjamin, translating these remarks, and a shudder seized the old man, who was chilled to the soul by Justinian's cold glances. He sensed resistance and hostility, so that he grew afraid that he would not prevail. Imploringly he raised his hand:

"Great Lord, bethink yourself, this is the only one of the holy treasures our people once possessed which still remains on earth. Our city did they batter down, our walls did they raze, our Temple did they destroy. Everything which we loved and owned and honoured has fallen into decay. One object only, this Lampstand, has lasted through the ages. It is thousands of years old, older than anything else on earth; and for centuries has it wandered homeless. While it continues to wander, our people will know no rest. Lord, have pity on us. The Lampstand is the last of our sacred possessions. Restore it to us. Think how God raised you from among the lowly to place you upon the seats of the mighty, to make you wealthier than any other man on earth. It is the will of God that he shall give to whom it has been given. Lord, what is it to you, this wandering Lampstand? Lord, let there be an end of its wanderings and let it go home to rest."

Whatever the interpreter translated, he translated with courtly embellishments, and hitherto the Emperor had listened indifferently. But when, through the mouth of the interpreter, Benjamin reminded him that he had been lifted from a lowly place to become the mightiest of the mighty, his face darkened. Justinian was not fond of being told that he, now accounted semi-divine, had been born the offspring of a poor peasant family in a Thracian village. He frowned, and was about to utter a curt refusal.

But with the watchfulness of anxiety, Benjamin was quick to perceive the signs of imperial disfavour, and already fancied himself hearing the dreadful, the irrevocable No. His fears made him eloquent. As if propelled by an irresistible force from within, and forgetting the etiquette which forbade him to advance beyond the white vein in the marble floor, to the alarm of all present he stepped briskly towards the throne and raised his hands imploringly towards the Emperor, saying:

"Lord, your rule, your city are at stake. Be not presumptuous, nor try to keep what no one yet has been able to keep. Babylon was great, and Rome, and Carthage; but the temples have fallen which hid the Lampstand; and the walls have crashed which enclosed it. It alone, the Lampstand, remained unhurt, while all around it fell in ruins. Should anyone try to seize it, his arm is broken and withered; and anyone who deprives it of rest will himself suffer perpetual unrest. Woe to him who keeps what does not belong to him. God will give him no peace until he has returned this sacred emblem to the Holy City. Lord, I warn you. Give back the Lampstand."

The onlookers were struck dumb. Not one of them had understood the wild words. But the courtiers had witnessed with terror how a suitor had ventured what none had ever ventured before; in the heat of anger he had drawn close to the Emperor, and, with impetuous words, had interrupted the mightiest in the world when about to speak. Shudderingly they contemplated this old, old man, who stood there shaken by the intensity of his pain, with tears glistening in his beard while his eyes flashed with wrath. The leader of the Jewish confraternity, greatly alarmed, had retreated far into the background; the interpreter, too, had withdrawn to a distance. Thus Benjamin stood quite alone, face to face with the Basileus.

Justinian had been startled out of his rigidity. He looked unsteadily at this wrathful old man, and impatiently bade the interpreter translate what had been said. The interpreter did so, toning the words down as much as he dared. Would His Majesty be gracious enough to pardon the aged stranger for a breach of etiquette, seeing that the Jew had in truth been driven beyond all bounds by anxiety for the safety of the Empire? He had wished to warn His Majesty that God had laid a terrible curse upon this Lampstand. It would bring disaster upon any who should keep it, and whatever town should harbour it would be ravaged by enemies. The old man, therefore, had felt it his duty to warn His Majesty that the only way of escaping this curse would be to restore the Lampstand to the land of its origin, to send it back to Jerusalem.

Justinian listened with bent brows. He was angered by the impudence of this irreverent old Jew, who had raised voice and fist in the imperial presence. All the same, he was uneasy. Being of peasant origin, he was superstitious, and like every child of fortune he believed in sorcery and signs. After thinking matters over for a few moments, he said dryly:

"So be it. Let the thing be taken from among the spoils of Carthage and sent to Jerusalem."

The old man quivered as the interpreter translated the Emperor's words. The joyful tidings illuminated his soul like a flash of lightning. His mission was fulfilled. For this moment had he lived. For this moment it was that God had spared his life so long. Almost unwittingly, he raised his left hand, the sound one, stretching it upward as if, in his gratitude, he hoped to touch the Almighty's footstool.

Justinian was quick to see how Benjamin's face was irradiated with joy, and a spiteful desire took possession of him. On no account would he permit the insolent Jew to go back to his own people with the boast: "I have persuaded the Emperor and have won a victory." He smiled maliciously, saying:

"Don't rejoice before you have heard me out. It is not my purpose that the Lampstand shall belong to you Jews, shall be restored to you as one of the implements of your false religion."

Turning to Bishop Euphemius, who stood at his right hand, he went on:

"When you set forth at the new moon in order to consecrate the church which Theodora has founded in Jerusalem, you will take the Lampstand with you. Not that it may have its lamps lighted and stand upon the altar. You will place it unlighted beneath the altar, that everyone may see how our faith is high above theirs and how truth transcends error. It shall be safeguarded in the True Church, and not by those to whom the Messiah came and who failed to acknowledge him."

The old man was terrified. Of course he had not understood the words spoken in a foreign tongue; but he had seen that Justinian's smile was ill-natured, and knew that the man of might must have said something intended to disappoint him. He wished to prostrate himself once more at the Emperor's feet and implore him to revoke whatever this last order could have been. But Justinian had already glanced at the praepositus. The latter raised his staff of office, and the curtains rustled together. Emperor and throne had vanished. The reception was over.

Benjamin stood dismayed, facing the partition. Then the master of the ceremonies, who was standing behind him, touched him on the shoulder with the golden wand, as a sign that he was dismissed. Aided by Jehoiakim, Benjamin tottered out, his vision clouded. Once more God had rejected him, at the moment when the sacred emblem was almost in his grasp. Again he had failed. The Menorah still belonged to those who regarded might as right.

When he had walked no more than a few paces across the square outside the palace, Benjamin, again sorely tried, staggered and was about to fall. The leader of the community and Jehoiakim had all they could do to get him safe into an adjoining house where they put him to bed. His face was deathly pale as he lay there scarcely breathing. They thought, indeed, that he was about to pass away, for even the uninjured arm hung flaccid, and the leader found it difficult to detect the beating of his heart, which fluttered irregularly. He remained unconscious for several hours, as if his last vain appeal to the Emperor had sapped the remainder of his vital forces; but, when night was falling, to the amazement of the two watchers, the man who had been so near to death came to himself and stared at them with a strange expression which suggested that he must be a visitant from the other world. Gradually recognizing them, he commanded (to their still greater astonishment) that they should remove him as speedily as possible to the synagogue in Pera, for he wished to bid farewell to the community. Vainly did they urge him to rest awhile longer until he had more fully recuperated; he stubbornly told them to do his bidding, and they had no choice but to obey. Hiring a litter, they had him carried to the Golden Horn and ferried across to Pera by boat. During the transit, he lay half asleep, without opening his eyes or uttering a word.

Long ere this had the Jews in Pera heard about the Emperor's decision. They had been so certain that the Lord would work a miracle that such a grudging return of the Menorah to Jerusalem could by no means satisfy them. This was an utterly inadequate fulfilment of their extravagant hopes. The trouble was not only that the Menorah was to be kept beneath the altar in a Christian church, but that they themselves were to remain in exile. Their own fate concerned them even more than that of the Lampstand. They looked like men stricken with apoplexy as they sat there gloomily, huddled up, and full of secret vexation. Hope told a flattering tale to him who was fool enough to believe it. Miracles were fine things to read about in Holy Writ and were as beautiful as the bow in the cloud which was a token of God's covenant made in the days when the Almighty was near to his creatures; but the time of miracles was over. God had forgotten his people, once the chosen, but now left unheeded in their sorrows and distresses. No longer did Jehovah send prophets to speak in his name. How foolish, then, to believe in uncertain signs or to expect wonders. The Jews in the synagogue at Pera had ceased to pray and ceased to fast. Morose they sat in the corners, munching bread and onions.

Now that the expectation of a miracle no longer made their eyes glisten and their foreheads shine, they had become once more the petty, plaintive beings they had been so long, poor and oppressed Jews; and their thoughts, which so recently had soared Godward, had again become commonplace and earthbound. They were traders and shopkeepers again, with minds according. The envoys openly asked one another of what avail it had been to make a long and arduous journey, which had cost a lot of money. Why had they spent so much upon fine clothes that were now travel-worn? Why had they wasted their time and missed excellent opportunities of doing business? When they got home again, the incredulous would make mock of them, and their wives would nag. And since the human heart is so constituted that it is ever prone, when hopes have been dashed, to show the strongest animus against all who awakened them, vexation was now concentrated upon the Roman brethren and upon Benjamin the false prophet. Sorely tried, was he? Well, he had been a sore trial. God did not love him, so why should they? When, after nightfall, Marnefesh turned up at the synagogue, they showed him plainly enough how their feeling towards him had changed. Not, as before, did they reverently draw near to him with cordial greetings. Deliberately they averted their countenances. Why should they bother themselves about him, the old, old Jew from Rome? He was no stronger than the rest of them; and God was as little interested in him as in their own sad fate.

Benjamin was quick to perceive the anger which underlay their aloofness; to perceive the discontent which alone could explain their cheerless silence. He was distressed to find that they looked at him askance, or would not even meet his eyes; and he could not but feel as if he must be to blame for their disappointment. He therefore begged the leader of the community to call them together, since he still had a word to say to them. Unwillingly, morosely, they came out of their corners. What more could he wish to say to them, the man from Rome, the false prophet? Yet they could not but feel compassion when they saw him rise with difficulty from his seat, and support himself on his stick, leaning forward, by far the oldest man in the company. He barely had the strength to speak.

"I have come once more, brethren, this time to take leave of you. Also to humble myself before you. Not of set purpose have

I brought you sorrow. As you all know, I did not wish to present myself before the Emperor, yet I could not but comply with your request. When I was only a little child, the elders of our Roman community took me with them, having snatched me from sleep, I not knowing wherefore or whither. Always, after that night, they continued to tell me and others that the whole meaning of my life was to redeem the Menorah. Believe me, brethren, it is terrible to be one whom God perpetually summons but to whom he never listens, one whom he lures onward with signs which he does not fulfil. Better that such a man should remain in obscurity where none can see him or hearken to him. I beg you, therefore, to forgive me, to forget me, and to make no further inquiries about me. Do not name the name of the failure who did you grievous wrong. Patiently await the coming of him who will, one day, deliver the Chosen People and the Menorah."

Thrice did Benjamin bow before the confraternity like a penitent who acknowledges his wrongdoing. Thrice did he strike his breast with his enfeebled left hand, while the other, the hand of the withered arm, hung motionless by his side; then he drew himself up and strode to the door. No one stirred, no one answered his words. But Jehoiakim, remembering that it was his duty to sustain the old man, hastened after him to the threshold. Benjamin, however, waved the youth away, saying:

"Return to Rome, and when the brethren there ask after me, say: 'Benjamin Marnefesh is no more, and was not appointed by God as a redeemer.' Tell them to forget my name and to say no prayers in memory of me. When I die, I wish to be forgotten. Go in peace, and trouble yourself about me no longer."

Obediently Jehoiakim refrained from crossing the threshold. Uneasily he looked after the old man, wondering why Benjamin, walking with difficulty and supported by the staff, took the uphill direction. But he did not dare to follow, standing his ground at the door to watch the bowed figure out of sight.

That night, in his eighty-eighth year, Benjamin, who never before had lost patience, for the first time arraigned God. Confusedly, regarding himself as a hunted man, he had groped his way through the narrow, winding alleys of Pera, not knowing his destination. His one wish was to flee from the shame of having led his people to entertain immoderate hopes. He would creep into some out-of-the-way corner where no one knew him and where he could die like a sick beast.

"After all, it was not my fault," he murmured again and again. "Why did they lay this burden upon me, expecting me to work a miracle? Why did they pick me out, me of all men?"

But these self-communings did not assuage him, as he was driven farther and farther by the fear that someone might follow him. At length he grew footsore, and his knees trembled with fatigue. Sweat-drops beaded his wrinkled brow, tasted salt as they rolled between his lips while others fell into his beard. His tormented heart beat fitfully, and his breath came in gasps. But like a hunted animal, the old man, still aided by his staff, mounted higher and higher along the steep path which led into the open, away from the houses. Never again did he wish to see or be seen by anyone. Away, away from dwellings and firesides, to lose himself, to be for ever forgotten, enduringly delivered from the persistent illusion of deliverance.

Stumbling along, as unsteady on his feet as a drunkard, Benjamin at length reached the open hill-country behind the town, and there, as he leaned against a pine which, though he knew it not, kept watch over a tomb, he rested and recovered his breath. It was early autumn; the southern night was clear; the sea shone brightly in the moonlight, showing silver scales like a giant fish; while, like a serpent, close at hand was the channel of the Golden Horn. On the other side of this channel, Byzantium slumbered in the moonlight, its white turrets and cupolas shining brightly. Very few lights were moving in the harbour, since it was after midnight; nor did there rise from the city any sound of human toil; but the breeze rustled gently through the vineyards, now and then detaching a yellowed leaf from the withering vines, a leaf that fluttered silently to the ground. Somewhere close at hand must be wine-presses and wine-vaults, for down wind came the sour-sweet smell of must. This smell reminded him of the past, and with quivering nostrils the weary old man snuffed the odour of fermentation. The vine leaves were sinking to earth, and would become earth again. Ah, could but he himself thus perish, be joined to earth as they were. Never did he wish to go back to live among his fellows, address himself to a fruitless task, torment himself anew. Let him be delivered, at length, from the burden of the flesh.

When, now, a sense of the prevailing stillness took possession of him, and he grew aware of being alone, he was more and more overmastered by the longing for eternal rest. Amid the silence, therefore, he raised his voice to God, half in complaint and half in prayer:

"Lord, let me die. Why should I go on living, being useless to myself, and a scorn and a trouble to all with whom I come in contact? Why should you spare my life when you know that I do not wish to live? I have begotten sons, seven of them, each one a strong man in his time and eager for life; yet I, their father, shovelled the first earth into the graves of them all. A grandson didst thou give me, young and fair, too young to know the desire for women and the sweetness of life; but the heathen wounded him unto death. He did not wish to die; he did not wish to die. For four days, though wounded unto death, he struggled against death. Then, at last, didst thou take him, who wished to live, while me, who long to die, thou wilt not take. Lord, what dost thou want of me which I am not willing to do? When I was a little child they snatched me from my bed, and obediently I went whither I was told. Yet now, in my old age, I have had to deceive those who believed in me, and the signs which led them to believe in me were false. Lord, let me be. I have failed, so fling me away. Eighty and eight years have I lived; eighty and eight years have I vainly waited to find a meaning in the length of my life and to do a deed which should prove me faithful to thy word. But I have grown weary. Lord, I am at the end of my strength. Lord, be content, and let me die."

Thus raising his voice, the old man prayed, with a yearning gaze directed heavenward, as he looked earnestly at the twinkling stars. He stood there, expecting God's answer. Surely an answer would come at last? Patiently he awaited this answer, but by degrees his uplifted hand sank slowly, and fatigue, intense fatigue, overcame him. His temples throbbed; his feet and knees gave way. Involuntarily he sank to the ground, in a pleasant lassitude. Not wholly pleasant, indeed, for he felt as if he were bleeding to death, yet there was pleasure in his overpowering weakness.

"This is death," he thought gratefully. "God has heard my prayer." Piously, tranquilly, he stretched his head upon the earth, which had the decaying odour of autumn.

"I ought to have put on my shroud," he thought, but felt too tired to seek for it in his scrip. Unconsciously he drew his cloak more closely around him. Then, closing his eyes, he confidently awaited the death for which he had prayed.

But not that night was death to visit Benjamin, the sorely tried. Gently he fell asleep, while his mind went on working in the imagery of a dream.

*

Here is the dream which Benjamin dreamed on that night of his last trial. Once more he was groping his way in flight after darkness had fallen through the narrow alleys of Pera; but that darkness was now darker than it had been before, while in the skies thick black clouds hung low above the hilltops and the peaks. He had carried fear with him into dreamland, so that his heart throbbed violently when he heard footsteps on his trail; again he was seized with terror at the thought of anyone following him; and as he had fled when awake so did he now flee in his dream. But the footsteps continued, in front of him, behind him, to right and left, all round him in the gloomy, vacant, black landscape. He could not see who those were that marched to right and to left, in front and behind, but there must be very many of them, a huge wandering company; he could distinguish the heavy tread of men, the lighter footsteps of women with clicking buckles on their shoes, and the pitter-patter of childish feet. It must be an entire people that marched along with him through the moonless, metallic night; a mourning and oppressed people. For continually he heard dull groans and murmurs and calls from their invisible ranks; and he felt convinced that they had been marching thus from time immemorial, being long since weary of their enforced wanderings, which led them they knew not whither.

"What is this lost people?" he heard himself asking. "Why do the skies lower over them, especially over them, in this way? Why should they never find rest?"

In his dream, however, he had no inkling who these wanderers might be; but he felt brotherly sympathy for them, and their yearning and groaning in the unseen impressed him more lamentably than would have loud complaint. Unwittingly he murmured:

"No one should be kept a-wander like this, always through the darkness, and never knowing whither. No people can continue to live thus without home and without goal, always afoot and always in peril. A light must be kindled for them, a way must be shown them, or else this hunted, lost people will despair and will wither into nothingness. Someone must lead them, must lead them home, throwing light on the path for them all. A light must be found; they need light."

His eyes tingled with pain, so full of compassion was he for this lost people which, gently complaining and already reduced to despair, marched onward through the silent and lowering night. But as he, likewise despairing, plumbed the distance with his gaze, it seemed to him as if, at the farthest limits of his vision, a faint light began to glow, the merest trace of a light, a spark or two, recalling the look of a will-o'-the-wisp.

"We must follow that light," he murmured. "Even if it be no more than a jack-o'-lantern. Perhaps, though it is a small light, we can kindle at it a great one. We must follow it and catch up with it, that light."

In his dream, Benjamin forgot that his limbs were old and feeble. Like an active boy, like the heathen god who was fabled to wear winged sandals, he speeded on his pursuit of the light. He pushed forward fiercely through the murmuring, shadowy crowd, which made way for him mistrustfully and angrily.

"Keep your eyes fixed on the light, that light over there," he called to them encouragingly. Nevertheless this depressed people moved on sluggishly, hanging their heads and groaning as they went. They could not see that distant light; perhaps their eyes were blinded with tears and their hearts enfeebled by their daily distresses. He himself, however, perceived the light ever more plainly. It consisted of seven little sparks which flickered side by side, looking like seven sisters. As he ran on and drew nearer while his heart throbbed violently with exertion and excitement, he saw that in front of him there must be a Lampstand, Seven-Branched, which sustained and fed these little flames. That was but a guess, for the Lampstand itself was not yet visible. Nor could it be standing still, for it, too, was a-wander, even as the people who surrounded him were a-wander in the darkness, mysteriously hunted and driven by an evil wind. That was why the flames that flew before him did not show a steady light, nor a strong one, but were feeble and flickered uncertainly.

"We must grasp it, must bring it to rest, the Lampstand," thought the dreamer, while the dream-image fled before him, "for it will burn brightly and steadily and clearly as soon as it is at rest."

Blindly he ran onward to reach it, and nearer and nearer did he come to the Lampstand. Already he could see the golden stem and the upstanding branches, and in the seven knops of gold the seven flames, each of them blown flat by the wind, which continued to drive the Lampstand farther and farther across lowland and mountain and sea.

"Stay! Halt awhile!" he shouted. "The people is perishing. It needs the consolation of the light, and cannot for ever and ever wander like this through the darkness."

But the Lampstand continued to advance, while its fleeing flames shone craftily and angrily. Then the hunter, too, grew wrathful. Summoning the last of his forces, for his heart was now beating furiously, he made a huge leap forward to grasp the fugitive Lampstand. Already his grip had closed upon the cool metal; already he had clenched his hand upon the heavy stem—when a thunderbolt struck him to earth, splintering his arm. He yelled with the pain, and as he did so there came an answering cry from the pursuing masses: "Lost! For ever lost!"

But see, the storm abated, the Lampstand ceased its wandering flight, to stand still and magnificent. Not to stand on the ground, but in the air, firm and upright as if on an iron pedestal. Its seven flames, which had hitherto been pressed flat by the power of the wind, now streamed steadily upward in their golden splendour, giving off a more and more brilliant light. By degrees, so strong grew this light, that the whole expanse of heaven into which it shone was golden. As the man who had been struck down by the thunderbolt looked up confusedly to see those who had been wandering behind him through the darkness, he became aware that there was no longer night upon a trackless earth, and that those who had been following him were no more a wandering people. Fruitful and peaceful, cradled in the sea and shaded by mountains, was a southern land where palms and cedars swayed in a gentle breeze. There were vineyards, too, teeming with grapes; fields of golden grain; pastures swarming with sheep; gentle-footed gazelles at play. Men were quietly at work upon their own land, drawing water from the wells, driving ploughs, milking cows, sowing and harrowing and harvesting; surrounding their houses with beds of brightly coloured flowers. Children were singing songs and playing games. Herdsmen made music with their pipes; when night fell, the stars of peace shone down upon the slumbering houses.

"What sort of country is this?" the astonished dreamer asked himself in his dream. "Is this the same people that groaned and lamented as it fled through the darkness? Has it at length found peace? Has it, at long last, reached home?"

Now the Lampstand rose higher in the sky and shone more gloriously. Its lights were like the light of the sun, illuminating sky and land to the very horizon. The mountain tops were revealed in its sheen; upon one of the lower hills gleamed white with mighty turrets a magnificent city, and amid the turrets projected a gigantic House built of hewn stone. The sleeper's heart throbbed again.

"This must be Jerusalem and the Temple," he panted. Thereupon the Lampstand moved on toward the city and the Temple. The walls gave way as if they had been water to let it pass, and now, as it flamed within the Holy Place, the Temple shone white like alabaster.

"The Lampstand has returned home," muttered the sleeper. "Someone has been able to do what I have ever yearned to do. Someone has redeemed the wandering Lampstand. I must see it with my own eyes, I, the witness. Once more, once more, I shall behold the Menorah at rest in God's Holy Place."

As the winds carry a cloud, so did his wish carry him whither he wanted to go. The gates sprang open to admit him, and he entered the Holy of Holies to behold the Lampstand. Incredibly strong was the light. Like white fire, the seven flames of the Lampstand blazed up together in one huge flame, so bright that it dazzled and hurt, and he cried aloud in his dream. He awoke.

Benjamin had awakened from his dream. But still the intense light of that flame glowed into his eyes, so that he had to close the lids to protect them from the glare, and even then the light shone through them sparkling and purple. Only as he raised his hand to shade them did he become aware that it was the sun which was scorching his forehead; that, in the spot where he had sought to die, he had slept until well on in the morning, when the sun was high; and that it was the sunlight which had wakened him. The tree beneath which he had fallen asleep had not been enough to protect him from the dazzling rays. Having risen to his feet with some difficulty, he leaned against the tree-trunk, looking out into the distance. There lay the sea, blue and boundless, as he had seen it when a child at Portus, even as he was now contemplating the

Euxine. Landward shone the marble and other stone buildings of Byzantium. The world displayed the colour and sheen of a southern morning. After all, it had not been God's will that he should die. In a fright the old man leaned forward and lowered his head in prayer.

When Benjamin had finished his prayer to the Almighty, who gives life at his will and does not end it until he chooses, he felt a gentle touch on his shoulder from behind. It was Zechariah who stood there, as Benjamin instantly recognized, being now fully awake. Before the old man could give vent to his astonishment—for he wondered how the goldsmith could have discovered him—Zechariah whispered:

"Since early morn I have been seeking you. When they told me in Pera that, on quitting the synagogue, you had wandered uphill through the darkness, I could not rest until I found you. The others were extremely anxious about you. Not I, however, for I knew that God still has a use for you. Come back with me to my home. I have a message for you."

"What message?" Benjamin had it in mind to say. "I want no more messages"—so ran his stubborn thoughts—"for God has tried me too often."

But he did not utter these refractory words, being still consoled by the wonder of his dream, and by the remembrance of the blessed light which had shone upon that land of peace—the light which seemed to have left a reflection upon the smiling countenance of his friend. Without refusing the invitation, therefore, he walked down the hill with Zechariah. They crossed the Golden Horn in a boat, and soon reached the walled quadrant of the palace. There was a strong guard at the gates, but, to Benjamin's amazement, they allowed Zechariah and his companion to pass freely.

"My workshop," the goldsmith explained, "adjoins the treasury, for there, in secret and fully safeguarded from danger, I can do my work for the Emperor. Enter, and blessed be your coming. There will be no one else to trouble you. We are and shall remain alone."

The two men stepped lightly through the workshop, which was full of artistically fashioned trinkets. In the back wall the goldsmith opened a concealed door, which led down two or three steps into an apartment behind, where he lived and did his more special work. The shutters were closed and heavily barred, the rooms being lighted only by a shaded lamp which cast a golden circle of light upon the table, at the back of which was an object hidden by a purple cloth.

"Sit down, dear Benjamin," said Zechariah to his guest. "You must be hungry and tired."

He thrust aside the work on which he had last been engaged, brought bread and wine and some beautifully worked silver saucers containing fresh fruit, dates, almonds, and other nuts. Then he tilted back the lampshade, so that the greater part of the table was lighted, as were the clasped hands of Benjamin—the gnarled and parchmenty hands of a very old man.

"Please break your fast," said Zechariah encouragingly. To Benjamin, the man sorely tried, the voice of him who had till so recently been a stranger came to his ears as softly as a gentle breeze from the west. He ate some of the fruit, slowly crumbled bread and took a few mouthfuls, washing it down with small gulps of the wine which shone purple in the lamplight. He was glad to hold his peace while collecting his forces, and was content that above the lighted table the room was in darkness. His feelings towards Zechariah were those which a man has to an old and trusted friend. Now and again, though Zechariah's head was in shadow, Benjamin studied what he could see of the face with thoughtful tenderness.

As if recognizing that his guest desired closer scrutiny, Zechariah took the shade right off. Thereupon the whole room was illuminated, and for the first time Benjamin got a clear view of his new friend. Zechariah's face was delicately moulded, and weary, as that of a man whose health left a good deal to be desired; it was deeply furrowed with the marks of suffering silently and patiently borne. When Benjamin looked at him, the goldsmith smiled responsively, and this smile gave the old man courage.

"How differently you feel towards me from the others. They are angry with me because I have not worked a miracle, although I implored them not to expect one from me. You alone are not incensed against me, you, who made it possible for me to have audience of the Emperor. All the same, they are right to make mock of me. Why did I awaken their hopes, why did I come hither? Why should I go on living, merely to see how the Lampstand wanders afresh and eludes us?"

Zechariah continued to smile, a gentle smile which brought balm and healing. He said:

"Do not kick against the pricks. Perhaps it was too soon, and the way we tried was not the right one. After all, what can we do with the Lampstand so long as the Temple lies in ruins and our people is still dispersed among the Gentiles? It may be God's will that the Menorah's destiny shall remain mysterious, and not be plainly disclosed to the people."

The words were consoling, and warmed Benjamin's heart. He bowed his head and spoke as if to himself:

"Forgive me my lack of courage. My life has grown narrow, and I must be very near to death. Eight and eighty years have I lived, so perhaps it is natural that I should lose patience. Since, as a child, I tried to rescue the Lampstand, I have lived only for one thing, its redemption and its return to Jerusalem; and from year to year I have been faithful and patient. But now that I am so old, what can I hope from waiting?"

"You will not have to wait. Soon all will be fulfilled."

Benjamin stared, but his heart beat hopefully.

Zechariah smiled yet more cheerfully, saying: "Do you not feel that I came to bring you a message?"

"What message?"

"The message you expected."

Benjamin quivered to his finger-tips.

"You mean, you mean, that the Emperor might receive me again in audience?"

"No, not that. What he has spoken, he has spoken. He will never eat his words, and will not give us back the Menorah."

"What, then, is the use of my remaining alive? Why should I wait here, plaintive, a burden to everyone, while the holy symbol leaves us, and this time for ever?"

Zechariah continued to smile, yet more confidently—a smile which made his face glow.

"The Lampstand has not yet departed from us."

"How can you tell? How can you say such a thing?"

"I know. Trust me."

"You have seen it?"

"I have seen it. Two hours ago it was still locked in the treasury."

"But now? They must have taken it away."

"Not yet. Not yet."

"Then where is it, now?"

Zechariah did not answer immediately. Twice his lips were tremulous with the beginnings of speech, but the words did not come. At length he leaned forward over the table and whispered:

"Here. In my dwelling. Close to us."

Benjamin's face twitched.

"You have it here?" he asked.

"It is here in my dwelling."

"Here in your dwelling?"

"In this dwelling, in this very room. That is why I sought you out."

Benjamin quivered. In Zechariah's tranquillity there was something which stupefied him. Without knowing it, he folded his hands, and whispered almost inaudibly:

"Here in this room? How could that be?"

"Strange as it may seem to you, there is nothing miraculous about it. For thirty years, more than twenty of them before Justinian began to reign, I have worked as goldsmith in the palace, and in all that time nothing has been placed in the treasury, nothing of value, without being sent first to me, for me to weigh it and test it. I knew that all the spoils brought back by Belisarius after he had overthrown the Vandals would take the usual path, and the first of them for which I asked was the Menorah. Yesterday the treasurer's slaves brought it here; it is beneath that purple cloth, and it is entrusted to me for a week."

"And then?"

"Then it will be shipped to Jerusalem."

Benjamin turned pale. Why had Zechariah summoned him? Only that he should once more have the Menorah, the sacred emblem, within his grasp for a moment—to pass anew into the hands of the Gentiles? But Zechariah smiled meaningly, saying:

"I should tell you that I am permitted to make duplicates of all the precious objects in the imperial treasury. Often they specially ask me to make such a replica, for they esteem my craftsmanship. The crown which Justinian wears is a copy of Constantine's, and of my making; in like manner Theodora's diadem is the duplicate of one which Cleopatra used to wear. I therefore begged permission to make a duplicate of the Menorah before it was sent to that church of theirs across the sea, and I actually began the work this morning. The crucibles are already heated, and the gold is made ready. In a week from now the new lampstand will be finished, so like our own that no one will be able to distinguish it, since it will be of precisely the same weight, will show no unlikeness in shape or ornamentation, or even in the graining of the gold. The only difference will be that one will be sacred and the other wholly the work of an ordinary mortal like myself. But as to which is the sacred Lampstand and which the profane, which one we piously cherish and which one we hand over to the keeping of the Gentiles—that will be a secret known only to two persons in the world. It will be your secret and mine."

Benjamin's lips no longer trembled. His whole frame tingled with the rush of blood, his chest expanded, his eyes sparkled, and a cheerful smile which was the reflection of Zechariah's lit up his aged face. He understood. What he had once attempted, this fellow-countryman of his would now achieve. Zechariah would redeem the Lampstand from the Gentiles, handing over to them one exactly alike in gold and in weight, but keeping back the sacred Menorah. Not for a moment did he envy Zechariah the wonderful deed to which he had consecrated his own long life. Humbly he said:

"God be praised. Now I shall gladly die. You have found the path which I vainly sought. God merely called me, but you hath he blessed."

Zechariah protested:

"No, you, and you alone must take the Menorah home."

"Not I, for I am so very, very old. I should be likely to die upon the journey. And then, once more, the Lampstand would fall into the hands of the Gentiles."

Zechariah answered, with a confident smile:

"You will not die. It has already been revealed to you that your life will not pass away until its meaning has been fulfilled."

Benjamin bethought himself. Yesterday he had wished to die, and God had refused to grant him his prayer. Perhaps his mission had, after all, to be fulfilled. He raised no further objection, merely saying:

"I will be guided by your promptings. Why, indeed, should I resist, if God has chosen me? Go on with your work."

For a week Zechariah's workshop was closed to all access. For a week the goldsmith did not set foot in the street nor open his door to any knock. Before him, on a lofty stand, was the eternal Menorah, tranquil and splendid, as of yore it had stood before the Altar of the Lord. In the furnace, the fire licked silently at the crucibles with tongues of flame, melting down rings and clasps and coins to provide gold for the beaten work. Benjamin spoke hardly a word during this week. He looked on while the precious metal fused in the melting-pot, whence it was poured into the mould, and hardened as it cooled. When, with great care, skilfully plying the tools of his trade, Zechariah broke away the mould, the shape of the new lampstand was already recognizable. Strong and proudly rose the stem from the broad base, and, thinning, this stem ran straight upward to the central chalice. On either side curved away three stalks from the main shaft, each ending in its own chalice to hold oil for a burning wick. As the goldsmith hammered and chiselled, the appropriate ornamentations began to show everywhere, the bowls, and the knops, and the flowers. From day to day the counterfeit came to resemble more and more closely the true Menorah. On the last, the seventh day, the two

Seven-Branched Candlesticks stood side by side like twin brethren, indistinguishable from one another, being exactly of the same size and tint, measure and weight. Unrestingly, with practised gaze, Zechariah continued to work at the counterfeit until, down to the minutest traces, it was a truthful representation of the true. At length his hands rested from their task. Indeed, so closely alike were the two lampstands that Zechariah, fearing that even he might be deceived, took up his graving-tool once more, and within the pistil of one of the flowers made a tiny mark to show that this was the new lampstand, his own work, and not the Lampstand of the Jewish people and of the Temple.

This done, he stepped backward, took off his leather apron, and washed his hands. After six days' labour, on the seventh, the Sabbath, he addressed Benjamin once more:

"My work is finished. Yours now begins. Take our Lampstand and do what you think best with it."

But, to his surprise, Benjamin refused:

"For six days you have worked, and for six days I have thought and have questioned my heart. I have grown uneasy with wondering whether we are not cheats. You received one Lampstand, and you will give back another to him who trusted you. It is not meet that we should return the false lampstand and keep, by crooked arts, that which was not freely given to us. God does not approve of force, and when I, as a child, tried to take the sacred emblem by force, he shattered my arm. But I am equally sure that God disapproves of fraud, and that when a man cheats, the Almighty will consume his soul as with fire."

Zechariah reflected, and answered:

"But what if the treasurer should himself choose the false lampstand?"

Benjamin looked up, to answer:

"The treasurer knows that one is old and the other new, and if he should ask which of the two is genuine, we must tell him the truth and restore him the genuine emblem. If God should so dispose that the treasurer asks no questions, considering that the two are precisely the same, because there is no difference in the gold or in the weight, then, to my way of thinking, we should do no wrong. If he, deciding for himself, chooses the lampstand which you have made, then God will have given us a sign. Let not the decision be made by us."

Zechariah, therefore, sent one of the slaves of the treasury to summon the treasurer, and the treasurer came, a corpulent and cheerful man with small but protruding eyes which sparkled above his red cheeks. In the ante-room, with the airs and graces of a connoisseur, he examined two saucers of beaten silver which had recently been finished, tapping each of them with his fingers, and examining the delicate chasing. Inquisitively he lifted one gem after another from the work-table, and held them against the light. So lovingly did he inspect piece after piece, both the finished and the unfinished work of the goldsmith, that Zechariah had to remind him he had come to see the lampstands, which were awaiting his judgment, the Menorah which was thousands of years old and the one which had just been made, the original and the copy.

All attention now, the treasurer stepped up to the table. It was obvious that, as an expert, he would have been glad to find some trifling defect or half-hidden inequality which would enable him to distinguish the newly made lampstand from the one which Belisarius had taken from the Vandals in Carthage. Lifting each in turn, he twisted them in all directions, so that the light fell on them from various angles. He weighed them, he scratched at the gold with his finger-nails. Stepping back and drawing near again, he compared them with increasing interest, acknowledging to himself that he could detect no difference. At length, stooping till he was quite close, and using a magnifying-glass of cut crystal, he studied the minutest marks of the graving-tool. The two lampstands seemed to him precisely alike. Outwearied by this lengthy comparison, he clapped Zechariah on the shoulder, saying:

"You are indeed a master goldsmith, being yourself the greatest treasure of our treasury. For all eternity no one will be able to tell which is the old Lampstand and which the new one, so sure is the work of your hand. You have made a superlative copy."

He turned indifferently away, to scrutinize the cut gems, and choose one of them for himself. Zechariah had to remind him.

"Tell me then, Treasurer, which of the lampstands will you have?"

Without glancing at them again, the treasurer replied:

"Whichever you like. I don't care."

Then Benjamin emerged from the dark corner to which he had discreetly retired.

"Lord, we beg you to choose for yourself one of the two."

The treasurer looked at the speaker in astonishment. Why did this stranger stare at him so eagerly, so imploringly? But, being a good-natured fellow, and too civil not to accede to an old man's whim, he turned back to the show-table. In merry mood, he took a coin from his pocket and tossed it high in the air. It fell and rolled along the floor, this way and that, but at length settled down towards his left hand. With a smile the treasurer pointed to the lampstand which stood to the left, and said: "That one for me." Then he turned, and charged the slave who was in waiting to carry this lampstand to the Emperor's treasure-chamber. Thankfully and courteously the goldsmith ushered his patron to the door.

Benjamin had stayed in the inner room. With tremulous hand he touched the Menorah. It was the genuine one, the sacred one, for the treasurer had chosen the replica.

When Zechariah came back, he found Benjamin standing motionless in front of the Menorah, looking at it so earnestly that it seemed as if he must be absorbing the sacred emblem into himself. When at length he turned to face Zechariah, the reflection of the gold gleamed, as it were, from his pupils. The man sorely tried had gained that tranquillity which comes from a great and satisfactory decision. Gently he uttered a request:

"May God show you his thanks, my brother. I have one thing more to ask of you, a coffin."

"A coffin?"

"Be not astonished. This matter, too, I have thought over during these seven days and nights—how we can best give the Lampstand peace. Like you, my first thought was that, if we should succeed in rescuing the Menorah, it ought to belong to our people, which should preserve it as the most sacred of pledges. But our people, where is it, and where its abiding-place? We are hunted hither and thither, only tolerated at best whithersoever we go. There is no place known to me where the Lampstand could be kept in safety. When we have a house of our own, we are liable from moment to moment to be driven out of it; where we build a Temple, the Gentiles destroy it; as long as the rule of force prevails, the Menorah cannot find peace on earth. Only under the earth is there peace. There the dead rest from their wanderings; if there be gold there, it is not seen, and therefore cannot stimulate greed. In peace, the Menorah, having returned home after a thousand years of wanderings, can rest under the ground."

"For ever?" Zechariah was astounded. "Do you mean to bury the Menorah for ever?"

"How can a mortal talk of 'for ever'? Who can tell, when man proposes, that God will dispose accordingly for ever? I want to put the Lampstand to rest, but God alone knows how long it will rest. I can do a deed, but what will be the upshot thereof I cannot tell, who, like a mortal, must think in terms of time and not of eternity. God will decide, he alone shall determine the fate of the Menorah. I intend to bury it, for that seems to me the only way to keep it safe—but for how long, I cannot tell. Perhaps God will leave it for ever in darkness, and in that case our people must wander for ever unconsoled, dispersed like dust, scattered over the face of the earth. Maybe, however, and my heart is full of hope, maybe he will one day decide that our people shall return home. Then—you can believe, as I believe—he will choose one who by chance will thrust his spade where the Menorah lies, and will find the buried treasure, as God found me to bring the weary Lampstand to its rest. Do not trouble yourself about the decision, which we shall leave to God and to time. Even though the Lampstand should be accounted lost, we, the Chosen People, fulfilling one of God's mysterious purposes, shall not be lost. Just as the Chosen People will not fade out of existence in the obscurity of time, so gold that is buried underground does not crumble or perish as will our mortal bodies. Both will endure, the Chosen People and the Menorah. Let us have faith, then, that the Menorah which we are about to inter will rise again some day, to shed new light for the Chosen People when it returns home. Faith is the one thing that matters, for only while our faith lasts shall we endure as a people."

For a while the two men were silent, their inward gaze fixed upon the distant prospect. Then Benjamin said once more:

"Now order me the coffin."

The joiner brought the coffin, which was, in appearance, like any other, as Benjamin had requested. It must not be of peculiar aspect so as to attract attention when he took it with him to the land of his fathers. Often the pious Jews bore coffins with them on pilgrimage to Jerusalem, in order to inter the corpse of some near relative in the Holy Land. He need have no anxiety about the Lampstand when it was hidden away in a deal coffin, for no one is inquisitive about the bodies of the dead.

Reverently the two men put the Menorah away in its resting-place, as reverently as if it had been a corpse. The branches were wrapped in silken cloths and heavy brocade, as the Torah is wrapped whenever it is put away, the vacant spaces being stuffed with tow and cotton-wool, that there might be no rattling to betray the secret. Thus softly did they bed the Menorah in the coffin, which is the cradle of the dead, knowing, as they did so, that unless God willed to change the fortune of the Jewish people, they were probably the last who would ever look upon and handle the Lampstand of Moses, the sacred Lampstand of the Temple. Before closing the coffin, they took a sheet of parchment and wrote thereon a statement to the effect that they two, Benjamin Marnefesh, known as the sorely tried, descendant of Abtalion, and Zechariah, of the blood of Hillel, had, at Byzantium, in the eighth year of the reign of Justinian, here deposited the holy Menorah, bearing witness to any who might, peradventure, one day disinter it in the Holy Land that this was the true Menorah. Having rolled up the parchment, they enveloped it in lead which was hermetically sealed by Zechariah, the cunning worker in metal, that the container should be impermeable to damp. With a golden chain he secured it to the shaft of the Lampstand. This done, they closed the coffin with nails and clasps. Not a word more did either say to the other about the matter until the bondmen had brought the coffin to Benjamin on board the ship which was about to set sail for Joppa. The sails were being hoisted when Zechariah took leave of his friend and kissed him, saying: "God bless you and guard you. May he guide you on your path and help you to fulfil your undertaking. To this hour we two and none others have known the fate of the Lampstand. Henceforward that fate will be known to you alone."

Benjamin inclined his head reverently.

"My knowledge cannot last much longer. When I am dead, God alone will know where his Menorah rests."

As usual when a ship enters port, a crowd assembled on the quay in Joppa when the boat from Byzantium came to land. There were some Jews among these onlookers. Recognizing by his appearance and raiment the white-bearded old Benjamin as one of their own people, and perceiving that the shipmen followed him ashore bearing a coffin, they formed up to follow in a silent procession. It was traditional among them, when such an event chanced, to accompany the corpse even of an unknown compatriot a few steps upon the last journey—to be helpful and reverent. When the news spread abroad through the town that an aged member of their people had brought the remains of a relative across the sea to be interred in the Holy Land, all the members of the community left work to join in the procession, which grew continually in length until the bearers reached the inn where Benjamin was to pass the night. Not until the old man had (strangely enough, as it seemed to them) arranged for the coffin to be placed on trestles beside the spot where he was to sleep, did these followers break silence. They invoked a blessing on the traveller, and then asked him whence he had come and whither he was going.

Benjamin was chary of words, being afraid lest tidings might have come from Byzantium and that one of those who had flocked together might identify him. The last thing he desired was to raise fresh hopes among the brethren. Nevertheless he could not bring himself to utter anything that was not absolutely true when he stood so near the Menorah. He begged them, therefore, to excuse his reticence. He had been charged to bring this coffin to Palestine, and was not permitted to say any more. To ward off further inquiries, he asked questions of his own.

"Where," he said, "shall I find a holy place in which I can lay this coffin to rest?"

The Jews of Joppa smiled proudly, and replied:

"This, brother, is the Holy Land, and every spot of ground in it is therefore consecrated."

However, they went on to tell him of all the places where, in caverns, or in the open fields (marked in the latter case only by cairns), were the tombs of their fathers and forefathers, of the mothers of the tribe, of the heroes and kings of the Jewish people; and they vaunted the holiness of these same places. Every pious member of their fraternity visited them from time to time, seeking strength and consolation. Since the old man's appearance inspired respect, they said:

"Gladly, brother, will we show you a suitable place, and go with you to join in prayer when the unknown dead is interred."

Benjamin, however, eager to preserve his secret, declined their aid courteously, saying that privacy for the burial was enjoined on him by the nature of his mission. Only when the visitors had retired, did he ask the innkeeper to find him someone who, on the morrow, for a good wage, would take him to a suitable place and dig a grave. A mule would also be needed to carry the coffin. The host promised that his own servant and his own beast should be ready at dawn to do whatever the visitor required.

This night in the inn at Joppa was marked by the last hours of painful questioning and of holy torment in the life of Benjamin the sorely tried. Once again he doubted; once again did his resolution fail. Once more he asked himself whether it could really be right for him to withhold from his brethren the news of the rescue of the Menorah and of its return to the Holy Land; right to say nothing to the members of the Jewish congregation in Joppa about the sacred emblem which was about to be interred here. For if the members of his afflicted race could draw so much consolation from visiting the tombs of their forefathers, what would it not mean to them, to those who were hunted and persecuted and blown hither and thither by all the winds of heaven, if they could but receive the slightest intimation that the eternal Menorah, the most visible token of their unity, was not really lost, but had been redeemed, and was to rest secure underground in the Holy Land until, in the fullness of time, the whole Jewish Congregation likewise would return home?

"How dare I withhold from them this hope and consolation?" he murmured to himself, as he tossed sleeplessly on his pallet. "How can I dare to keep the secret, taking with me into the tomb information which might give joy to thousands? I know how they thirst for comfort. What a terrible fate is it for a people to be kept in unceasing expectation, feeding upon thoughts of 'some day' and 'perhaps'; relying dumbly upon the written word, and never receiving a sign. Yet only if I keep silent will the Menorah be preserved for the people. Lord, help me in my distress. How can I do right by the brethren? May I tell the servant whom my host has placed at my disposal that we have buried a sacred pledge?

Or should I hold my peace, that no one may know where the Lampstand has been laid to rest? Lord, decide for me. Once before thou gavest me a sign. Give me another. Relieve me of the burden of decision."

No voice of answer came through the silence of the night, nor would sleep visit the eyes of the man sorely tried. He lay awake hour after hour, his temples throbbing, as he asked himself the same perpetual round of unanswerable questions, and became more and more entangled in the net of his fears and sorrows. Already light was showing in the eastern sky, and the old man had not yet decided upon his course, when, with troubled countenance, the innkeeper entered the room, to say:

"Forgive me, brother, but I cannot provide you with the servant I spoke of yesterday, the man well acquainted with the neighbourhood. He has fallen sick during the night. Foam issued from his mouth, and now he has been smitten with a burning fever. The only man available is my other servant, a stranger from a far country, and dumb to boot. It has been God's will that since birth he has been able neither to hear nor to speak. Still, if he will serve your turn, he is at your disposal."

Benjamin did not look at the innkeeper, but raised his eyes gratefully heavenward. God had answered his prayer. A dumb man had been sent to him in sign of silence. A stranger, too, from a far country, that the place of burial might remain for ever hidden. He hesitated no longer, and answered the host, saying thankfully:

"Send me the dumb man. He will suit me excellently, and I shall be able to find my own way."

From morn till eve, Benjamin, with his dumb companion, crossed the open country. Behind them came the patient mule, with the coffin tied across his back. From time to time they passed wayside huts, the dwellings of impoverished peasants, but

Benjamin did not pause. When he encountered other travellers, he shunned conversation, merely exchanging the usual greeting of "Peace be unto you". He was eager to finish his task, that he might know the Menorah to be safe underground. The place was still uncertain, and some mysterious intimation withheld him from making his own choice. His thoughts ran as follows:

"Twice I have been given a sign, and I will await a third."

Thus the little procession moved on across the darkling land. The sky was obscured by clouds; though fitfully, through breaks in these, the moon glimmered, nearing the zenith. It was perhaps a league from the next village, where rest and shelter might be found. Benjamin strode on sturdily, followed by the silent servitor who shouldered a spade, and behind the pair walked the mule with its burden.

Suddenly the beast stopped short. The man seized the bridle and tugged, but the mule, planting his forefeet, refused to budge. "I have had enough of it," he seemed to say, "and will go no farther." Angrily the attendant lifted the spade, intending to belabour the animal's flanks, but Benjamin laid a hand upon the raised arm. Perhaps this balking of the packmule was the sign for which he had been waiting.

Benjamin looked around him. The dark, rolling landscape was abandoned. There was no sign either of house or of hut. They must have strayed aside from the road to Jerusalem. Yes, this was a suitable place, where the interment could be effected unobserved. He thrust at the earth with his staff. It was soft, not stony, and would be easy for the digger. But he must find the exact spot.

He glanced uncertainly to right and to left. There, to the right, a hundred paces or so away, stood a tree, recalling the one beneath which he had slept on the hill above Pera, and where he had had the reassuring dream. As he recalled that dream, his heart was uplifted. The third sign had come. He waved to the dumb man, who unbound the coffin from the beast's back, and, on the instant, the mule, relieved of the burden, trotted up to him and nuzzled his fingers. Yes, God had given him a sign. This was the place. He pointed to the ground, and the servitor began to dig busily. Soon the grave was deep enough. Now there remained only the last thing to do, to commit the Lampstand to its tomb. The unsuspecting deaf-mute lifted the burden in his strong arms and carefully lowered it into the grave. There lay the coffin, a wooden vestment for the last sleep of its precious golden contents, soon to be covered by the breathing, life-giving, ever-living earth.

Benjamin stooped reverently.

"I am still the witness, the last," he mused, trembling beneath the burden of his thoughts. "No one on earth save me knows the secret resting-place of the Menorah. Except for me, no one guesses its hidden tomb."

At this moment, the moon shone once more through the clouds. It was as if a huge eye had suddenly appeared in the heavens, lidded by dark vapours. Not like a mortal eye, perishable, and fringed by lashes, but an eye that was hard and round, as if chiselled out of ice, eternal and indestructible. It stared down, throwing its light into the depths of the open grave, disclosing the four corners of the tomb, while the white pinewood of the coffin shone like metal. No more than a momentary glance, and the moon was again obscured; but a glance that seemed to come from an enormous distance before the eye was hidden as the clouds regathered. Benjamin knew that another eye than his had espied the burial of the Menorah.

At a fresh sign, the servitor shovelled in the earth, and made all smooth above the tomb. Then Benjamin waved to him to depart, to return home, taking with him the mule. The man wrung his hands, and showed reluctance. He did not wish to leave this aged and fragile stranger by night in so solitary a place, where there was danger of robbers and wild beasts. Let him at least accompany Benjamin to some human habitation, where there would be rest and shelter. Impatiently, however, Marnefesh commanded the underling to depart. It irked him till he should be alone here beside the tomb, when man and beast should have vanished into the darkness, leaving him by himself beneath the expanse of heaven, to the emptiness, the incomprehensibility, of the night.

When his wishes had been obeyed, he bent his head beside the grave to utter the prayer for the dead:

"Great is the name and holy is the name of the Eternal in this world and in other worlds and also in the days of the rising from the dead."

Strongly did he desire, in accordance with the pious custom, to lay a stone or some other recognizable indication upon the freshly shovelled earth; but, reminding himself of the need for secrecy, he refrained, and walked away from the tomb into the darkness, he knew not whither. He no longer had a purpose or a goal, now that he had laid the Menorah to rest. Anxiety had departed from him, and his soul was at peace. He had fulfilled the task laid upon him. Now it was for God to decide whether the Lampstand should remain hidden until the end of days and the Chosen People should remain scattered over the face of the earth, or whether, in the end, he would lead the Jews home and allow the Menorah to arise from its unknown grave.

The old man walked onward through the night, beneath a sky in which the clouds were dispersing, allowing moon and stars to shine. At each step he rejoiced more and more heartily. As by a charm, the burden of his years was falling from him, and he felt a sense of lightness and renewed energy such as he had not known since childhood. As if loosened by friction with warm oil, his aged limbs moved easily once more. He felt as a bird may feel flying free and happy over the waters. Head erect, shoulders squared, he marched joyfully like a young man. His right arm too (or was he dreaming) was again hale, so that he could use it as he willed—the arm that had been useless for eighty years since that morning at Portus. His blood was coursing with renewed energy, as the sap rises in a tree during the springtime; there was a joyous throbbing in his temples; and he could hear the noise of a mighty singing. Was it the dead under the earth who sang a brotherly chorus to him in greeting, to him the wanderer who had returned home; or was it the music of the spheres, was it the stars that sang to him as they shone ever more brightly? He did not know. He walked on and on, through the rustling night, upborne by invisible pinions.

Next morning some traders on their way to market at Ramleh caught sight of a human form lying in an open field close to the road which led from Joppa to Jerusalem. An old man, dead. The unknown lay on his back, with bared head. His arms widespread, seeming ready to grasp the infinite, he had his fingers likewise opened, as if the palms were prepared to receive a bounteous gift. His eyes, too, were wide open and undismayed, his whole expression being peaceful. When one of the traders stooped, with the pious intention of closing the dead man's eyes, he saw that they were full of light, and that in their round pupils the glory of the heavens was reflected.

The lips, however, were firmly closed, as if guarding a secret that was to endure after death.

A few weeks later, the spurious lampstand was likewise brought to Palestine, and, in accordance with Justinian's command, was placed beneath the altar in the church at Jerusalem. Not long, however, did it there abide. The Persians invaded the Holy City, seized the seven-branched candlestick, and broke it up in order to make golden clasps for their wives and a golden chain for their king. Time continually destroys the work of human hands and frustrates human design; and so, now, was the emblem destroyed which Zechariah the goldsmith had made in imitation of the Holy Candelabrum, and its trace for ever lost.

Hidden, however, in its secret tomb, there still watches and waits the everlasting Menorah, unrecognized and unimpaired. Over it have raged the storms of time. Century after century the nations have disputed one with another for possession of the Land of Promise. Generation after generation has awakened and then has slept; but no robber could seize the sacred emblem, nor could greed destroy it. Often enough a hasty foot passes over the ground beneath which it lies; often enough a weary traveller sleeps for an hour or two by the wayside close to which the Lampstand slumbers; but no one has the slightest inkling of its presence, nor have the curious ever dug down into the depths where it lies entombed. Like all God's mysteries, it rests in the darkness through the ages. Nor can anyone tell whether it will remain thus for ever and for ever, hidden away and lost to its people, who still know no peace in their wanderings through the lands of the Gentiles; or whether, at length, someone will dig up the Menorah on that day when the Jews come once more into their own, and that then the Seven-Branched Lampstand will diffuse its gentle light in the Temple of Peace.

AVAILABLE AND COMING SOON FROM PUSHKIN PRESS CLASSICS

The Pushkin Press Classics list brings you timeless storytelling by icons of literature. These titles represent the best of fiction and non-fiction, hand-picked from around the globe – from Russia to Japan, France to the Americas – boasting fresh selections, new translations and stylishly designed covers. Featuring some of the most widely acclaimed authors from across the ages, as well as compelling contemporary writers, these are the world's best stories – to be read and read again.

MURDER IN THE AGE OF ENLIGHTENMENT
RYŪNOSUKE AKUTAGAWA

THE BEAUTIES
ANTON CHEKHOV

LAND OF SMOKE
SARA GALLARDO

THE SPECTRE OF ALEXANDER WOLF
GAITO GAZDANOV

CLOUDS OVER PARIS
FELIX HARTLAUB

THE UNHAPPINESS OF BEING A SINGLE MAN
FRANZ KAFKA